THIS ABOVE ALL

A NOVEL BY

LINDSEY ROTH CULLI

CURIOSITY QUILLS PRESS

A Division of **Whampa, LLC**
P.O. Box 2160
Reston, VA 20195
Tel/Fax: 800-998-2509
http://curiosityquills.com

© 2016 **Lindsey Roth Culli**
http://www.lindseyrothculli.com

Cover Art by Eugene Teplitsky
http://eugeneteplitsky.deviantart.com/

All rights reserved, including the right to reproduce this book or portions thereof in any form whatsoever. For information about Subsidiary Rights, Bulk Purchases, Live Events, or any other questions - please contact Curiosity Quills Press at info@curiosityquills.com, or visit http://curiosityquills.com

ISBN 978-1-62007-340-7 (ebook)
ISBN 978-1-62007-348-3 (paperback)

*For MJ Peters
and all the English teachers*

CHAPTER ONE

This is the part where I'm supposed to imagine them all in their underwear. Or naked. Or... something.

Except I'm standing by myself on this stage, and the darkened auditorium is basically empty so there's not really anyone to imagine naked in the first place. Not that I would want to. Adam and Eve were ashamed for a reason. And anyway, the only person here is the school's new drama teacher, Mr. Brooks, and maybe one of his gofers. Trust me, imagining Mr. Brooks in his skivvies soooo would not help right now. I mean, if he has that many wiry hairs sprouting from his ears, just think what the rest of him could look like.

Err... on second thought, don't.

So, it's just me up here beneath one wicked hot spotlight on a lonely stage, staring out into the darkened auditorium where a disembodied voice with a thick British accent says, "When you're ready."

Mr. Brooks is from London and apparently takes his Shakespeare quite seriously. How he ended up in Podunk central Illinois is beyond me, but our school's production will be better for it. He insisted on a tragedy, *Romeo and Juliet,* despite the head of the English department wanting something lighter and more playful like *A Midsummer Night's Dream.*

Now, there's nowhere to hide, and I have to choose: open my mouth and say the words I've practiced a hundred times, or bolt. But there's this thing that happens any time I try to speak in front of large audiences, or any audience, really—my heart races and my palms sweat, the room starts to seem bigger and hotter, and my mouth stops working. Like my tongue, my lips, everything. Won't. Work.

I clutch the paper with the words I've memorized, the words that at this point, I know as well as if they were my own. They aren't my words, of course. They're Juliet's, and I'm supposed to bring them to life. Right now. If I could only make my mouth open.

The problem is, aside from appearing as "Lesbian 1/AIDS Girl" in our church's annual Hell House—a spin on the haunted house that demonstrates many predominant sins in skit form—my experience with acting and theater is rather limited. I've been told I rocked the performance last fall, and a couple people cried one night. That's pretty rare. The glaring difference here is playing Lesbian 1/AIDS Girl was specifically *for* Jesus, to win souls for Him. Playing Juliet or pretty much anyone in a Shakespearean play? If I asked my dad's permission, I know just what he'd say: "How does this influence the Kingdom and glorify God?"

And my answer? Well, I'm not sure it does.

Which is why I technically didn't ask his permission. He thinks I'm at an after-school meeting. I don't make it a habit of lying to him since there's no telling what he'd do if he found out the truth. At the very least, it would probably involve a lot of Scripture memorization drills. There are like seventy verses about disobedience. I'd have to recite them all while I kneel on grains of rice. But then, that's only if he finds out. And he won't.

I hope.

Until now, this has all been a non-issue because our school tends to favor musicals to dramas since they generally require larger casts and therefore are more inclusive. I can't sing, so I could never muster up the courage to show up to those auditions. I signed up last year, but bailed at the last minute when I found out auditions were open, which would mean even if my acting were passable, I would probably get laughed off the stage after two bars of "We love you, Conrad." That, and open auditions meant word would probably get back to one of my eleven siblings somehow and, consequently, my dad.

The fact they're even doing Shakespeare at school this year seems like a gift from my mom. Thanks to her, I grew up on a steady diet of Shakespearean sonnets. The story goes when I was a baby, "Mary had a Little Lamb" or "Twinkle, Twinkle" wouldn't cut it for my colicky self so in a fit of desperation or maybe sleep deprivation, my mom resorted to reading me bedtime sonnets from one of her old school books she brought with her from Trinidad. Her reverence for the classics like Shakespeare or Dickens almost rivaled the scriptures. Almost. What I wouldn't give to hear Mom read Shakespeare (or anything, really) now. *Love is not love which alters when it alteration finds.*

Even though I know my dad would think I can better spend my time studying the word or witnessing or at the very least, joining FCA instead (never mind I'm not an athlete in any sense of the word), I love the theater and everything about it—from the chance to be someone else and transport the audience someplace else for a couple of hours, to the costumes and makeup, right down to the musty smell of the upholstered seats in the auditorium. I can measure the last few years of my life by the plays I sneaked out to see at the Theatre Center downtown, my own personal way to escape the weighty cloak of grief, which seemed to envelop our house after my mom died.

It only seemed appropriate that I sought refuge in the theater. It was *Evita* and *Annie* when I was fourteen, *Waiting for Godot, Anything Goes* and *Rosencrantz and Guildenstern are Dead* when I was fifteen, and this year, *Macbeth* and *Picasso at the Lapin Agile*. Actually, I'm pretty sure my dad knew about my habit. Or if not what I was doing, that I was doing something. The last time, when I went to the University to see *Picasso at the Lapin Agile* there was a mysterious $20 in a blank envelope nestled on top of the clothes in my dresser drawer. Dad never said anything, but I figure it had to come from him. My siblings might loan me money, but they wouldn't be anonymous about it, and they'd definitely charge me interest.

I've also spent more hours than I care to admit watching Kenneth Branaugh or Idina Menzel's Broadway clips on YouTube (when I was supposed to be cataloging church media hits) and then mimicking their techniques back to myself in the mirror.

I adore the theater, but can I actually *do* theater? Or more importantly, should I do theater? I'm supposed to be in the world and not of the world, but sometimes, it's hard to tell where the line falls.

I try to shake the myriad thoughts from my head and replace them with just this one: worst-case scenario, I totally stink, get laughed off the stage, and my family finds out about this *indiscretion*. It's not as if my dad would pull me from public school immediately and send me to live with my aunt and uncle back in Kansas, like my cousin Becky a couple years ago. She went from Texas to Kansas to "visit" them. For approximately nine months. Dad would be mad, and I'd have to spend a lot of extra time memorizing and reciting Scripture, but that's probably it. Just auditioning doesn't mean I'm breaking any major rules. Not technically.

"Miss Ryan, when you're ready," Mr. Brooks repeats.

There's a heaviness in his voice, and I can tell he's low on patience. How many auditions has he watched today? How many other people have butchered—or maybe worse, nailed—their monologues? I'm probably stupid for ever thinking I could do this. For letting my best friend Jodi convince me I might be able to try.

But I'm already up here. And I'll never know unless I do it, right?

Right.

Breathe. Breathe. Breathe. I will my lungs to fill with air and my heart to slow. I squeeze my eyes shut for a moment, open them again, and then I'm off.

"*Shall I speak ill of him that is my husband?*" The paper falls from my hands as I continue, traipsing around the stage. In this moment, I am not myself, not a middle daughter of the Ryan family, not a church going, Bible reading, long-skirt wearing good girl. I'm Juliet, and she is me. Her tragedy has become my own. I try to think of the actors I've seen, emulate the way they would allow themselves to be consumed by a role so the audience would forget they were watching an actor. I think of the moment right before I knew my mom died, and then the moment just after. All that confusion, anger, helplessness? The feeling of being absolutely surrounded by people—my massive family, of course, but also Mom's boisterous extended family members who'd flown to the States from Trinidad to be there—and still feeling so hopelessly alone. I try to channel all of it into Juliet's words.

"*In that word's death; no words can that woe sound.*"

As I finish the soliloquy, I drop my hands to my sides and stand there waiting, but for what I'm not sure. I don't expect applause exactly, maybe just some kind of acknowledgement of my presence. At the very least a "thank you." Something.

But there is nothing. Nothing but silence that stretches on for what feels like an hour. Oh no, am I that awful? How stupid can I *be* to think Hell House is comparable to real theater? I'm an idiot. As I walk to the stairs on stage left, the squeaking of my flats is the only sound in the entire auditorium, but it seems to fill the space as completely as my voice did mere moments ago.

Right as I am about to descend, a voice calls out across the expanse. Mr. Brooks. "Miss Ryan, I wonder, would you be so kind as to read the first monologue? There on the table?" I step over to the table at the base of the stairs and pick up a page from the first stack. I can hardly read it in the dim light, but it looks like Romeo's famous soliloquy: *What light through yonder window breaks?*

"The, uh, Romeo one?" I ask, holding it up. Maybe I'm looking at the table from the wrong angle. Maybe he means the first from the other end.

"That's the one," Mr. Brooks says. "Take a moment to look it over. Then, when you're ready, I'd like you to give it a go."

When I'm ready I should give it a go? As Romeo? Umm, okay, I guess. Maybe he ran out of copies of the other female characters' monologues. I scan it over once, twice. Where the Juliet bit needed movement, emphasis, the clear marks of a grief escalating to madness, it's obvious Romeo needs subtlety. Quiet. A hush. For one thing, he's hiding in a bush. And for another, he's talking about beauty and love, not death and destruction. My voice should feel like it's barely above a whisper. A gentle hum.

I clear my throat and then start, slowly. *But soft.*
"What light through yonder window breaks?"

I try to dig as deep as I can, try to find a seed of longing somewhere. It will never match Romeo's, but I haven't had a lot of time to study up on him as a character. And since I'm not a *homo*, it is a little hard to identify with him longing for a woman. I know I stumble over a few of the lines, but I do my best to pay less attention to the actual words than the weight behind them. When I get to the line about vestal livery—her virginity—I freeze.

I can't do this. I so cannot do this. What was I thinking? Shakespeare secular, obviously, but I guess I selectively blocked just how vulgar he can be. And just reading or not, I'm a girl talking about another girl's body, affections, and sexuality? Like I'm what, a dyke?

Nope. It's wrong on so many levels it almost makes me physically sick.

My face burns and the spotlight feels like it's getting hotter, brighter. I open my mouth to speak, to apologize for my mistake but I can't do anything. I just stand there like a total idiot. "Miss Ryan, are you all right?" Brooks asks, his voice shaking me from the trance. I drop the paper and run off the side of the stage, praying the stage left doorway isn't locked so I can make a clean exit.

"Miss Ryan?" Mr. Brooks calls behind me in his thick accent.

I don't look back; I can't look back. This was a mistake, and I want to just forget the entire thing.

CHAPTER TWO

Friday morning creeps by in a foggy jumble of nerves and anxiousness. My insides feel like lumpy, undercooked oatmeal. The cast list is going to be posted before lunch and honestly, it's all I can think about even though I know, after my performance, my name will not be on it. I shouldn't even want my name to be on it. But I do.

In English, Mrs. D is talking about haikus, introducing our next reading, and though I keep my eyes forward, I'm not there. Not really. She turns her back to the class to write on the board and I feel a piece of paper smack the side of my face. This is not exactly a rare occurrence. I suppose if I were allowed a cell phone, I'd get texts instead. I uncrumple the paper expecting to see the usual lame insults or attempts to shock me with badly drawn phalluses, but I find it reads, "Do not fret my pet/When it is all said and done/ You'll be Juliet." There are little smiley faces over each 'i' which means it could only have come from one person: Jodi. She's sitting there, wide-eyed and smiling.

I didn't tell her about how the audition ended, about how I ran off stage halfway through my second reading. I'm embarrassed, sure, but I also feel like maybe she'd be disappointed since she's been so unwavering in her support. Also, I know she wouldn't understand why I feel so guilty.

Jodi kicks her foot out to get my attention so she can offer another encouraging grin. I return it weakly, grateful for her enthusiasm even when I don't feel it myself. After my mom died, my dad wasn't about to pick up the homeschooling for the twelve of us, so my siblings and I were thrust into the public school system. Jodi had just moved here from Antwerp or Amsterdam or something. She was an outsider. I was an outsider. Even though she's not really religious, somehow we bonded. My dad doesn't exactly approve of our friendship, but he doesn't disapprove, either. "God's put Jodi heavy on my heart for a reason," I've told him. It's not even a lie.

I glance at her paper again. *"You'll be Juliet."* I don't know if I'd even want to be Juliet anyway. And that's not sour grapes talking—it would just be so complicated. Figuring out how to attend rehearsals but not letting my family know. To say nothing of the fact that I'm not stupid enough to believe there's no difference between delivering Kenneth Branagh's version of Hamlet's famous soliloquy in front of my bathroom mirror and delivering Juliet's death speech in front of hundreds of people in the school auditorium. I might be so paralyzed by stage fright I would make a terrible Juliet. Juliet the mute? This is Shakespeare. The words are everything.

Another note hits my face. This one says, "If your name isn't on the list, you can be Rosaline. In spirit, anyway." Rosaline. The character only spoken of, the one who never really appears on stage. Maybe that's fitting.

Later, after Calc is over, I decide to avoid the English wing and the drama room altogether, since that's where the list will be posted. The wing is in the same direction of the commons, but on a different floor so not too hard to bypass it. Right now, in this moment, my name might be on a cast list, and I want to dwell in the possibility for a while longer before reality comes back around to smack me in the face.

Actually being cast in the play would require me to ask my dad's permission or maybe worse, do it behind his back. I've never circumvented his authority before. I've never even considered doing that and, to tell you the truth, I feel a little bit guilty now for even thinking about thinking about it. To say nothing of the fact that I completely botched my audition.

I guess I could always volunteer to help with props or costumes or something just to be there. It wouldn't be the same exactly, but kinda like with Jodi and the track team—she tried out for and made the distance short-list which means she gets to practice with the team and may even get to dress for a couple of meets and sit on the bench. It's better than nothing. Also, less likely to break any of my dad's rules.

And ohmygosh, I've walked right toward the drama room without even noticing. I must have cut over instead of going all the way down the main staircase. There's a cluster of students running their fingers up and down the list. Above the paper is a bright orange sign announcing in big, bold letters that the first mandatory cast meeting is after school. Today.

I chew the inside of my cheek and am about to just keep walking when a few people step away from the list, giving me a clear enough view to read it. One guy gives me a solemn little half-smile, but I don't want to let myself think about what it could mean. Better luck next time? Probably.

Enough already. I've gotta know. I step forward and scan it over, starting at the bottom of the list, where the smaller roles are listed. My eyes search frantically for my name. Piper Ryan. Piper Ryan. Piper Ryan. I pause for a minute on Ryan, but it's a first name. Whoever he is, he got Friar John.

Finally, I get to Juliet and see Chloe "I-practically-starred-on-Broadway-when-I-was-five-and-I-won't-let-anyone-forget-it" Wennert's name. Can't say I'm surprised.

I'm not on the list. It's okay. Really. It's okay. I'm almost relieved, actually. It makes things so much less complicated. I take a deep breath and start to step back when I notice one more name on the paper. Above Chloe's name.

Romeo. And next to it, Piper Ryan.

Wait, what?

CHAPTER THREE

I squint to make sure this is not some hallucination. That in my fit of wanting something so hard, I've tricked myself. Or at least tricked my eyes into seeing something that's not there. I squeeze my eyes shut and open them again.

Nope. I'm not dreaming, my name really is there, next to the part of Romeo.

Well, that has to be a mistake. Romeo is a dude. And since I'm missing the small but crucial detail of a Y chromosome, it can't be meant for me. I check to see that all of the other female characters have female names next to them, spoiling my theory that maybe my name was accidentally inverted with someone else's. Someone slides up next to me, linking her arm in mine. Jodi.

"So?" she asks.

I shake my head, and her face falls.

"No?" Jodi lets go of my arm and steps to the list herself. "Shut up?!" she squeals. "Piper, your name is definitely up there."

"I know, but it's next to Romeo. That can't be right."

"The list was put together by English teachers. How much you want to bet they proofread it first? C'mon let's celebrate!" She grabs my hand and tugs me down the hall, toward the school store where she loads me up with an armload of sugary snacks—all the junk she usually avoids and that I can never have at home.

"This calls for a chocolate feast!" she says as she hauls the candy bars and me toward the commons. She's practically skipping. But all I can think about is whether or not I should go to the meeting after school today. Show up so I can be laughed at? Ugh. No thanks.

Our friends are scattered around our usual table. Ridgedale is not immune from standard high school lunchroom politics. The further your table is from the cafeteria, the higher your rank on the popularity food chain. We sit by the Pepsi machine, which is a middle of the pack kind of location. Exactly the kind of location I like. My only brother, Peter, usually sits on the opposite side of the room, really close to the cafeteria and with the rest of the *churchy* kids—most of them were either formerly homeschooled, too, or went to Kingsway Christian before it shuttered. I'm totally breaking rank by not sitting with all of them. I don't have a good excuse why except I find the smell of greasy hamburgers wafting through those doors nauseating.

To our left and several rows over is the table reserved for the seniors who are the current and future prom kings and homecoming queens. People like Chloe Wennert. Juliet.

"So?" Jodi's friend Stef looks up from her book, which is kind of amazing since the girl is always reading something and rarely ever pauses, even when she's having a conversation with you, which can be really annoying. She reads a non-required book a week, at least. Probably more. She pushes her glasses up her slightly upturned nose and tucks a strand of her dark curly hair behind her ear. We're always swapping notes on the latest and greatest hair products for curls. Hers are usually more bouncy and silky than mine. Somehow, she navigates humid 105-degree heat index summers with nary a rebellious flyaway. At first, she was standoffish toward me, which I can't say I blame her for. My family and our church are rather notorious around here, and I think most everyone expects me to proselytize all the time. When I proved that wasn't really my thing by not mentioning Jesus even once, she warmed up a bit. I obviously don't tell them that I pray almost daily for their salvation.

We don't hang out on the regular, but she doesn't mind me sitting with them. I think the fact that I choose semi-trendy pencil skirts over my sisters' pleated monstrosities probably helps my case. I don't stand out. Too much.

"Well..." I flop down next to Jodi, who has already started opening a Kit Kat bar, her favorite. She tosses me a package of Reese's cups, my favorite. I rarely get to have them, so today, I can't resist.

"Spill it!" Jodi says between bites. She has this thing where she nibbles the edges of each Kit Kat stick, then the chocolate off the top, and then she separates the crunchy layers one by one with her teeth, kind of like a rabbit.

"I umm, got Romeo," I say. "I think it's probably a mistake." It's definitely a mistake. There is no way on God's green earth that it's not a mistake.

"Romeo?" Serene sets her tray next to me. She's got a salad, an apple, and a frou-frou vitamin water, same thing she has every day. "That's a guy isn't it?" Serene is more Jodi's friend, and that's mostly because her family is Korean so they reached out to Jodi's mom just after Jodi moved to town. It's a tight-knit community, I guess.

"Yeah. Which is why I'm just sure it's a—"

Jodi shushes me by shoving a peanut butter cup in my face. "You are Romeo. Maybe it's unorthodox, but I, for one, think it's really freaking cool."

"Are you even allowed to do drama stuff?" Serene asks. "I mean, you know they have s-e-x in *Romeo and Juliet*, right? Shakespeare was a dirty old man."

"He wasn't old," I say. And at least Shakespearean plays hold to Elizabethan sensibilities. *Romeo and Juliet* is a love story, sure, but there's no love until after marriage. That's a huge plot point. And it's one of the reasons I let Jodi talk me into finally auditioning. It's beneath the indecency threshold, but just barely. Or it was, anyway, until my name was on the cast list as Romeo. Now, I'm not so sure.

"He's the lead so that's kind of a big deal," Stef says. "Who got Juliet?"

"Chloe Wennert." I glance in the direction of her table and see she's smiling and her crowd has gathered around her, like they want her freaking autograph or something.

My gaze flicks over them all, watching the guys especially. I find myself studying the way they carry themselves. The way they use their bodies. They seem awkward and stiff, as if they haven't quite figured out how to use their necks and arms and legs. Shoulders hunch over the table where arms support the weight of bodies, and knobby-knuckled hands shovel food into mouths. Sitting forward in my chair I try and square my shoulders and hold my head low the way they do. I crinkle my nose. It's awkward, and I get the feeling that if I held the pose too long, my neck would seriously cramp up. Why am I even doing this? I don't need to imitate a male because I am not one. I will never be one. Ridiculous.

I turn away from the jocks, and instead, my gaze falls on the table across the main aisle. The *artistes*. They're the group at school who flit effortlessly between slacker and hipster. Some of them look like they've tried really hard to look like they haven't tried at all. And some of them, like that guy, Dylan Miller, seem to just *be*. He's exactly the type of person I should keep my thoughts from—a fornicator at worst, a pervert at best—and yet I can't seem to. There's something magnetic about him. He's just so completely comfortable in himself which is rare anywhere, and in my experience, rarer still in high school.

I watch as a grin spreads across his face, starting with his eyes. He cocks his head to the side and knocks against his friend with his shoulder, which, I note, though square is not nearly as angular as the jocks. Dylan leans back and lets his arm drape across the empty chair to his right. He runs his other hand through his hair—chestnut brown and at least three shades lighter than his facial hair, which is strange but in a good way. It's long enough that it rests against his chin, so he usually pulls it back in a low ponytail at the nape of his neck or else throws some kind of cap over it. Right now, he's wearing it down so that he has to shake it from his eyes every now and again. Or brush it away with his hand.

Without even thinking, I mimic the pose, pushing my hips forward in my chair so that the space between my shoulder blades presses against the chair back to support my weight. It's not comfortable, but it's less uncomfortable than the jocks' way of hunching. I'm squirming to adjust myself into the pose when I feel eyes on me and look back up to see Dylan watching me. I quickly look away, the heat rushing to my face as I remember the other time I locked eyes with him. *A fornicator at worst, a pervert at best.*

A simple article in the newspaper last summer had my father convinced that teenagers in town turned the trails of the local parks into, in his words, "cesspools of fornication," and he was determined that we exterminate the problem. That three girls from Phoebe's class had babies within a few months of receiving their high school diplomas only served to stoke the flames. When local law enforcement refused to crack down as firmly as he'd hoped (i.e. they didn't put the fornicators in jail), my dad took matters into his own hands. Every Friday night for pretty much the entire summer, he brought a handful of us with him on "trail raids."

We stationed ourselves at the two mouths of the most popular trail, the one with the lookout point that hovered above the two-fingered pond. It was kind of a perfect place to make-out. Better than the back of a crusty old car at least. Probably.

Not that I would know.

At exactly 9:30, each group made its way into the thicket, until we reached our designated spots about fifty yards apart on either side. My sister Pammy blinked her little flashlight once and the other group (usually Penelope, Paula and my dad) flashed theirs back.

We counted to ten Mississippi-style and then a couple of us blasted the foghorns.

Paula flipped on her flashlight, and Peter and I turned on the megawatt camping lights, which, with the help of some Duct tape and Kraft paper had become makeshift spotlights.

My father shouted into his megaphone. *"'I say unto you, that whosoever looketh on a woman to lust after her hath committed adultery with her already in his heart!' I have seen thine adulteries, and thy neighings, the lewdness of thy whoredom, and thine abominations on the hills in the fields."* He raised his voice higher on the word whoredom.

Then he shrieked and wailed into his megaphone while half-dressed kids caught in the gaze of our spotlights scrambled to their feet.

We'd whoop and holler as the teens rushed past, shining our flashlights, symbolic of the light of God's truth, on them as they ran. My father chased behind them with his megaphone, calling out verses of Scripture and praying for the "heathens" and their "whoredom."

The kids would run out the two ends of the trail into the waiting arms of the park police, who still wouldn't throw them in jail like Dad wanted, but who would call their parents and/or issue them citations for public indecency.

Since it was so dark and it all happened so quickly, I usually didn't recognize the kids as they ran past. Mostly they were blurs of flesh and bits of denim and fleece.

Until one night when I did.

Dylan.

He was fully clothed, but the girl he was with grabbed her discarded shirt and clutched it in front of her as she peeked out from behind him. Beneath the beam of my flashlight, a bold tattoo bloomed on her shoulder. Dylan held a scratchy wool blanket in his hands. For one brief second, we stared at each other. I could hear my father whooping behind me in the trees and the crunching of underbrush as he approached.

Before I could even think, I shooed Dylan and the girl away. "That way," I whispered. I pointed out the unblocked path up the hill with the flashlight then spun around on my heel, giving them the cover of darkness.

Dylan glanced over his shoulder and winked at me before grabbing the girl's hand and scrambling off into the night.

Seconds later, my dad came up behind me, whooping as he chased a couple other kids off into the thicket. I just stood there and watched the figures shrink away, disappearing into the night.

My cheeks flare as I shake the memory away. I don't know much about him except that he's a senior, he's in art club, and the plaque by the door says he designed the mosaics that now adorn the otherwise boring white cinder block walls of the commons. I've heard he works at the coffee shop down on Ash Street, but I've never seen him there. We're not really supposed to drink coffee, so it's not exactly a place I frequent.

Of course, I'm not supposed to sneak out to the theater or be in school plays, either.

"Romeo, Romeo, wherefore art thou Romeo?" someone behind me says. And I'd recognize the cattiness in that voice anywhere. Chloe.

I spin around and look at her.

"Sorry about the mix-up," she says as her boney, perfectly manicured fingers plunk some quarters into the Pepsi machine next to our table. "Imagine *you* as Romeo! But on the bright side, you'll have your afternoons free." She shoots me a wicked little smirk and raises her soda can to me, a sort of a toast. Then she swaggers away, sipping her Diet Pepsi through a straw. Where in the world did she get a straw?

I'm determined now. If they did mess up, they at least owe me an explanation. To my face.

CHAPTER FOUR

I'm sitting in the drama room with the rest of the cast. Tony De Luca AKA the Italian Stallion, grabs the seat behind mine and leans in close. "I can't believe you got Romeo." I expect to see him laughing, but when I turn he's smiling. "I'm so jealous." He shakes his fists toward the ceiling.

"I'm pretty sure it's a mistake," I mumble. It has to be.

Tony starts to reply but Mr. Brooks walks in. His arms are loaded down with a stack of papers, and as usual, he seems flustered. It's like he's always a day behind or something. He sets the stack on the lectern, but half the sheets slip and scatter across the room.

"Oh for pity's sake," he huffs stooping to gather them. Since a bunch of them fluttered close to my feet, I slip out of the chair to help pick them up.

I'm crouched down eyeing the papers I'm trying to collect. Some of them look like schedules with dates and names printed on them, and some look like permission slips. Re-collating all of them is going to be fun. Not. I reach for a rogue paper under the bookcase and smack my head into the desk. Or not the desk. I've smacked my head into Dylan Miller's. He straightens, rubbing his temple with one hand while clutching a small stack of papers in the other and looking back at me. He's wearing a brimless knit hat, the kind that covers all of his hair and still sorta hangs loose at the back. The kind he's not allowed to wear during actual school hours.

"Ouch," he says.

"Sorry, I uh, didn't see you there." I reach for the stray paper at the same time he does, and we almost smack heads. Again.

"Go ahead," I stammer, backing up, my head throbbing. As he reaches for the paper, the sleeve of his shirt lifts, and I can see the edge of a tattoo on his wrist. Exposed tattoos are against school dress code, which totally explains why he always wears long sleeves. Completely normal now in February, but kinda weird in, say, May. Of course, I'm the expert on dressing against the norm.

My face is in flames as I sit back down in front of Tony. The papers are all jumbled, but I don't care, I wouldn't know how to organize them if I wanted to. Mr. Brooks comes by and shuffles them so they're at least all facing the same direction.

"Let's get started." He eyes the room while taking attendance on his cast list, calling off cast members alphabetically by last name. When he gets to the Rs, I hold my breath, waiting for my name to get passed over. Instead I hear, "Piper Ryan?" He looks at me and nods before making a check in his book.

So I *am* supposed to be here? As Romeo?

I want to raise my hand and ask since, judging by the sideways looks and muffled whispers that fill the room, everyone is wondering the same thing. I avoid eye contact with the lot of them but especially Chloe Wennert who's sitting at her desk brooding.

Mr. Brooks either doesn't notice or doesn't care. He continues talking about the production schedule, the importance of commitment and a few other orders of business I barely hear. I'm too busy sneaking glances at Dylan. The girl next to him whispers a question, and I watch the way he shrugs, slow and deliberate. Involuntarily, I mimic his movement, trying it on for myself. As he glances back down, his gaze flicks to mine again, and I know: he's caught me. Embarrassed, I stare down at the desk and the list of cast members. The cast list includes all the parts, but Dylan's name isn't there. So what is he doing here? Then I realize there are a few people whose names aren't on the list, either.

As if he read my mind, Mr. Brooks says, "Mr. Miller is designing our set for us. He'll be assisted by Miss Garrett on props, and Miss Johnson is in charge of makeup and costumes." The three of them give little waves or nods. The two girls are dressed alike. Skinny jeans, black Vans and well-worn vintage concert t-shirts. The Sex Pistols and The Pixies. Dylan's in a matching screen-printed t-shirt with a long-sleeved white tee underneath. His jeans are dark but not skinny. I bet he could rock some skinny jeans though. If he wanted to.

Kim Johnson leans over Dylan's desk and starts doodling something in his Moleskine notebook. She giggles and he smiles as he scratches at his bushy sideburns.

"All right, a few pieces of business first," he says. "I'm passing around a rehearsal group list and a schedule, whenever your group or groups are listed on the schedule, you're to be here, understood?" He doesn't wait for us to answer, his eyes searching over each of us from beneath his scraggly eyebrows that look like mini-versions of his mustache.

"If for some reason you feel you are unable to commit to our rigorous rehearsal schedule"—he says schedule like a true Brit: shed-u-all—"then please let me know now. You've been chosen for these roles because we want you here; however, you are not irreplaceable. You should also note that next Monday we have a full day rehearsal. Be in the auditorium by 9 o'clock a.m. sharp ready to work."

Next Monday, we don't have school thanks to one Casimir Pulaski, a Polish Revolutionary War hero to whom loads of Illinois public school kids owe an obscure but much appreciated day off in early March. The first Monday of March, to be precise. Except I guess we won't be having a day off after all. How on earth would I hide that from my dad?

Mr. Brooks eyes each of us, as if he's daring someone to groan, but no one does. "Also, I'm passing out a permission slip. In two weeks, the senior AP English students will be going to see the Chicago Shakespeare Theater. This year, they're performing *King Lear* not *Romeo and Juliet*, but that is beside the point. The point is to see Shakespeare performed. To watch actors try on and live in new skins." He's practically bouncing. "It's an overnight trip and will also include a visit to the Art Institute. The department has invited you all to attend if you'd like. However, if you wish to go, and I strongly recommend that you do, you must return this permission slip tomorrow as well as the trip fee. If the money is a problem for anyone, please let me know and we can work it out."

"All right. Now that that's taken care of, no time to waste." Mr. Brooks drops a binder on my desk. The thwack of it startles me, and I jump to face forward. "Scripts." He passes them out to everyone.

Someone has used a label-maker to print my name on the top of my binder. And next to my name: Romeo. I press my index finger over it to see if it smudges off.

"Today we're going to read through the first two acts, and I'd like the stage crew to stick around to get an idea of who's who among our cast. Circle up." Mr. Brooks pushes the lectern back and spins a desk around.

I'm lost in a sea of scooting desks and creaking chairs. I stand and move my desk to the wall next to the chalkboard. Tony sits next to me.

We open with the prologue, which Mr. Brooks reads. It sounds so much better with his British accent anyway. Then we start. Apparently, Mr. Brooks and student-director-Scott have done some minor tweaks to the original text.

"We haven't added anything, of course," he says. "Only made a few snips for the sake of flow and vision for the play."

"Baz Lurman got there first," Tony whispers to me. I wonder who Baz Lurman is but I get the feeling I *should* know, so I don't ask.

And then my mind travels to what I know about *Romeo and Juliet* and that one scene. Where Romeo and Juliet are in bed. IN. BED. It's bad enough to pretend to be a guy, but to pretend to be a guy being *with* a girl, in the biblical sense? Holy cats. And I can't help it, while Gregory and Samson and Benvolio are arguing about thumb biting, I flip ahead to Act III, scene V. But there is no mention of a bed. In fact, the stage directions say "at the window." Oh, thank God. Because miming a love scene with anyone, much less with Chloe Wennert? No way.

Wait. Will I have to kiss her? Surely not, right? I've never even kissed a boy. But kissing a girl? On stage? Forget excommunicated, I'd be disowned. To say nothing of what God might do to me.

I steal a glance at her. The diamond-crusted cross around her neck bobs between her cleavage as she tries to suppress a laugh. It gets quiet, and I look up to find everyone's eyes on me. Including Dylan's. He's staring at me from across the circle, chewing the corner of his cheek.

"Miss Ryan?" Mr. Brooks says. "That's your cue."

I've lost the page, and Tony slides his binder closer while I get my bearings. He points to my line. To Romeo's first line. Uh. It's just a read through, right? I can do that. Maybe after I do, they'll see how ridiculous this is, how absolutely un-Romeo I am. *"Is the day so young?"*

Benvolio, AKA John, answers.

I've said the line. It's Romeo's line and I've read it and no one batted an eye. They all look to me expectantly moments later and so I continue. *"Ay me! Sad hours seem long. Was that my father that went hence so fast?"*

I try to focus on the words, on what Romeo is saying, but it's difficult for one thing because I still feel like a poseur. And for another, because he's speaking in riddles. Also, I notice, he's really putting the emo in Romeo.

The read-through continues until we hit the end of Act II. Or at least the abridged end. Mr. Brooks says he envisions the wedding will be blocked while we hear the Friar's speech as a voice over.

"Marvelous. We'll stop there for today and pick up where we left off tomorrow afternoon. Do remember your permission slips if you intend to go to Chicago. And those of you with lots of lines might want to get a head start on memorizations. We've got eight weeks, people."

Everyone clears out of the drama room, but I take my time collecting my things and hang back.

"Mr. Brooks?" I ask as he's sitting at his desk, shuffling through some papers.

"Miss Ryan?" He looks surprised to see me, as if we haven't just spent the last few hours together and he can't put together why I'm in his room.

"I can't do it," I blurt. "I can't be Romeo." Once I've said it it's such a relief, a burden literally lifted from my shoulders. Even though I really do want to be in the play, homosexuality is wrong, and I cannot have any part in glorifying or even condoning it. I shift my weight from one foot to another, waiting for him to ask me why or beg me to stay or something. Instead, Brooks just studies me, unblinking.

"I mean, are you sure I am supposed to uh, play Romeo? It's kind of..." I can't think of the appropriate word.

"Unconventional?" He asks.

"Yes. Exactly. That." A lot more, really, but unconventional is a start.

He takes a deep breath, so deep it whistles through the whiskers above his top lip. "Miss Ryan, the play is called *Romeo and Juliet* which means we can't have a play without a Romeo and we can't have just anyone in that role. The part demands the best and, quite simply, you were the best." He folds his hands. "Even with your rather dramatic exit halfway through the soliloquy, you ran circles around every other potential Romeo. It would be a shame to waste your potential."

My expression must give away that I am unconvinced. His voice softens, and he combs his index finger through his mustache. "You know, in Shakespeare's day, all of the parts were played by men. Even Juliet." I've heard that before, but I'd forgotten it. The first Juliet was a guy. Huh.

"Oh." I can't help but think about my dad's go-to demonstration, with two power cords. The way that men and women were created to complement each other. The wrong ends together don't work. Likewise this—me as Romeo—wouldn't work. *Would it?* I ask Mr. Brooks.

"I don't think you playing Romeo has anything to do with sexuality. We're merely reversing the precedent. You're still playing a *character* who's male opposite a *character* who is female."

What he's saying makes sense, I guess. But I worry about what could happen if my dad and our church hear about this. I've seen firsthand how far they'll go for their cause. And sexual morality is one of their— one of our—biggest pet issues. I'm not sure they'd see it the same way. Worse, this could put me square in the middle of it all, caught in my own family's crosshairs. Am I really prepared for that, all over a silly play? To say nothing of how it's not a very big leap between this, what Brooks is saying about the characters' sexuality not being changed, and the fact that at the end of the day it would still be me, a girl, and Chloe, a girl. On a stage. Pretending to be in love.

Mr. Brooks' brow furrows. "Miss Ryan, why don't you focus on memorizing your lines and being the best Romeo you can be and let me worry about the rest of it?"

"But will I have to—I mean..." I'm not even sure I can say what I mean without blushing, but it hasn't escaped me that this is a tragic love story. Emphasis on love. That is a line I will not, simply cannot, cross.

His face softens a bit. "There are all sorts of stage tricks we can employ. You and Miss Wennert won't be asked to do anything that would make you uncomfortable, same as if you were playing opposite a gentleman instead. Besides, it's not so much about what happens on stage as what the audience *believes* happens off. Your job is to convince them. Are you up for the challenge?"

Am I? I don't know. I want to be the sort of person who is, but I don't know if I actually am. I wonder if that is enough? "Umm, I guess so."

Mr. Brooks narrows his eyes. "You're going to have to do better than that, I'm afraid."

"I'll try?" As long as I don't have to kiss her, I can try, right? No harm in that.

Brooks considers this and nods once. "Fair enough."

Wait. I've just agreed to stay in the cast. How did that happen? I try to retrace the steps of our conversation, but even as I do, I feel that familiar tickle return to my stomach. Nausea, yes, but laced with excitement, too. I want to be in the play, but I don't want to go against my family or our beliefs. Why is this so complicated?

We part ways at the end of the hall, but as I'm heading down the stairs, Mr. Brooks calls after me, "Don't forget your permission slip tomorrow. I would really like you to go on this trip."

THIS ABOVE ALL

Miss a day of school, go to the city, and see professional Shakespearean actors? In Chicago? My dad would never let me go. I know I shouldn't even want to go—too many temptations and potential pitfalls. But I do. Just as I *want* to be in the play... even if it means playing a guy.

CHAPTER FIVE

"Hey, kiddo. How was the..." Dad looks up from the mound of files. "Was it a meeting?" With so many of us, it's no wonder he can't keep all of our comings and goings precisely straight. I was counting on this when I made up the small white lie about the meeting in the first place. It was mostly a lie of omission but a lie just the same. My ears burn as I think of it.

"Oh, uh, fine," I say. The guilt I've been trying to keep at bay resurfaces, and I wonder if my dad can see my sin like an aura. Even if being in the cast isn't technically a sin, lying about it surely is. The Ninth Commandment. Also, the Fifth is about honoring your parents and straight up lying to your father pretty much goes against that. I implied that I wouldn't need a ride today because of a planning meeting for SYATP, or See You At the Pole, which doesn't happen again until next September. Basically, it's a day where believers around the country meet at our schools' flagpoles to pray. "You know, a pretty standard meeting."

He won't press me for more information, not about this. If we were talking about the SATs or a Calc test or my scripture memorizations, he might ask for details. Really, he thinks SYATP is too secular since it involves all believers, not just those who believe as we do, so he probably doesn't care much at all, actually.

"Good. Good." And his gaze returns to the files. He's the pastor, the head of our church, and is therefore never not working. Usually, he has papers spread out all over the dining room table, says he works best when he's in the middle of things, in the heart of the home. "Christ is the heart of the church, the table is the heart of the home," he's always saying. Yellow legal pads filled with his chicken scratches, file folders laden with post-its, and an assortment of different annotated translations of the Bible that look like they could do some serious damage if they ever fell on your toe.

Moose, our black pug that sounds like he's got a perpetual sinus infection, dances around my feet. He was supposed to be a short-term lesson to my brother about responsibility and how he wasn't ready for it, but then my dad fell in love with the dog and so here he is. I reach down to pet him, but he steps away from my outstretched hand because that's not what he wants. What he wants is inside the dog-shaped cookie jar on the counter.

"Win any souls yet?" He reaches into his bucket of Red Vines—his one vice—and pulls one out then thinks again and takes out another, handing it to me.

"Working on it." I smile, taking the licorice and nibbling it slowly. With the exception of Dad's Red Vines, we never have junk food in the house. And my dad hardly ever shares with anyone. Except me.

Dad licks his bottom lip and scrunches his nose, a gesture I've inherited despite his instance that I don't do it. "You'll ruin your pretty little face if you get wrinkles like me." Wrinkles or not, he's handsome, my dad. One of those people who looks like he's sporting a perpetual suntan. No matter the season, his skin is coppery and warm. My mom's was the same way, only a touch darker. More like raw honey.

I didn't get so lucky. I'm technically a quarter Trini but where my mom—daughter of a local and a missionary—was rocking that gorgeous Indian/African blend, my skin is pale as paste probably thanks to my Irish grandmom. And that doesn't really ever change, even in the summer. Instead, my freckles get darker, especially the ones across the bridge of my nose. Angel kisses, Grandmom always called them. When I was little, Peter had me near convinced that I was adopted, since I look nothing like the rest of my family who all have easily tanned skin, dark eyelashes, and thick chestnut hair. But there's no denying I've got my mom's eyes.

Moose is relentless. When the dancing around fails, he just sits there looking from me to his "cookie" jar to me again as if to say, "See what a good boy I am? Don't you want to reward me?" And I'm a totally sucker where small furry things are concerned, so I step over to the counter and grab him one. As soon as I lift the head-lid, the thing makes a fake barking sound, and Moose goes nuts. With a dexterity that rivals a snake's, his tongue grabs the biscuit from my hand, and he scoots off down the hall.

I palm the rest of my licorice when a few of my younger siblings race through the kitchen and out the back door. One of them—Paige—is holding a football. All of my siblings have names that start with "P." I don't really know why P in particular, something to do with a dream my mom had. The angel appeared to Joseph in a dream and told him to name his son Jesus, and Mom said an angel told her to go with P. All told there's Penelope, Phoebe, Pearl, Peter, me, Paula, Paige, and the last, Pammy. I can't hardly keep 'em all straight, either.

"Pearl's choice for dinner tonight," Dad says. Her birthday was last week and normally when it's your birthday, you pick the meal either at home or out, but Pearl was sick last week. So I guess tonight is her rain check. He catches me eying the Red Vines and hands me another. "Don't tell your siblings." He winks.

'In a bit' means I've probably got at least an hour. And since most of my other siblings are off doing homework, practicing instruments, or apparently playing hopscotch out back, I figure I've got free rein over the girls' bathroom. After spending the day a sweating ball of nerves, nothing sounds better than a long, hot bath. Especially since they are exceedingly rare around here.

I sprinkle some of my mom's lavender bath salts in the water. I found them when I was going through the hallway closet after she died and have been rationing them out ever since. Anytime I need a little boost or a reminder of her, I let myself use a pinch. Today it's especially appropriate since it's her love of Shakespeare that helped me get into this whole... thing. Unbeknownst to my dad, Mom kept reading Shakespeare to me until I was nine or so, and I declared I was too old for bedtime stories. Paula used to listen, too, but even though she's younger than me by about eighteen months, she outgrew bedtime stories long before I gave them up.

"Shakespeare is nonsensical," Paula says now. Pretty much anything secular is foolish in her mind.

I slide into the tub, taking care not to get my hair wet. It's so curly that if I wash it, it will take ages to dry, even with a blow drier and a diffuser. I got my dad's hair color (auburn so deep that it's almost brown) and my mom's texture (super thick and curly), which makes for a lot of fun in the humid Midwestern summers (picture a frizzy poodle that mated with an Afghan Hound. Now dye him deep auburn-red and sit him atop my head). Today at least, it's not so bad.

When we were little, we used to get haircuts every summer but then somewhere along the way Dad decided that we should keep our hair long. "*If a woman has long hair, it is her glory*," he said, quoting from the Bible of course. "Besides, don't want anyone to get the *wrong idea* about you beautiful jewels." He gave my sister Phoebe the side-eye, probably thinking of the time when she got a near pixie cut, and he was convinced it meant she was a lesbian, or at least that people would think she was one. Long hair is all well and good for my sisters and their stick-straight hair. But mine's a mess of curls that takes me ages to tame each morning.

Gah. My hair. How on earth would I be able to be Romeo with this? I pull my hair back off my face, as flat to my head as I can get it. Even with a whole can of hairspray, it wouldn't stay this way, I know. Probably not with a thousand bobby pins, either. Plus, I still look like a girl.

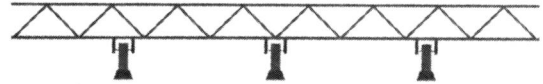

Jesus came to me as a cloud once.

It was shortly after my dad moved us all from Kansas to Ridgedale because God gave him a vision that here was where he should establish

Mt. Zion Baptist Church of the Elect. The university in town meant it was a cesspool of sin filled to the brim with homosexuals, idolatry and the like, a slew of sinners crying out in need of a savior. A modern day Nineveh only unlike Jonah, my dad would never run away from God's decree, no matter how intimidating that command may be.

I told my dad I'd seen Jesus' face while I was picking tomatoes in our yard. My mother's idea of a garden was a small patch of dirt and some tomatoes, planted in early May and allowed to grow upward or outward at whim. We took turns watering the plot, never weeding or staking them, even when the plump green globes pulled the vines down, trailing them along the dark soil.

"Just water and sunshine's all they need," Mom would say.

On this particular day, Peter and I made our way out to the plot armed with gardening gloves and two large metal mixing bowls to collect ripe ones. Plush clouds raced across the sky, blocking the sun here but not there, so that Peter who stood a few yards away would be shaded and I would not. When they passed, we'd both be caught up in the sun's direct gaze again. I paused from my chore to watch them drift over, wondering how they could dance across the sky so smoothly and yet down on earth we felt almost no breeze at all.

And then I saw Jesus.

His face was just the way I had remembered seeing it in my father's study, where his portrait hung squarely on the wood-paneled wall behind the desk. His skin, as creamy and smooth as my mother's lone place setting of china, appeared to glow from within. His eyes, turned upward, were intent upon someone or something just off the canvas. Though they never shifted, I would watch those eyes follow me every time I moved about the office.

Cloud Jesus didn't say anything, he just looked at me with those same eyes I'd seen in the painting, the ones that searched you over like they were looking into you and through you at the same time, shining their light into all the dark places of your heart, the places you'd tried to hide from everyone. Like they were drilling through all that darkness and muck to get to the truth. And that's how I knew it was really Jesus.

THIS ABOVE ALL

Who else could see into your soul like that?

Peter thought I was crazy and told me as much, but when I told him, my dad insisted, almost giddily, that it was a revelation.

"You're just like Paul!" he'd said. "Remember? On the road to Damascus, Saul was struck down by a vision of Christ in the sky. God turned his hardened heart, and he became the Apostle Paul."

Peter rolled his eyes.

Dad continued, undeterred. "Jesus has never revealed himself so visibly to any of the rest of us. That means He must have big plans in store for you."

The following Sunday, I was baptized.

"Piper Hope Ryan, do you renounce Satan and all forces of the underworld that rebel against God?" my father asked me as I stood before a crowd of twenty of our church's congregants who'd gathered at the YMCA's swimming pool for the occasion, since our church didn't have a proper baptismal fount.

I wore a threadbare t-shirt to cover my fire-engine-red one-piece swimsuit a season too small. I could smell the fried chicken and my mother's homemade cheese potatoes topped with cornflakes wafting in from the adjoining fellowship room. She and my older sisters had busied themselves all morning making sure everything was all set up for the pitch-in lunch afterward. They swatted the younger children's hands as they tried to steal tastes from beneath the tented aluminum foil.

I licked my lips. "I do."

My father motioned for me to enter the shallow end of the pool and wade over to where he stood. The water, clouded by a recent shock of chemicals, splashed up at my armpits and was so cold it sent a shiver reverberating down my spine. Through iron lungs and a clenched jaw, I struggled to take a breath. In an instant, goose bumps covered my whole body.

"Do you renounce all sinful desires that draw you from the love of God? The lust and hatred in your heart, the wandering of your eyes, your self-righteousness and your own iniquity?" my father asked. He placed a heavy hand on my shoulder. I searched his eyes, a bit unsure of what I was agreeing to. "Do you?" He gave a solemn little nod as if to encourage me on. I nodded. "If so, say 'I do.'"

"I do," I said.

"Do you turn to Jesus Christ and accept him as your Savior?"

"I do."

"Do you promise to trust and obey the Lord your God all the days of your life?"

"I do."

"And do you promise to yield yourself to the leadership of the Church, of which God has appointed me its righteous earthly spiritual head?"

"I do."

"Do you pledge to obey and follow the teachings of this church until Christ returns or the Lord calls you home?"

"I do."

"Piper, because you have made a public profession of your faith, I baptize you in the name of the Father, the Son, and the Holy Spirit."

I brought my hand up to plug my nose, closed my eyes, and waited to feel my father's rough, knobby fingers behind my neck. My dad placed one hand there and another on my chest and tipped me backward. I plunged beneath the water and hoped I'd be able to feel it as the evil and sin melted away from my body.

What would it feel like to be pure and clean? Would I actually feel any different at all? All of my older siblings had been baptized already, and as far as I could tell, not much changed in them from before they'd been dunked. Phoebe was still self-righteous, and Peter had his mean-streak.

Still, I hoped it would be different with me. That cloud-Jesus would clean me from the inside out.

I expected to rise back up quickly, but moments passed, and I found myself still suspended beneath the surface. I stopped trying to feel the cleansing process and instead, started to panic. I let go of my nose and thrashed my arms upward, clawing at my father's torso. My dad held his hand firmly against my chest and dug his stubby nails further into the scruff of my neck, catching a bit of my ponytail in his hand as he did.

I tried to grab at his forearm to pull myself up. I kicked and bucked. But the tangy water silenced my screams as it entered my mouth and lungs. My chest ached, and my nostrils burned.

I opened my eyes. For a moment, I could see the figure of my father above me, his face blurred and distorted by the surface of the pool. Soon, it was as if my body was shutting down. I felt my heart lull and my legs relax. I stopped fighting it and allowed myself to go limp with fatigue and resignation. I was certain it was all over for me, that I would be meeting the real Jesus in the clouds very soon.

Then I felt myself being lifted up. Higher and higher I rose, leaving the water behind to lap at my ankles and kiss my toes. When I felt the air rush against my face, I sucked it in through my clenched teeth, greedily filling my lungs with as much they could take. As soon as I opened my mouth, I started to cough, and the sound bounced off the walls of the natatorium, growing louder and more vibrant in its echoes. I realized the sound had come from clapping, not my coughing.

"Yes indeed," Dad said. "God had big plans for you."

Somehow I doubt being Romeo is what my dad—or God—had in mind.

CHAPTER SIX

At Salvatore's, Dad tells me to go in ahead to put our names down for a table while he and other siblings unload from the van. I'm waiting by the host stand when I find I'm eye level with a familiar face. Tony is standing there, rolling silverware into maroon cloth napkins. I know at least half a dozen girls in our class who have a crush on him because they talk about him or giggle around him constantly. He shakes his hair from his eyes and smiles when he sees me, a killer white grin that spreads across his whole face. It's like something out of a Crest commercial.

Okay. I get it. Studying him up close like this, I have to admit somehow when I wasn't looking, he grew up, but in my head, he's still the scrawny kid who cried when he messed up his solo in "Pie Jesu" as part of the Ridgedale Municipal Children's Choir (him) and Orchestra (me). He's just more chiseled now. And has a deeper voice.

"Piper?" he asks.

Of the dozens of times we've come here, I've never seen him, and he never mentioned seeing me, either. "Hey, Tony. I didn't know you worked here."

"It's a new development. As of last week, actually. My uncle is *the* Salvatore so nepotism is alive and well." He glances behind me. "Table for... one?"

"Uh," I mentally run down the list of who's coming. "Eleven. My dad and the rest of the family are right behind." My siblings, a couple of their spouses and dad. It takes them forever to unload from the vans. "A few tables near each other is fine."

Tony reaches beneath the host stand and grabs a stack of menus though none of us will need them. Half the reason Salvatore's is on the acceptable eat-out list is the family style pastas. Two large orders of spaghetti and meatballs is miraculously enough to feed all of us. Like Jesus' loaves and fishes, we're really good at making food stretch.

"So I guess we'll be seeing a lot more of each other now, huh?" He picks up a specials flyer and stacks it atop the menus.

"You know, I went out for Romeo, but Brooks had me read for Mercutio instead."

I glance at the door to make sure my family is still outside, out of earshot. "Well, I tried out for Juliet and, well..."

The corner of Tony's mouth curls into a faint smile. "Romeo is kind of critical to the play so Brooks will only want the best of the best."

I roll my eyes. "That's not me. Definitely, not me. Honestly, I don't know why he cast me. At least I wasn't laughed off the stage." Yet.

"Laughed off what stage?" Peter asks coming up behind me. He's got Paula and Pearl with him and Dad and my older sisters and a couple of their husbands follow with the rest of the kids.

"Oh, nothing." I shoot Tony a desperate glance, and the way he stops talking tells me he understands.

Tony's gaze flicks to Peter and back to me. I could swear there's a hint of pity behind his eyes. "I'll show you to your tables."

Dinner is as it always is: a jumble of forks, spilled ice water, balled napkins, and Dad praying over the food for so long that by the time the pasta bowls are filled, the spaghetti's gone cold. Dad gives our effeminate server the side-eye more than once and talks loudly around the subject of sexual sin whenever the server's within earshot. It's his brand of "subtlety."

"You should finish your salad." Peter eyes my half-eaten portion.

It takes everything I have not to roll my eyes. "Yes, Mother," I mumble. He's fourteen months older than me but constantly harping on everything I do. Or don't do. Eat this, do this, stand up straight. He thinks I'm intimidated. Usually, I'm just annoyed. "How about you worry about the *log* in your own eye?" I snap, nodding toward his untouched meatball.

Oblivious, Dad keeps going on and on about the stuff he's been researching for his latest sermon series. I take a sip of my water, but don't touch my salad at all. Instead, I try to tune them all out, thinking about what Tony said earlier. *Brooks wants the best of the best.* That couldn't possibly be me. Could it?

I've never been in love myself; I'm not even sure I believe in a love like Romeo and Juliet's, the kind you'd literally risk everything for. Could I even do him justice? And what's more, I'm a total newbie. How could I convincingly portray one of the greatest lovers of all time?

And... opposite a girl?

CHAPTER SEVEN

We spend the first week of play rehearsals reading through the script, but by Monday for our full-day workshop, Mr. Brooks is ready to start getting serious. My dad thinks I'm volunteering at the nursing home today, but in reality, Mr. Brooks has other plans.

"The first thing we've got to get you all to do is learn how to fight." He introduces Mr. Ferreira, the dude who is an expert in Capoeira—some type of Brazilian martial arts and dance hybrid. He's going to teach us how to move our feet.

Chloe and a few of the other girls stand in front stage watching as Mr. Brooks calls us up. "Ladies, you, too."

"But who am I going to have to stage fight?" Chloe asks innocently. She crosses her arms.

"No one. But the drama department is paying Mr. Ferreira to be here, so we're going to get our money's worth. If nothing else, think of this as a team building exercise."

Chloe huffs and climbs the stairs. The other girls follow her, but I notice Ashley looks kind of excited as she steps up next to me. She smiles at me and takes the stance Mr. Ferreira suggests.

After an hour of learning the *ginga* and how to pivot on the balls of our feet and rock back and forth defensively and offensively, Mr. Ferreira says we're ready for the *Roda*. We circle up as he beats a drum and Mr. Brooks shakes a tambourine.

"I will call off your numbers two at a time," says Mr. Brooks, "and those people will step forward and sort of challenge each other."

Umm. What? We just learned how to do this, and I still don't even understand what, exactly, we're doing, but I don't have time to dwell on it because all of a sudden, he's calling out my number and I'm in the circle with... Chloe.

Fan-freaking-tastic.

She tries to bob and weave, keeping time with the music, and I have no choice but to follow her. She goes left so I jut right. She comes forward, and I step back. It's tricky in a skirt and that gives Chloe a slight advantage over me. We bob and weave around each other and all I can think is thank God we aren't really holding daggers or rapiers because the look she's giving me makes me want to take her out. She scrunches her nose every time I get close and never have I so badly wanted to knock someone off of her feet.

Chloe steps left, and I'm not prepared to change directions; I lose my balance, falling on top of her. The circle of onlookers gives way, and we tumble off the apron.

"Omph," I grunt. My shin slams into the edge of the stage.

Chloe screams. Or shrieks, really. "I think my elbow is broken!"

Brooks hops to the stage and pulls us both up, checking out Chloe's arm. "It's only your funny bone. Hurts like a beast, but you'll be right as rain in a moment."

Chloe holds her arm protectively and glares at me. "You did that on purpose, *lesbo*," she sneers, barely above a whisper.

After the Capoeira session, we're all exhausted, but Mr. Brooks tells us to rub some dirt on it. "The theatre is hard work. Plan accordingly." He gives us forty-five minutes for lunch and then says we're going to get into blocking. "And the props and sets crew will be here to get started on their bit." Which means we'll have an audience.

Everyone scurries off to lunch, and I'm left alone in the auditorium with my smashed peanut butter sandwich and home-bagged pretzels. I'm about to plop down in the corner when Tony asks if want to head over to the burger place across the street.

"Me?" I ask, eyeing the backs of a handful of other cast members with whom he's probably friends. They're pushing their way out the front toward the row of fast food spots across the street.

"No, the other Romeo behind you. Of course you. Come on."

I ditch my smooshed sandwich in the trash can and follow him.

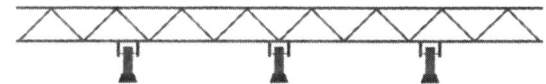

"That was brilliant," Tony says, dipping a fry into some Siracha mayo.

"What do you mean?"

"Going after Chloe, like that. Throwing her off balance. Who needs swords?"

"I tripped. I didn't do it on purpose."

Tony eyes me and licks his lips. "Sure you didn't. I'm sure it was completely innocent."

I open my mouth to protest, but he's laughing so I drop it.

"You're not at all like they say, you know?"

"Like what who says?"

He waves his hand. "You know. People." He eyes me steadily. "Come on, you have to know your family is a bit... notorious around here. I'm just saying you seem different somehow. Were you always like this?" His lips purse to the side, and he taps his chin. "You seem more *progressive*."

I stop mid-bite. Progressive? If I were Catholic, I'd have to make the sign of the cross right now. "Get behind me Satan." I smile broadly so Tony knows I am, in fact, joking. Satan can take on many forms, but I don't actually think Tony's one of them.

"So what does your family think about you being Romeo?"

"Oh. Umm."

"Wait, they don't know?"

I press my lips together. "Not exactly. I'm going to tell them. I mean, I have to tell them. But when the time's right."

Tony nods slightly, but he can't hide the pity in his eyes. "It must be tough."

"What?"

"Pretending to be one way for your family's benefit when you're really something else."

"I'm not pretending. I'm just not sure what I'm supposed to be." Or if what I'm supposed to want and what I actually want are the same things anymore.

"Ah, so questioning, then?" Tony asks.

"Asking questions, sure," I say. Some of which, I'm pretty sure, there are no good answers for. "So Mercutio, huh?"

"Yeah. I get to play your loyal sidekick. Your BFF." He rolls his eyes. "Not the most amazing role, but at least I get a kick ass fight out of it."

"I read once that Shakespeare said that he had to kill Mercutio or else Mercutio would have killed him."

"Meaning?"

"Mercutio had to die or else he'd have stolen the whole show."

"I guess I've got my work cut out for me."

"You and me both."

"You'll be great," Tony says. I can't tell if he's just saying it to say it or if he really means it, but either way, I appreciate it. "You planning to study theater in college?"

I nearly choke on my French fry. "Ha. Funny."

"How is that funny? You are planning to go to college, right?"

I nod. Well, I hope so. Dad would have me go to a Bible college, but I'm not so sure that path is for me. Not that it wouldn't be great to get a solid biblical education, but so far, all of my sisters who've gone end up finding husbands and dropping out after a year. I feel like there's a lot of things I want to do before all of... that.

"Let me guess, Wheaton? Olivette?"

I thought about Wheaton, and it would definitely be a good compromise. A real college with a strong foundation of faith. "Northwestern is my top choice." It's the first time I've actually said it out loud.

"Impressive." Tony nods approvingly. My gaze flicks to his, but he's not looking at me anymore, he's looking behind me. Staring is more like it. I turn to see what's caught his attention. Some guy picking up a greasy sack of burgers and fries. He nods at Tony before making toward the door.

"You know him?" I turn back.

Tony shakes his head and shrugs, dipping another fry in the mayo. "Nope."

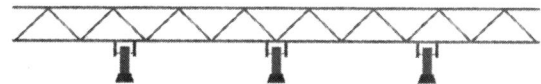

After lunch, we spend a while working on a few scenes that don't include me so I get some time to read my book for English and work on the Calculus homework I've been putting off. But by mid-afternoon, Mr. Brooks decides he's ready for me. Well, for Romeo.

"People, people." Mr. Brooks comes up the center aisle clapping his hands. "Take your seats; we've got loads to get through this afternoon."

Jenn bursts through the back doors. "Sorry, I'm late," she mumbles.

"Ah, Miss Thompson. Decided to finally grace us with your presence?"

She smiles awkwardly and starts down the center aisle toward the apron.

Brooks holds up a hand. "You may leave for the day."

She stops mid-stride. "What?" Her arms fall limply to her sides. "Are you serious?"

"As a heart attack. Come back when you are also serious."

Whoa. Brooks mentioned punctuality before, but clearly, he means it. I make a mental note to not be late. Judging by my castmates' faces, they're thinking the same thing.

"Now, where was I?" He explains that we might as well tackle the most difficult scene now. We all assume that means the Romeo and Juliet death scene, and I glance at Chloe. She keeps her eyes forward and her face firm, still cradling her arm. At least no one can say she's not dramatic. "Ah, right. Thanks to the dramatic irony, the final death scene is the most difficult for the audience, but the most difficult for the players is Mercutio and Tybalt's death scenes."

I've read through the scene of course, we all have. We spent the last week doing nothing but reading and memorizing. But what strikes me is that the bulk of the action is nuanced not scripted. Sure, there are some famous lines—'a plague on both your houses' comes from this scene. But most of what happens is internal and the result of each player not knowing what the other knows. Mercutio and Tybalt don't know about Romeo's marriage to Juliet and for whatever reason, he chooses not to tell them. Or he tries to, but they don't really hear him. So they make all these assumptions and it doesn't end well.

Mr. Brooks calls us to the stage. It's me, Tony, and this kid Robert, who is Tybalt. Plus the Montague crew.

Mr. Brooks explains his vision for the scene and how he wants us to use the space. "First, we'll read through the scene and tentatively walk through it. Then we're going to go off-book as best we can and fully engage with the material. I want you start thinking about the physicality of your characters. And you can try and put your Capoeira training into use with these." He passes out some fake daggers, the kind where the plastic blade is spring-loaded and retracts when you press it against something. I'm not sure how to grip mine properly and Tony shows me where to put my hand.

"It's a knife, not a spoon." He laughs.

The read through was fine because we were all so focused on the words themselves and making them right that it doesn't really feel like acting. Not yet, anyway. But when it comes time to drop the book and try it for real, I'm a ball of nerves.

"Take it from Benvolio's line," Mr. Brooks says. Which is great because it means I don't have to go first. In fact, there's a whole heap of this scene before Romeo ever appears. So I watch the others maneuver about as they recite their lines. I can tell everyone is approaching the scene timidly. Like they're intimidated maybe, but trying.

"*Here comes my man,*" says Robert. Er, Tybalt.

My *man*? Man. Right, man. I'm a man.

I close my eyes for a moment, trying to push my nerves aside and focus on the scene, on getting into the mind and heart of Romeo and going with it. As if no one else is watching. Not Tony. Not Mr. Brooks. Not Chloe. And especially not Dylan who's standing over there with the prop people, sketching out the space and putting bits of blue painter's tape on the floor. I don't think he even knows who I am at this point. Probably completely forgot about the park incident altogether.

Anyway, I know that if I let myself think of him, of any of them, really, I'll totally freeze up.

So I don't. I think of nothing except what Shakespeare would have me think of. Which is 1) Juliet 2) not killing Tybalt and 3) blind rage. And once I let go of everything else, I'm off. When I release of all the other voices in my head, it's surprisingly easy to slide into Romeo's psyche, and I find it doesn't matter if he's a guy. He could be a leprechaun or a horse, and it wouldn't change much.

As I'm saying the lines, I try to determine exactly where Romeo is in his head. How much he loves Juliet, how the love is mostly lust, and how it all at first sets him free and then at some point he realizes that his love for her has in some ways emasculated him. And some combination of that anger and his fury over his best friend's death propels him into this ridiculously intense moment where he gives up the control he was trying so desperately to sustain and instead gives in to his fury. Allows it to overtake him.

We dart around the stage, modulating our emotions as the script calls for it. Tybalt scampers off, and I give chase, not even worrying about whether my skirt flips up a bit above my knees. I watch as he writhes on the stage and "dies." I take a step back and think about what just happened. I look at Romeo's hands, now bloodied. "*O, I am fortune's fool!*" I scream, pulling from the depths of myself, channeling something inside of me that feels primal. It comes out raspier than I intended and when my knees hit the stage, it kind of hurts.

I think I nailed it. Maybe?

But if I nailed it then why is it so quiet? I open my eyes and see everyone staring at me.

Mr. Brooks is silent. Tony, who's supposed to be lying dead, is propped on his elbows looking at me. Robert, who is also supposed to be dead is sitting there wide-eyed. Even Chloe is staring at me. Is that shock on her face? Horror?

Oh, no. I got too into it, and now Mr. Brooks is probably trying to figure out a way to remove me from the cast for overacting or something. I chew my lip. Why won't anyone say anything? Even the set crewmembers have fallen absolutely silent. All of their eyes are trained on me.

Finally I hobble to my feet and laugh nervously. "Umm, are we stopping there?"

"Let's take a five minute break," Mr. Brooks mumbles. He's eying me, but his expression is indecipherable. That mustache.

So, I turn and bolt from the stage before anyone can say anything to me. I push through the side door to the hallway and make a break for the water fountain, which, right now, is absolutely screaming my name. It's as if I have something lodged in my throat.

Like maybe a giant ball of inadequacy.

Tony chases after me and smacks me on the back when he catches up. "Holy shit!"

It startles me and my face goes too far into the stream of water.

"What?" I wipe the drips from my chin with the back of my hand. "Was I really *that* horrible?" I kind of want to disappear, like if I turned into a pillar of salt right now, maybe that would be okay.

"Horrible?" Dylan asks from behind me. I spin around; he's leaning against the doorway to the stage watching Tony and me. "Umm, you were really good." His gaze finds mine for the first time since the incident in the park and he offers me a little half smile.

"Really good," Tony adds. "Really freaking good."

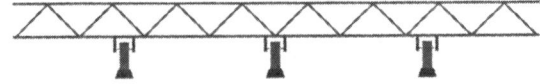

Part of living in Central Illinois means we're in close proximity to a bunch of colleges and universities. For the better part of my childhood, our church has traveled around to them, focusing on outreach and evangelism or even protesting when the situation warrants. It was a lot easier when we were homeschooling, so the past few years, I haven't gone along as often.

"Centers of higher education are cesspools for fornication. The Lord is calling us into Nineveh so we can call them to repentance. To tell them to turn from their vile and wicked ways," my dad says.

This afternoon we're at the branch of the State University in town. We set up shop in front of the student union. Dad has Peter dole out various signs with Scripture emblazoned on them and the rest of us are to chant and sing while students walk past us on their way to and from class. Well, I hold the sign and move my lips, but today I can't bring myself to say anything at all.

At the point when he feels we've reached a critical mass of a hundred or so onlookers, my dad begins to preach, engaging students in debate. He smiles and rocks back on his heels. "You know what the Bible says? It says you all can go to hell." He points to the sign I hold. It reads 'Roman 6:23.' "It's what you've earned, after all. What, with your wickedness and hatred and lust." He pays special attention to a couple girls in *hijab*, but they get up and leave.

A few students scoff and mimic him, but he is wholly unfazed. Actually, I think it adds fuel to his fire. Like the more they mock him, the louder his preaching gets.

"*Who hath woe? Who hath sorrow? Who hath contentions? Who hath babbling? Who hath wounds without cause? Who hath redness of eyes?*" he sings, gesturing to a kid who is, obviously, high as a kite. The kid is wearing a Che Guevara t-shirt and looks like he hasn't bathed in a few days. "*Woe unto their soul! For they have rewarded evil unto themselves.*" He continues on a tirade against the perversion of college campuses slamming the fornicators and Greek houses and the plethora of abortions committed in the name of personal liberty.

"You are not free. You were purchased at a price!" One of my siblings chimes in.

My dad peppers the students with verses. Pelts them, really. About homosexuality. Lust. Greed. Wrath. Sin.

Bam! Bam! Bam! Judgment in staccato!

I can hear his voice ricochet off the buildings. It pops and splatters, covering the whole crowd with snippets of his exhortation. Soon, a couple of students hone in on my dad. They taunt him, flaunting their sexuality by lifting their skirts higher or pressing their chests out. One guy kisses another guy.

I lower my sign and head to the side of the makeshift barricade.

"Oh no you don't," my dad says, leading me by the shoulder and guiding me toward a crowd of students sitting there, minding their own business and enjoying a break from class. He grabs Peter and Paula, too. "It's high time you teach your siblings how to evangelize properly." Dad winks at me as he ushers me toward a group of onlookers.

"Show 'em what you've got," he whispers in my ear.

I step toward the crowd and even though I don't really want to do this. I also don't want to disappoint my dad who's standing there, beaming at me. "You there," I call, gesturing to a couple guys in baseball hats. "Do you know that you're going to hell?"

"No, I'm not," the one guy says. He's wearing a black hat with a cursive 'O's' on it. "I'm Catholic."

Peter smiles and gives me a knowing look. Just like my dad, he's waiting for me to lay into this guy.

I reach into the folds of my mind and try to think about the scriptures I know that specifically condemn Catholic dogma. "Uh, it is written, *For the law appoints as high priests men in all their weakness; but the oath, which came after the law, appointed the Son who has been made perfect forever.*"

It's an obscure passage from Hebrews. At least, I think it's Hebrews. Or is it Ephesians? Truthfully, I'm not even sure what it means except that Jesus is greater than the priests. I don't know a whole lot of Catholics, but I doubt they would contest that. Right now, it's all I got. I widen my stance and try to stare the guy down. Maybe he'll be intimidated enough to back off and then this whole thing can be over.

The kid chews the corner of his thumb and glances at his buddy. "Yeah, well, the Bible also says." He pauses, pulls a Bible out of his backpack, and flips it open, searching for the exact verse he wants. It's so small, it pretty much fits in his palm. Either the writing had to be tiny or the Bible incomplete. Maybe it's an abridged version. For my sake, I hope it is. For as many demonstrations as I've participated in, I've never seen someone challenge my father with an actual Bible in hand. Great.

Dad nods encouragingly, and I notice Peter is covering his mouth with his hand, trying to hide his smirk.

"It says, *But God demonstrates his own love for us in this: While we were still sinners, Christ died for us. Since we have now been justified by his blood, how much more shall we be saved from God's wrath through him! For if, when we were God's enemies, we were reconciled to him through the death of his Son, how much more, having been reconciled, shall we be saved through his life!*"

Romans 5. I know it.

The kid closes the Bible on his finger and sits back, watching and waiting for my response. I don't have my Bible on me, but I've memorized so much Scripture that I should be able to come up with a rebuttal. I search the recesses of my brain, comb through the memories there. All the hours we spent memorizing Scripture, often under duress as we knelt on unpopped popcorn kernels until we got it right. I've got... nothing.

Paula taps my calf with the stick of her sign and jerks her head, as if to say, "Say something."

Dad's face darkens and his eyes seem to plead.

The Catholic guy and his buddies just sit there. Staring. Finally the guy's friend says, "Well, don't you have a response?"

I sigh and look at my family and then back to the guy. "Not really, no. The Bible does say that."

"So you still think we're going to hell?"

Before I can respond, Phoebe swoops over and I can almost feel my dad's shoulders relax in relief. "Yes. You are going to hell."

The kid reads it again. "So, what does that mean to you?"

Phoebe rolls her shoulders back, puffing her chest out just a bit. "*For all have sinned and fall short of the glory of God.* And I don't have to tell you that the 'wages of sin is death.' It's right there. Romans 6."

The kid smiles. "But finish that verse."

She gapes at him and puts her hands on her hips. "It is finished."

He turns the page. "No. Finish the verse. It continues and says, *But the gift of God is eternal life...*"

"*In Jesus Christ our Lord,*" she says. "That's how it finishes. And if you don't have Jesus, you don't get eternal life, either."

"How can you tell me I don't have Jesus?" the kid asks. By now, a small cluster has formed around him, mostly students eager to see if their comrade can beat us at our own game. Peter, Paula, and I step back along the side, watching her engage in the debate that I could not.

As I listen to the guy debate with my sister, I find myself agreeing with his points. Or at least, understanding them. Dad's always been so insistent that these campuses would be full of fornicators and heathens that I'd practically expected to see blood dripping from their mouths. But in all our years doing this, I'd never really seen anything like that, had I? And this guy had a Bible in his backpack. That he carried around with him. To class.

That means something, doesn't it?

"The book of Isaiah says, *Woe to those who call evil good, and good evil; Who put darkness for light, and light for darkness; Who put bitter for sweet, and sweet for bitter!*"

"But how can you say that I do that? You don't know me from... from Adam."

Phoebe rocks back on her heels and smiles. "You're here, aren't you?"

The kid shakes his head and rises to his feet. "Yeah, I suppose I am. But you know what? So are you."

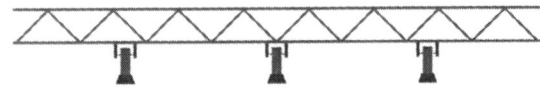

When we get home this evening I think about that permission form I have hidden between the pages of my Chem notebook. I know after this afternoon's disappointment, I can't ask for my Dad's permission, or if I do, I know he won't grant it. But somehow, I also know that I absolutely have to go. Even if I am a sheep among wolves.

So I do the only thing I can: I forge my dad's signature and turn it in to Mr. Brooks.

CHAPTER EIGHT

The charter bus has like fifty seats, but there are only about forty of us, Mrs. D's AP English students plus the twenty or so members of the cast and crew, but there's some overlap. We have to meet up in the school parking lot at 6 a.m. to make it to Chicago in time for an early lunch and the matinee of *King Lear*. I throw my stuff down in a window seat and avoid eye contact with anyone. Most people will have to double up, but it would be great if I had a row to myself. But no, Tony plops down next to me before I can protest.

"Seat taken?" He grins.

I shake my head. Okay, I guess I can handle sitting next to the Italian Stallion. If I must. I catch a glimpse of him in profile and even though I'm not attracted to him like that, I can see why other girls are. Strong jawline and lashes that go for days. To say nothing of how he's clearly spent a lot of time in the gym. His bicep flexes as he pushes himself forward, and I feel my cheeks flare at the inappropriate turn my thoughts have taken.

Thankfully, Tony doesn't seem to notice. "So how'd you convince your parents to let you come?"

Oh, that. My small lie and bigger rebellion. "I, uh, told them I'm going to a lock-in with Jodi that starts right after school." When I told him, Dad had been so thrilled that Jodi is going to a church event of her own volition that he didn't even care when I said it was Korean PCA.

"At least they're reformed," Phoebe had said.

Tony smiles. "You won't get busted?"

"I hope not." I am weaving a dangerous web. Tug one string and the whole thing could unravel.

"You know, I've been reading up on Mercutio, and you were right. I read there are some productions that never recover after he dies."

Yikes. "Hopefully not ours. No offense."

He laughs. "None taken. And no, something tells me that won't happen with ours." He winks, pulls out an e-reader, and flips on the tiny reading light above his seat. While we wait for the stragglers to load up, he steals my *Newsweek* so I grab his e-reader and check out his book choices. Lots of stuff by someone named Michael Cart and something called *Hero* by Perry Moore. Also, some David Levithan, including *Boy Meets Boy* and *Lover's Dictionary*, neither of which I've read.

"Any good?" I ask.

He flashes me a sheepish grin and shrugs. "Yeah. You could say that."

The last few people make their way down the aisle toward the back of the bus. I don't know why anyone prefers the back of a charter bus. You're near the bathroom.

Dylan slips down the aisle and when our eyes meet, he nods at me. And was that a smile? He slides into a seat next to some other senior guy in the row in front of us. The other guy keeps his shoulders squared, his legs wide so that he takes up the entire seat, even though he doesn't really need it. Do all guys do that? I look at my own crossed legs, the way I fold myself up so I seem to take up less space. Hmm.

Dylan relaxes into the seat and his leg bends so that part of it is sticking out in the aisle. I try the same, stretching my legs out into a wide, protruding V. I'm wearing shorts under my skirt today, so it's not like I'm being indecent or anything. I relax my arms so that my elbows press into my thighs. It's eleven kinds of awkward and completely uncomfortable, but I wonder if I look like a boy?

"You're doing it wrong," Tony says. I snap my attention back to him and away from Dylan. A grin spreads across his face. "Relax your shoulders and lean forward a bit, like you're arching your back out."

I do as he says and smile self-consciously back at him. "Better?"

"Now, let your hands hang over, like this." He demonstrates and I have to admit, it looks more relaxed and natural than when my hands were sticking out over my knees. "You've got to take up more space, adopt an assertive pose."

I try it and he sighs. "No, no, no. You're Jack Lemmon when you should be Dustin Hoffman."

"What?"

"*Some like it Hot*? Jack Lemmon dressed in drag? Terrible impersonation of a woman. But Dustin Hoffman in Tootsie? Awesome."

"I haven't seen either of those."

He waves dismissively. "Forget it. Just, move your shoulders down more."

"Like this?" I press my shoulders wide, elbows out.

He nods. "There you go. Now if you scratch your balls, you'll be spot on."

CHAPTER NINE

The Courtyard Theater is impressive. It's on the back end of Navy Pier. Or maybe it's the front end? Whatever end is furthest out in the water, that's where the theater is. Out past the shops and the giant Ferris Wheel.

It's a thrust stage like the original Globe, which means it juts out into the audience, and the seats sort of wrap around it so that if you were down in front, the actors would practically be in your lap. And the auditorium is also a lot like the Globe Theater, where many of Shakespeare's plays were originally performed, only I imagine this is much nicer. For one thing, there's no hay on the floor. For another, everyone gets to sit. In Shakespeare's day, the commoners like us would be down below in a bunch of hay, standing for the entire performance.

We're in the dress circle or mezzanine level. Because our group was originally only the AP students, we're split up and seated in two sections across from each other. This means I can watch as Frank Green makes stupid faces at his buddy Curt Mueller. Great.

"Dude, we can all see you," Tony whispers shaking his head.

He's sitting next to me in the front row of our section. They're pretty good seats, really. And the theater is packed mostly with other school groups. Mrs. D is excited because she plans her syllabus around what the Chicago Shakespeare Theater's performing and she loves *Lear*. Apparently, *Romeo and Juliet* was last year's tragedy.

Soon, the lights dim and Kent and Gloucester are on the stage, talking. I lean forward to watch as King Lear himself makes his entrance.

King Lear is arguably Shakespeare's dramatic masterpiece and certainly, Lear is one of his greatest characters. Though I've read of his descent into madness (thanks, Mrs. D), this is the first time I've ever gotten to watch it unfold on stage. And the actor who plays Lear is talented like whoa. Halfway through the act, I have to remind myself I'm watching an actor and not some actual guy named Lear. As the scenes progress, his whole physicality shifts from a strong, self-assured leader to a self-conscious rogue, and I know his descent is far from finished.

"So what do you think so far?" Tony asks as the lights come up for intermission.

"Amazing," I say. I can't really think of how else to describe it.

"The nature of human suffering," he says.

"What?"

"Probing it like that. Unflinching and all. Shakespeare was a badass."

"Yeah," I say. It wasn't exactly what I was thinking, but I guess it fits.

We're quiet for a moment before Tony whispers, "Yeah well, and that Kent is pretty hot."

Wait, what? Did I hear him right? Tony keeps his eyes forward and doesn't look at me for a long moment. He glances over. I can tell by his blank expression he's waiting for my reaction.

"Err..." I'm trying not to react, not to let my eyes bug out or shift away from him or gasp or turn red or any number of things my body wants me to do because I know being homosexual—simply being attracted to members of the same sex—is not inherently a sin. But homosexual behavior? Actually acting on those desires? That's a whole other ball of wax. The Bible is pretty clear on that front.

I steal a glance at Tony and wonder if he has acted on them. Because that would definitely change things, wouldn't it? Associating with a known homo is like associating with a fornicator. Or an idolater. In the Paul's second letter to the Corinthians he said, *"Do not be yoked together with unbelievers. For what do righteousness and wickedness have in common? Or what fellowship can light have with darkness?"* Or as my dad would summarize, if you lie down with dogs, you're bound to wake up with fleas. Not that Tony is a dog. Far from it. Of all the people in the cast, he's basically the only one who's given me the time of day. And I think about that last bit. 'What fellowship can light have with darkness?' I'm not trying to argue with the Bible or anything, it's just light cannot exist without darkness nor darkness without light, can it? One reveals the other. Maybe that's the task God's putting before me. Maybe the entire reason I'm in this cast, spending so much time with Tony is to minister to him. To be the light that helps him recognize his darkness.

Tony shifts in his seat away from me as if to give me space, and I try to take a deep breath without seeming like I am. Why Tony would confide in me of all possible people is a bit of a mystery. Or maybe he's already out and I didn't know? Although I doubt it since about six different girls who are at present lusting after him. Like Chloe Wennert who's across the galley and keeps making these weird noises and flipping her hair every time she looks his direction. She's been watching Tony this entire time.

I glance up to see her staring at us. And two rows in front of her is Dylan. And he's staring, too. But at me, I think. I look away quickly; when I glance back up, he's still watching me, like he's studying me. This intense gaze that makes me feel like a specimen or something.

It's kind of creepy. But I realize it's exactly what I've been doing to him lately, studying his movements, trying to mimic the way he carries himself. Pretty much every time I'm around him, I can't help but watch the way he shifts and fidgets. The way he hinges and unhinges his jaw when he's thinking. The way he hunches his shoulders forward or rolls them back, depending. That's different though.

It's research.

I'm grateful when the lights go back down. He might still be watching me, but at least I can't see him. Also, I hope Tony can't see when I shift uncomfortably in my seat. He's not contagious, I know. And I also know it's not like his homosexuality means he has AIDS or something. At least, not definitely. I move my hands from the armrest and into my lap.

The last three Acts are mind-blowing, which is a welcome distraction. The stage design is cool—modern and minimalist, which, I think, is what Mr. Brooks is hoping to do with our production, too. But when the storm comes in Act III, Lear is wandering around upstage and a hundred light bulbs on strings drop from the ceiling, flickering and swaying. The effect is like a lightning storm only cooler. Definitely more abstract.

Lear himself is amazing. So much so that when he comes out for his curtain call, I spring to my feet, clap wildly and drag Tony to his feet, too. Because Lear is that good.

Mr. Brooks' words flood into my head. "I really want you to see it." Holy Moses, I hope he doesn't expect that level of a performance from me. I mean, for one, I'm completely new to this. Two, I'm in high school, not a professional actor. That guy probably trained with the Royal Shakespeare... something. I scan the playbill. Yup. Shakespeare Theater Company's Academy for Classical Acting.

After the play is over, we're instructed to stay in our seats and wait for our group to leave together. I rest my hands against the rail and watch the tops of the heads below as they shuffle out the door. One kid puts his arm around a girl's shoulder and she squeals. Another pack of girls all whisper and giggle at something else. My eyes drift higher, and I'm watching Dylan again. What is it about him that I can't seem to look away from? He's got a pencil behind his ear and another in his hand and he's writing something in a notebook. He pauses for a minute, scratches his head, and keeps writing, chewing the corner of his cheek so that he pulls to the side. Today he's wearing pseudo-skinny pants and, I've noticed, he can indeed rock them.

He looks up and catches me watching him, but this time he's smiling. I return it with a little grin, a raised eyebrow and an unspoken question. "What gives?"

"Idea," he mouths tapping his forehead and nodding toward the set, I think. He goes back to his notebook and a single strand of hair falls forward against his cheek.

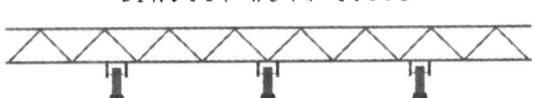

Since we're in Chicago, we have to go for pizza. It's like a law or something, I think. And we opt for Giordano's. So it's not the *very* best deep dish in Chicago, but it's pretty good and maybe more importantly, they're able to accommodate our massive group. The catch is, we have to go to dinner at four. It's okay though, because the pizzas take like an hour to cook anyway.

"People, people," Mrs. D says above the noise and hubbub as we congregate in the restaurant's lobby and a few of us spill out onto the street. "Here's the deal: as a table, you may order one large pizza to share between you. You can also order one appetizer for the table and sodas. Capiche?"

Tony sticks close to me. I keep thinking about his confession from earlier. "Don't tell anyone though," he said quickly. "I'm not *there* yet, you know?"

"Of course," I said. "It's none of my business anyway." It isn't any of my business, but truthfully, I'm not really sure what to do with it or how to process it. Or even why he told me. It's safe to say he knows who my family is. What we think. And what we *do*.

It doesn't change who he is; I know that. But it is weird to always think something is one way and discover it's been something else all along. Like when you drive by the same park your whole life and one day, realize there's a statue or something there. It's always been there you just weren't paying attention. Or it was hiding behind a tree. Or whatever.

I glance over and watch as Chloe flirts with him. He flashes her that grin and I'm struck by what that really means. I'm pretending to be Romeo for a few weeks. Tony's been pretending for most of his life. Difficult as that would be, it's still probably easier than the alternative.

My dad says there are places for people like Tony where they can get counseling, intense therapy to help them either channel their sexual urges into complete celibacy or else to realign their instincts toward a healthy, God-approved expression of their sexuality. According to him,

"All things are possible with Jesus."

But, honestly, I wonder how that can be. Why God would create homosexuals if he didn't want them to be homosexual? Is it possible that my dad is wrong? Or, if not wrong, at least not entirely right?

CHAPTER TEN

When they lead us into the dining room, Tony separates himself from Chloe by grabbing my arm and tugging me toward a four-top near the back of the section. I slide into the booth, and he takes the chair opposite me. Chloe turns her attention to Dylan and follows him into the dining room. She's not touching him, exactly, and yet somehow she's clinging to his side. How does she do that? He sits down, and she grabs the chair next to him, frowning at some kid whose hand was on it.

Just as I'm wondering if, and kind of hoping, someone will join us, Jenn AKA the Nurse steps over. "Can I sit here?" Her gaze darts back and forth from Tony to me. She's quiet, but she seems nice enough.

"Absolutely," Tony says. He pats the seat next to him so she sits and tucks a strand of her chin-length white-blonde hair behind her ear. She's not smiling; she's beaming.

We're scoping out the menu, and I'm trying to ignore this thing that's hanging there between Tony and me when someone slides into the booth next to me. I lower the menu to see Dylan staring back. He blinks, but otherwise, his deep brown eyes are locked on mine.

"So what'd you think?" he asks, finally.

No, "Hi."

No, "Can I sit here?"

"Umm, what if that seat was being saved?" I ask. But my smile gives it away.

"It wasn't," he says. "Besides, it's been ages since I've had real Chicago-style pizza and Chloe says she wants thin crust because of the carbs or something and that won't do." He hooks his thumb over his shoulder toward the empty seat next to Chloe. I look over to find her scowling back at me. "We've got to get the spinach. It's the best."

Tony lets the menu flop down. "Sounds great to me. Since it seems like you're the expert, how do you feel about the garlic cheese bread?"

"I feel good about it," Dylan says. "You haven't been here before?" Dylan glances back and forth between us. Tony and Jenn shake their heads. "Wow, seriously?"

People who aren't from Illinois often forget that there is more to our state than Chicago, but even downstate sometimes we forget, too. There's "the city" and then there's everything else. And truly everybody comes up for a weekend now and again, to catch a show, go to Wrigley, do some shopping.

Of course, while I've been here several times for church events and a few protests, I've never come to the city for any of those sorts of things. But even when we're here to do the Lord's work, we usually make a stop for pizza, too.

"I've been," I say. "But Giordano's definitely isn't the best Chicago-style pizza in town." It's decent, but a total tourist trap.

Dylan runs his tongue over his teeth and cocks his head. "Oh? Gino's East?"

I shake my head. Like Giordano's, Gino's is all right. "My favorite is Lou Malnati's."

"You're a connoisseur then?"

My lips search for the straw in the water the waitress set in front of me. "Something like that."

"So is that why you want to go to Northwestern? So you can have it anytime you want?" Tony asks.

"Northwestern, huh?"

"Uh, maybe."

"What for?" Jenn asks.

"Umm. I have no idea." I haven't gotten that far yet. I only know I want to go to a real university. It doesn't much matter what I study.

"Not theater?" Tony asks.

I laugh and choke on my water. "Funny."

"If you wanted to pursue it, I think you totally could."

"Nah. That's just for fun. I don't have any formal training or anything." So far, everything I know about being Romeo has come from spying on people like Dylan, and trying to mimic him. Not exactly Royal Shakespeare material.

"Exactly. Which is what college is for." Tony stares at me like it's some sort of challenge.

"How about you all?" I ask. I know Tony's a junior like me, but Dylan's a senior so he's probably accepted somewhere already. Jenn is a sophomore, I think. She's got to have ideas about college, right? I mean, I did.

Jenn shrugs. "Maybe the U of I, but I don't really know yet." U of I is the standard answer for most people at our school, which is precisely why I'm not interested in going there. "I want to take some time off and work or travel or something though."

We look at Tony as if he's somehow next in the queue.

"Butler," he says. "In Indianapolis? If I get in, anyway. I want to study music and minor in dance."

Dance? Really? I had no idea he was a dancer. Although as I think of it, he did take to the Capoeira really well. For one thing, he didn't knock anyone off the stage.

"I'm going to Columbia College here in the city," Dylan says. "Hopefully studying graphic design."

"Why hopefully?" Tony asks, echoing the thought in my own head.

He shifts in his seat. "My parents don't think there's much of a future in it. They want me to study business and follow in my dad's footsteps."

"But you don't?"

"I'd rather make my own path. Besides, my dad has really small feet."

Tony laughs. He has a really great laugh that starts as a low grumble and accelerates to this full-bodied chuckle. And oh man. He's eying

Dylan, resting his head against his palm while Dylan talks about his last visit to Chicago. I know that look. I'm guilty of that look.

Wait, is Dylan a homosexual, too?

He smiles at me, this sort of crooked thing he does. And I just *know*. Nope. Definitely not a homo. Sorry, Tony.

Our pizza comes and Dylan reaches over me to grab the red pepper flakes. His hand brushes against mine for like .2 seconds, but it's enough to send sparks all the way to my pinky toes. I look away when he smiles at the contact.

"Pardon my reach." He douses his piece with spice. I'm watching him intently and he catches me. "Some like it hot." His voice is a low rumbling whisper, his words for me only.

My gaze snaps back to my plate. I lower my eyes and hope that my face isn't really as red as it feels. I cut off a bite of the cheesy goodness and lift my fork to my mouth, avoiding Tony's grin.

CHAPTER ELEVEN

"People! Some ground rules." Mrs. D claps and motions for us to gather around her in the lobby near the reservation desk.

"Holy shit," Tony whispers behind me. "This is a *hotel*."

It's true. I was expecting Motel 6 in Schaumburg or something. Not a four-star hotel downtown, right off the river and two blocks off Michigan Avenue.

Apparently, someone's dad is in with the hotel's parent company and got us a sweet deal. Clearly, because this hotel is not the kind of place a group of public school kids from down state would ordinarily stay. As evidence: the pristine lobby with its soft lighting and plush furniture and marble floors polished so they shine like mirrors.

"Now, you're free to hang out in the lobby, visit the pool, whatever. But by 10 p.m. you are to be in your rooms, no exceptions," Mrs. D continues as Mr. Brooks hands out our room keys. "We'll be coming around then to check in on you. No room service and no pay per view, understood? It shouldn't work anyway, the hotel doesn't have an incidentals account for any of your rooms."

We gather our bags, and I study the room key envelope in my hand. Room 810.

"I'm one floor down, in 716. Want to meet back down here in a bit?" he asks as we climb onto the elevator.

"Ten minutes?" Dylan asks, pressing the button for floors 6 through 10. Wonder how he knows we need those floors? He winks at me in the reflection of the closing elevator doors.

Tony steps off with a couple of girls and Greg. They must be roommates, and my mind wanders to the two of them alone together in a room. Is Greg gay, too? I don't get that vibe from him, but then I didn't get it from Tony either. I hope and pray that he isn't so Tony isn't tempted to do anything that he'll regret. If my dad were here, he would say that if Tony hasn't acted on his homosexual urges yet, then there's still hope. If Tony has, well, it will probably be a lot more difficult for me to help him. Not impossible, but difficult. But my dad's not here.

Also, I'm not sure trying to change Tony is what God would actually want.

Dylan and I both step off on eight along with a handful of other students, mostly guys, but also Chloe, Jenn and Ashley. At least one of them is my roommate and I hope hope hope it's not Chloe.

But only Ashley stops in front of 810 and puts her key in the lock.

"Hey, Roomie," she says when I step up beside her and hold up the envelope with my key card and "810" written on it.

The door opens to reveal a pair of double beds, made up with fluffy white down comforters and more pillows than one person could possibly use.

"Heaven." Ashley flops down on one.

I agree. This is a small taste of heaven. At home, I share a room with basically all of my sisters, and at various times in my life that means sharing an actual bed. I throw my book bag on the other and make for the bathroom. At dinner, I felt like I had to keep doing something to avoid fidgeting next to Dylan so I drank five glasses of water.

The bathroom is as welcoming as the room itself. Tons of towels and tiny little bottles of yummy smelling shampoos and lotions. I study my face in the mirror. I look a little tired and the lighting in here makes me look extra pale, but at least I'm having a good hair day. My curls are soft and bouncy, even without extra Argan oil.

Gah! Why do I even care? Still, I primp my hair a bit and put some of the moisturizer on my hands.

"So, here's the thing," Ashley says when I come out of the bathroom. "My boyfriend is here." I glance around the room then and she laughs. "Well not here, here. Not yet. But he's in school at DePaul. And he was going to come by tonight." She bites her lip and searches my face.

"Okay?" I'm not sure what she's asking exactly.

"Well, he was going to come in a bit and then hide out downstairs during the room checks. And I figured you were probably going to go hang out right now anyway, so I was wondering if that's okay."

And I know this is my test. Am I a cool kid or a total dork? My dad would probably want me to spend all night witnessing to her—to them. Warning them about the perils of their sinful behavior and the slippery slope of lust like we do on campuses. But honestly, I find the thought exhausting. It would be so much work to get her riled her up and then hit her with the truth. Plus, I've only ever really done the confrontational thing in large groups where people are inherently removed, not close quarters with one person.

"As long as he doesn't get caught," I say before I can think better of it. It probably goes without saying that I'm a bit of a rule follower, but I'm actually kind of enjoying not being *that* girl all the time. Hey, I can be like the nurse in *Romeo and Juliet*, enabling young love. And then this thought: I am about to be like Romeo, going downstairs to spend time with forbidden, er, company.

"Thank you, thank you, thank you," she squeals, hugging me. She jumps up and down, pulling me with her. "It's been sooooooo long since, well... you know."

Since what, I wonder? And then I put it together and try not to let my eyes go wide. This isn't about young love. I'm enabling fornication. But before I can backtrack or withdraw my consent, Ashley says, "You're not at all like I thought you'd be. I mean you're actually kind of... cool."

Cool? I'm pretty sure that no one has ever called me cool. But I know if my dad could see me now, he wouldn't think my behavior today was cool. On the contrary, at this point he'd be extremely disappointed in me.

But am I disappointed in myself?

I can't think about it further as there's a knock at the door and Ashley jumps up and giggles.

"Well, I guess I'll head downstairs now," I say. "I'll be back up right before ten so, erm...."

"We'll take our uh, intermission then," she winks.

Wait, intermission? What will they do after ten? I don't get the chance to ask because as soon as the door opens, Ashley and her boyfriend are so caught up in each other that they don't seem to realize that they aren't even alone yet.

Tony, Dylan, Jenn, and a couple other people camp out in the lobby playing cards. Some game called Golf that has nothing in common with its namesake except, it turns out, that I suck at both. When our group grows, we switch to Gin Rummy. For someone who's never played cards (though I definitely don't admit that to anyone), I'm not too bad at Gin. Although once again, I have to quiet the nagging voice in the back of my mind that can't believe I'm playing a game named after an alcoholic beverage.

At about nine thirty, Tony's roommate Greg gets a call. "Uh huh." He snaps his fingers and eyes Dylan. "Okay. There will be... ten of us?" Dylan does a quick finger count then nods. "Yeah. Ten. Okay. Great."

"All set?" Dylan asks when he hangs up.

"Game. Set. Match." Greg smiles.

"What's set?" I ask.

Dylan leans in and the whole table of us follows suit. "At 10:15 on the dot, meet downstairs, conference level by the back door. We're going out."

"Out?"

"Yeah, you know. *Out?*"

My mind is racing. Bending the rules for Ashley is one thing but specifically going off the hotel premises into the city? That is something altogether different.

"Where?" Tony asks. "I mean I don't have an ID with me. My, uh, fake is at home." The way he says this tells me there is no fake ID at all. Maybe that I clearly don't have one either will be excuse enough for me, too. If they're planning to go someplace where a fake ID is even potentially required, I'm out. I don't know what I'll do as an alternative since my room is occupied, but I'll ride the elevator all night or something.

"Not necessary." Greg eyes me for a long few seconds before glancing at Tony and Jenn.

"I'm not going to a bar," I say, apparently a bit too loudly, because it earns me an elbow to my ribs courtesy of Jenn. "Umm. I can't," I whisper.

"It's not a bar," Tony says although the tone of his voice leads me to think he's lying.

"Just out. We'll definitely stop into that big church. The stone one on Michigan." Greg says, nodding too vigorously.

"You're lying."

Tony puts his hands up. "Nope. We're just going out to have some fun. What would Romeo do?"

I did notice the church earlier today and wondered what all that stained glass would look like lit up at night. "How will we get in? To the church?"

Tony's eyes widen and Greg steps in. "I know a guy."

"You know a guy?"

"Jesus, Piper. Either come or don't, your choice." Greg says.

I narrow my eyes at him and press my lips together. He's right; Romeo would go out and seek the thrill. But I am not Romeo. I'm not even supposed to be in Chicago right now, much less roaming the streets after curfew. If something happens and we get caught? I will be grounded for life. Like, literally. For life. Maybe even eternity.

I shake my head. "Guys, I can't."

They all gang up on me, pleading and heckling, trying to soften my resolve. I remember what waits for me in my hotel room. Ashley and her boyfriend. I may be a virgin, but I can probably guess what they're doing, and that I definitely don't want to see. Or hear.

"You want to get into Romeo's head, right?" Tony asks. "What better way than to have an adventure?"

I glance at Dylan whose eyes seem to plead with me. Tony smiles encouragingly and so does Jenn and even Chloe. "Come on, Piper. Have some fun."

"Fine," I say. "But so help me if we get caught…"

"We're not going to get caught." Dylan says. "Have a little faith."

"And if we do?" I ask.

"It's not gonna happen. But if it does? I'll take the fall." He's so calm and relaxed, like he's untouchable. He's the one who's like Romeo. "Okay. Now, 10:15, downstairs and wear walking shoes." Dylan lifts an eyebrow and stares at each of us girls one by one.

Everyone looks pointedly at Chloe.

"What?" She smiles.

You don't have to tell me twice. I never wear heels if I can help it, and certainly wouldn't to walk around Chicago. With my luck, my heel would get caught in the bridge way just as it's being raised for a passing boat. And then I would die, thus proving my long-held theory that heels truly are deadly.

We trickle off back upstairs. Dylan is on the eighth floor with me and we ride the elevator together. He watches as I pause outside my room and knock softly.

"What's going on?" he asks and I shake my head.

No explanation is necessary because some giant of a kid wearing entirely too much cologne bursts out of the door. His shirt untucked, pants undone, and shoes in hand, he runs toward the elevator.

Dylan cracks up as he opens the door to his room.

My room smells like over-sexed boy. Eww. I flip on the bathroom fan and notice Ashley's sitting on her bed in only a T-shirt. Thankfully, my bed near the window is still untouched. Because if they have sex in my bed so help me.

Moments later, there's a knock on the door. Ashley bounds over to open it. "Goodnight girls." Mrs. D says as she peeks into the room. I bite the nail of my ring finger and hope she doesn't smell Ashley's boyfriend's Axe overdose. Ashley tried to cover it up with her fruity body spray, which means our room smells like a Bath & Body Works crashed into a guy's locker room.

"Goodnight," we singsong in unison. I'm holding my pajama pants like I'm about to make for the bathroom. She eyes me steadily and I realize I'm wearing lip-gloss and probably looking much too put-together than I should be for someone going to bed.

"Be downstairs tomorrow at 9 a.m. sharp." Finally, she tugs the door closed behind her. "And keep the deadbolt locked."

Ashley stretches and yawns. "So, if it's okay, Jesse is probably going to stay tonight. You keep my secrets, I'll keep yours." She winks.

I don't really have any options. "Fine." As long as no sex happens while I'm *in* the room.

I shove the PJ pants back in my book bag and go to the bathroom to check my hair. Again. I know I shouldn't care, that it doesn't matter, that vanity is also sinful, but I can't help myself.

"So where you guys going?" she asks.

"I'm not entirely sure. Someone knows someone somewhere. They mentioned the stone church maybe someplace else? I'm kinda just following the pack."

She clicks her teeth. "Well be careful. And don't look away from your drink for a minute. Keep a napkin over it or something."

What? My drink? Why? I ask and she tells me something about her sister's sorority sister getting drugged. "He slipped it into her drink when she wasn't watching and then…." Her voice gets quiet.

That sort of thing actually happens? I always assumed it was a story my mom had told us to keep us in line. Now I won't just worry about making a fool of myself, or getting lost, or getting my foot caught in the causeway. I'll have to worry about date rape drugs in my Sprite. But one glance at Ashley and her oversized t-shirt tells me my alternative is sitting in the hallway while she and her boyfriend fornicate all night.

Here goes nothing.

CHAPTER TWELVE

It's not a church. It's actually the kind of place that comes to mind when you hear the word, "pub." Not at all what I've pictured from my dad's sermons on debauchery. I imagined drunken people flailing all over each other, booze being poured down their throats by cocktail waitresses in tight leather bustiers. Instead, it's a bunch of laid-back people in jeans and t-shirts. I can't help but wonder if my dad was so off base about this, what else could he have been wrong about?

In the middle of our table, there's this huge tower of beer. Seriously, four feet of beer with a spigot. I watch everyone else relax into their bar stools, chatting and drinking and having a good time and though I want to join in, I'm also nervous and can't shake the feeling that what we're doing is wrong. That we're going to get caught and expelled and then my dad will hate me forever. This is exactly what my dad is so afraid of—that the second we're off on our own we'll be wooed by the world, succumb to its glamor, and make poor, potentially deadly (at least spiritually) choices.

Some tinny hipster-bluegrass type music starts up in the background and quiets the thoughts in my head just a smidge. Apparently, the drummer is Greg's cousin and the one who got us all in.

"They've got a meeting with Columbia next week," Greg shouts in my ear, gesturing toward the makeshift stage. It's pretty much a small area near the back where they cleared out some tables and chairs and set up some amps.

"College?" I ask.

"No. Records."

I nod as if this is impressive because I get the sense it is supposed to be, but truthfully, it doesn't mean much to me. I've heard secular music occasionally on the radio in Jodi's car or in stores or whatever, but I wouldn't say I listen to it.

Tony takes a shot of something and winces. He holds a small glass to me and I shake my head.

Jenn grabs it from his hand and throws it back without flinching. She bites into a lime and when she catches our shocked expressions, she shrugs. "What? I like tequila."

Tony keeps reassuring me that we won't get caught. "Piper, live a little. They can't expel the entire senior class."

"This is not even close to being the entire senior class," I say, but it falls on deaf ears. Plus, several of us are juniors. At any rate, I'm pretty sure that the school wouldn't hesitate to expel ten of its students for sneaking out to a freaking bar. Tony just grins and hands me a pint glass. He flips the spigot and before I know it, I'm holding a beer just like the rest of them. I consider lifting it to my lips to drink, but think better of it. I'm at a bar. That's enough limit stretching for now. Probably for life.

"Wise choice. That cheap stuff tastes like cold, fizzy, piss." Dylan laughs. He leans in. "Don't worry, I'm good at keeping your secrets."

"Likewise, as you know." I think of that night last summer when I caught him in the woods. With all the time we've been talking lately, it's the first time I've ever alluded to that. Maybe he doesn't even know that's what I mean, but the way his eyes widen tells me he knows exactly what I'm referring to. "I mean. Obviously. I wouldn't... I don't." Oh man. I almost want to take an actual sip of the beer just to fill the awkward space. I sniff it instead. He's right. It smells disgusting, calling to mind some of the early Saturday mornings I've spent handing out tracts in front of the campus bars, when the sidewalks haven't been sprayed down yet from the night before. People actually want to drink this stuff?

I lean back against the wall and he scoots his stool closer, so he's out of the way of Jenn, who is simultaneously flirting with Greg and challenging Tony to a drink off. At least from my vantage point, they both seem to be drinking a lot though admittedly, I'm not really much of an expert.

"It's better cold." He clinks his pint glass to mine where it rests on the table. "Cheers." He lifts the glass slightly before taking a long drink.

Chloe comes up behind Dylan and tousles his hair. "Hi," she slurs.

The way his jaw clenches, I can tell touching his hair must be a big no-no, but he doesn't say anything. He awkwardly maneuvers himself away from her reach, so that he's practically in my lap since I'm in the corner spot. Chloe, oblivious, moves around the other side of the table and starts to dance up against some other guy, a senior I don't know.

Dylan runs his hand through his hair to smooth it back out and smiles self-consciously when he catches my eye.

"Particular about it, are you?" I ask.

He laughs. "At least I don't own a blow drier."

"Liar," I say. We fall quiet, listening to the music for a bit. The beat doesn't seem like dancing music, but isn't really relaxed either. And it's kind of loud. Tony waves at me from across the bar and starts to make some weird gesture that I think is meant to mean something to me, but he's drunk and his appendages aren't working as well. I laugh and Dylan spins my stool toward him and leans in.

"So what's it like?" he asks.

What's what like? I lick my lips and consider. "Being the daughter of one of the region's most notorious evangelists? Disobeying my dad at practically every turn these days?" Feeling simultaneously empowered and crushed by guilt? Trying and failing to balance the weight of expectation and the realities of being a modern teenager?

He tosses his hair again and smiles. "Being a female Romeo, I mean. What's it like?"

Oh. That. "Umm, well jury's still out I guess. I've only been, uh, him for a couple weeks. And I have to be Romeo to freaking Chloe Wennert's Juliet so that sorta…"

"Blows?"

"Stinks," I say.

"I take it you two don't get along?" The corner of his mouth lifts slightly.

Snort. "That's a gross understatement." I watch her wiggle and writhe up against the senior guy. He bobs his head to the music, but otherwise his feet are planted.

"She doesn't seem *so* bad." Dylan stares.

"Ahh, but see I'm immune to her breasts." And I so completely am. This I know—as much as I've been trying on the male persona, I'm not attracted to Chloe, platonically that is. Not even a little bit. Truthfully, she kind of repulses me. Which my dad would say makes her an 'extra grace required' person for me, one that I should be praying over a lot. But for some reason I just... can't. I don't want to.

It's Dylan's turn to snort. He gags on the sip of beer he just took. Is he blushing? He lowers his eyes to the glass now resting between his hands.

It's true though. And she uses her assets wherever and whenever possible. Case in point: the senior she's dancing against is now dancing with her. Well, his feet have moved a bit. He's shuffling, at least. She knows how to move her body to use it to get guys to respond. No wonder I'm the Romeo to her Juliet.

"Anyway, it's only acting so it doesn't matter who I'm opposite, right?" I say.

"And how are you finding the physicality of it? Of impersonating someone, well, someone like me?" He grins.

Oh no, have I been caught?

I blink several times and I'm sure the color drains from my face. "Piper, relax. It's cool. I appreciate that you're trying for accuracy."

"Accuracy?" I whisper.

"You know. Whenever guys impersonate girls, they throw their voices all high and flick their wrists and act ridiculous. I've never seen a girl actually act like that. Ever. So I assume it's like that. Or, the opposite I guess."

I press my lips together and stare at my hands. I cannot believe he's on to me.

"Piper, seriously. Don't worry about it. I'm flattered that you want to use me as your *muse*." He laughs.

"Muse? Who says you're the only one I'm imitating?" I snap, a bit more gruffly than I intend.

Dylan just smiles. "You have multiples, then? Okay, Piper. Okay." He lifts his glass to his lips.

The truth is, when I think about playing Romeo, the only person I want to emulate is Dylan. There's just something about him. In fact, I could wear a bracelet that asks, "WWDD?" That might not be a bad idea. My dad probably wouldn't even notice the D instead of J. Well, except that no one really wears those anymore. Not even my family. It's not what Jesus *would* do, it's what He *did* do, my dad always says. What he still does.

"Dudes, drink up." Greg sticks his head in between Dylan and me, reaching his arms around our shoulders. The Tower O' Beer has at least two feet to go which means we've only drained half of it. Ugh.

"I'm good." I gesture to my still-full beer.

"Oh come on. We're just wandering around the Art Institute tomorrow. You don't need to be coherent for that."

"I'm pretty sure that puking on 'American Gothic' is a capital offense," Dylan says.

Greg is impervious and fills my cup to the brim anyway.

"*Romeo I come! This do I drink to thee,*" he quotes the line Juliet says before she downs the friar's drug. He's grinning at me. "Now, seriously, drink up."

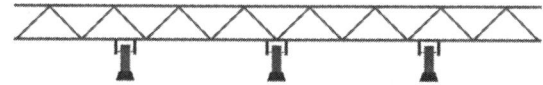

It's well after one o'clock when we stumble from the pub, back toward the hotel. Greg and Tony and Jenn are totally tossed. I obviously don't feel anything at all because when the others weren't looking, I poured some of my glass into theirs and spread it around little by little. Of course, this means Dylan and I pretty much have to carry the rest of them home. I link Jenn's arm across my back and hold her at her waist. Dylan does the same with Greg and Tony, one arm supporting each of them.

We pass by that church Tony enticed me with and I pause for a minute to admire the backlit stained glass windows in the front. But I can't stop long because Dylan at the front of the pack turns around to check on why we're delayed.

"Come on, you guys. Still got a ways to go."

A few others from our group scurry in front of us, whooping it up. Chloe has basically forgotten about the senior guy, though, and is instead trying to entice Dylan. Fortunately, he's too distracted trying to keep Greg and Tony on the path to notice her boobs. Which is sort of remarkable since the top she's wearing is stretched over her chest. Tight. She keeps tugging the hem to keep it that way. We hobble along for what feels like miles even though it's actually just a few blocks. City blocks, but blocks.

"This is the river?" Jenn asks, teetering against the railing. I tug her back. Drunk plus unsteady plus a bridge is not a good equation. I try to steady her and goad her to keep walking. When we're within sight of the hotel, Jenn does the unthinkable.

"I'm gonna be sick," she says. Or she starts to say. But before she can finish warning me, she pukes. And it's all over me. I mean everywhere. In my hair, on my coat. My shirt. Somehow, it's even on my shoes.

She looks horrified. "Piper… I'm so…" and then she pukes again.

On me.

CHAPTER THIRTEEN

The back door we came out of is locked, so one of us will have to go around front and hold it open. We decide it should be whoever will appear the most inconspicuous, which could have been me five minutes ago, but now I'm covered in puke and that's not something the staff or any guests would be likely to ignore. So Dylan goes.

"Give me one minute," he says before dashing around toward the front of the hotel.

It is the longest minute of my life. I'm freezing because, of course, the puke is wet and the wind whipping off Lake Michigan is frigid. Jenn is crying because she's embarrassed. And drunk. And Greg is cooing and cajoling and practically ready to make out with her as they stumble backward. The hotel is right up against the Chicago River, so stumbling backward could end badly. Really badly.

"Stop it," I hiss. I sound like a kindergarten teacher. "Stand there and be still. Keep your hands to yourselves. One more minute and you can be inside where it's warm and safe, okay?" Plus, Jenn should probably brush her teeth like twelve times before she thinks about kissing anyone. Or anyone thinks about kissing her.

Dylan appears at the glass door and holds it open. "Come on."

I give him a wide-eyed look. "What took so long?"

"Sorry. Mr. Brooks is definitely at the lobby bar."

"What?"

"Gin and Tonics and a blonde." Dylan laughs and shakes his head. "So, we have to sneak up to the lobby level and use the far elevators." Together, we corral everyone to the far elevators, shushing them all the while. I start praying that no one gets on at the lobby level.

As the elevators rise, so does my stomach. I hold my breath as we approach the lobby, but when we keep going up without pausing, I sigh a little bit louder than I mean to in relief. Jenn and Greg are still holding hands, oblivious to anything else. Tony has this dopey grin plastered on his face. And by now, the whole elevator smells like vomit. Thanks to me. No, thanks to Jenn.

Dylan and I ride up to ten to make sure Jenn and Greg at least make it that far, and once they stumble off to their rooms, we head back down to eight.

"Sorry I stink." My voice is a low whisper that gets caught in the back of my throat.

Dylan laughs. "It's not exactly your fault."

"I still stink."

We step off the elevator and head to our respective ends of the hall, he to the right and me to the left. I'm so ready to crawl into bed at this point; I don't care if there's also a boy in my room. Or if he's naked. Just give me some soap, some clean clothes and a pillow.

I ignore the "Do Not Disturb" door hang and push the key card into the slot. The green light flashes, but when I go to open the door, I find it's dead-bolted. It won't budge.

And I'm stuck mere feet away from my bed covered in puke. Cold, boozy puke.

I knock. "Ashley?" I whisper. "Ashley?!" I can't yell, of course, because Mr. Brooks or Mrs. D could hear me. They could be staying on this very floor.

"Ashley?" I pound a little harder. This is so not happening. "Ashley?"

Do not cry. Do not cry. Do not cry. I lean my head against the door and nearly shriek when a hand touches my shoulder.

"Fudge buckets!" I whisper-screech. But it's just Dylan.

"Fudge buckets?" He smiles. I am not in the mood and I think my face must show it because then he softens. "What's wrong?"

"Ashley dead-bolted the dang door."

He pounds his fist against it, slightly harder than I did.

"You've got to be kidding me," I groan. "I'm covered in someone else's vomit, I'm tired and I have no place to go." I lean against the wall because I need it to hold me up. I've lost the will. But soon, I give up slink down to the floor. I'm going to sleep in the hallway tonight. Awesome.

Dylan pounds a few more times, jiggles the handle and whispers Ashley's name. "Do you have her cell number?"

I shake my head, so Dylan pulls out his cell and starts dialing someone. Wait, who's he calling? Ah, the front desk and they must put him through to the room because he beams at me. He's a genius! Then I hear the phone in the room—my room—ring. And ring. And ring.

And ring.

Pick up. Pick up. Pick up. My lips mouth the words, a mantra, as if it will help. It doesn't though, because eventually, the phone stops ringing and the door never opens.

"They're probably having sex. In my bed!" I groan. "And I'm going to sleep in a freaking hallway."

Dylan grabs my hand and pulls me to my feet. "C'mon. You're not sleeping out here." He leads me down the hall back toward the elevator.

"The lobby, then? That's not much of an upgrade. Plus, Mr. Brooks will see me."

"No, not the lobby. You can stay with me." He tugs me past the bank of elevators and toward his end of the hall.

What? I stop walking and my feet plant firmly in place. He laughs at me standing there. "Chill out. I can sleep on the sofa or the floor or something." He stops in front of what must be his room.

Even though what he proposes sounds heavenly compared to a night spent on the hard, very public hotel hallway floor, a part of me—a very large part—is screaming 'no, no, no.'

But if I'm being completely honest, another part, a quieter part, squeals, 'yes!'

"What about your roommates?" I whisper.

He unlocks the door and flips on the light, revealing that apparently, he doesn't have any. There's one massive king sized bed and a small sofa by the window. "It shouldn't be a problem."

"But I don't have any of my stuff. Like non-puke covered clothes."

"You wouldn't have that if you'd slept in the hallway, either." He does have a point. "Look, you can shower and borrow a t-shirt and shorts."

He reaches into a bag and pulls out a t-shirt and shorts. "Seriously, I'll take the couch. No worries."

"How did you get a single room?" I thought I'd lucked out only have to share with one person since some students were in threes or fours.

His hand runs through his hair again but one strand still hangs in his face, curling against his cheek. "Let's just say I know a guy."

Uh, what the heck does that mean?

"My dad. He works for the company."

"Ah, so you're the one, huh?" I heard the rumor that someone's parent scored us a deal. Not someone, it seems, but Dylan.

"Dad's up here on business all the time. Like, weekly. We have a condo over on Dearborn. Well, he does."

"Why don't you all just live in Chicago then?"

Dylan pulls at a thread hanging from his sleeve, twirling it between his fingers. "When my mom left, my dad wanted to keep things stable for my sisters and me. Or as stable as possible, I guess. So we stayed in Ridgedale and he commuted whenever he had to."

"But you said your *mom* earlier." I think back to dinner and our discussion about parents and families.

"I said parents. And I meant my step-mom, Gina. My mom left when I was like six. My dad's wife, Gina, has been my 'mom' for a while now. So I just call her that."

"You have sisters?" I ask. I don't know why I should be surprised. The self-assured way he carries himself around girls says yes.

"I've got three older sisters. Sylvia is in law school, Emily's at U of I and Mackenzie's a senior at IMSA. She's only older than me by like a month, though."

Wait. Older by a month? "How is that even...?"

"Stepsister. Technically."

"And your real mom... where is she?"

"Who knows?"

I want to press him for details, but the way he crosses his arms and looks toward the window tells me I shouldn't. So instead, I head to the bathroom to take a shower. I let the water get scalding hot and it turns my skin pink as I stand under it. But even after using up half the bottle of hotel-provided shower gel stuff, I still think I smell like the inside of a bar toilet. Yuck. Yuck. Yuck. Also, my hair is going to be a total mess tomorrow. I'll probably more closely resemble a freaking poodle than myself, but there's not much I can do about it right now.

While I'm drying off, I take to scrubbing my clothes. Fortunately, my skirt made it out of the ordeal pretty much unscathed. Thank God, because that was the only one I brought on the trip. There's a spot on the right just above the knee, but some serious bar soap and water seems to help. The shirt is done for though, so I tuck it into the drawstring plastic bag the hotel provided for just such a purpose. Well, I doubt they anticipated this particular situation. But my clothes are dirty and that's what it's for.

I tug Dylan's shirt over my head. It smells like clean laundry and boy, and, strangely like baked goods. A sweetness—almonds or something? Whatever it is, I like it.

I'm out of the shower and standing in the doorway when I see Dylan is definitely asleep on the far side of the bed. The overhead light is still on but the bedside lamp is switched off. He holds a pencil and his book is open in his lap. I inch closer and crane my neck to look at what he was reading and instead notice my face reflected back at me from the margin. Well, my head is turned to the side, but it's definitely my profile. My face.

I'd ask him why, but he hasn't moved.

He's also wearing a short-sleeved t-shirt, revealing not just a tattoo on his arm, but a full sleeve that starts at his wrist and goes at least as high as his bicep. It's the kind where every time you look at it, you'll probably see something new and different. I can make out some type of fish, a sun and some vines. There's an abstract-looking flower along the inside of his forearm—a rose. The whole sleeve is all black ink, but the rose stands out in the center because it makes use of the negative space, more flesh than ink. His arm moves slightly, hiding rose from view.

Should I wake him? He did promise to take the couch. But then I think I'm being a bit ridiculous. It's his room. His bed. His blankets and pillows.

I make my way toward the stiff-looking decorative sofa across the room, flipping the overhead light off as I do. I've never slept in the same room as a boy before. I mean, a boy I'm not related to. And even then, that was different.

So very, very different.

I climb onto the sofa and as my eyes adjust to the dim lamplight, I can't help but watch him sleeping. I think about the scene I'll have as Romeo where I'll have to lay on the altar next to Juliet as though in the sleep of death. I haven't really thought about it before. Is "masculine" sleep so different? The way his chest rises and falls, the way his head rests against the pillow. It's in the shoulders, I think. The way they stay squared off instead of rounded in, like mine probably would. I lie against the seat cushion and tighten my back, squeezing my shoulder blades together. It's totally uncomfortable, but it might just work. And I won't have to hold the pose for more than a few minutes. Just long enough to play dead.

I sit back up and switch off the last lamp, this time lying back down as myself. It doesn't matter that I'm on sofa and not the hard floor because I'm so wired that I get zero sleep. Thanks to the blackout curtains, I can't really see a thing. Not the shape of him on the bed or even the expanse of the room itself. Between the buzzing in my head and the thumping of my heart, sleep is clearly not in the cards for me. Nope, I am wide-awake.

So instead I listen.

To the weird humming of the hotel, the way air whooshes through the vents every now and again. The droning of the neighbor's television. The sounds of the city streets below. The muffled voices that pass in the hallway. And, mostly, I listen to Dylan sleep. The rhythm of his breath. The way he sighs and shifts.

And, eventually, the massive thud as something in the room hits the floor, and I nearly jump out of my skin.

CHAPTER FOURTEEN

"Omph," **Dylan says. A gentle swooshing follows, likely the** comforter sliding from the bed as he scrambles around to get up. "Sorry about that," he whispers. "I fell off the bed."

"Oh." I lay back against the sofa.

"I guess I fell asleep," he says. "Sorry, I know I promised to take the couch I can just... uh... switch, if you want."

"It's fine." I feel a rush of heat to my face and I'm thankful for the cover of darkness. "I mean it's no big deal. I'm good."

"Are you sure? You don't even have a blanket."

"It's fine. I'm fine. Thanks."

Shuffling moves across the room. When his voice breaks the silence again, I can tell he's close. "You"—he yawns—"smell better." A thick lump of plush fabric falls onto my legs. His arm brushes mine as he tugs the blanket toward my chin, not quite tucking me in, but close.

"Thanks," I say. I'm too afraid my voice will squeak if I try to say anything more. Not that there's anything else to say, really.

He sighs and shuffles away. The mattress rustles as he flops down on it. He groans quietly and I lay there for a bit listening to the sound of his breathing and the sound of him shifting around. A few moments later, he shifts again. Then again. I find myself thinking of his broad, squared shoulders. But this time, not for research purposes.

"You asleep?" he whispers, after a while.

"No. You?" I ask. Gah. Of course he's not asleep. He's talking.

"Nope. That fall sorta jolted me awake. Got the adrenaline pumping." He shifts and the mattress rustles again. "I was dreaming that I was standing on the glass balcony on the observation deck of the Sears Tower—or Willis Tower now, I guess. Then I fell out of bed."

"Creepy."

"Seriously. Must have been what I was reading before I feel asleep."

"A horror novel?"

"Ha. No. Poetry."

"Poetry?"

"A collection of my mom's favorites. That's where my sisters and I got our names."

"Dylan? I assumed your parents were fans of sixties folk music or something."

I can almost hear him smile. "Dylan Thomas. Emily is either Emily Browning or Emily Dickinson, we're not really sure which. And Sylvia is after Sylvia Plath."

"Oh, uh. That's nice." Naming your kid after a suicidal poet?

"I know, I know. Some legacy, huh? But *the poetry*." He groans. He's quiet for a moment and then I hear something. Is he humming?

"'Maybe she'd give me a bath, how I wish I had a Sylvia Plath...'" he sings. "You know that song? Ryan Adams?" He continues humming the melody for a bit and comes back in with the chorus.

"You sing?" I ask when he quiets.

"Not really. Sometimes."

"That's a depressing song," I whisper.

"Picky picky." He takes a deep breath. "'Is this the real life? Is this just fantasy,'" he croons. I feel like I'm supposed to know this, so I smile and bop my head but then I realize he can't see me so I laugh instead.

"I'm just a poor boy!'" His voice grows more impassioned and his pitch, higher. Then all of a sudden he stops. "You aren't singing along."

"Oh. I. Umm."

"No. No, no, no. I refuse to believe that you do not know 'Bohemian Rhapsody.' Queen? Freddie Mercury... Seriously?"

I bite my lip and shrug even though I know he can't really see me.

The sheets rustle as Dylan leaps out of bed and plods over to the small chest of drawers. "Well, that will not do." A small square glows brightly, illuminating his furrowed brow.

I glance away and then a moment later, back again. He took off his shirt? When did that happen? The light reflects off his chest, which is way more muscled than I would have guessed. Broad shoulders, toned abs. He comes off all artsy, but he clearly spends some time in a gym. Or on a field. Something. I look away again.

"All right. Here we go. Allow me to pop your Queen… uh. Never mind." He shakes his head. "'Bohemian Rhapsody' in all its glory."

Seconds later, a strange set of voices come on, like Autotune or something. The voices blend and harmonies twist in beneath. Soon, a languid piano accompaniment joins in. "Is this some kind of rock opera?" I ask when we hit the bridge. Or what I assume is the bridge. Hard to tell as the music is all over the place.

"Come on." Dylan reaches for my hand. "It's about to get good."

He pulls me up on the bed and we're both standing there waiting for something, my hand in his because he hasn't let go. The music goes on but he still doesn't release mine. My hand is sweaty and so is his but I don't want to let go if he doesn't.

I'm still just standing there awkwardly in the dark, holding Dylan's hand listening to this bizarre song. So, not quite how I'd pictured my first night alone with a boy. "This song isn't really funny though, is it?" I ask. The guy is singing about killing someone and facing what— prison? Death?

"Shh—here comes. Okay, ready?" The flash of the light from the screen illuminates his broad grin. The music changes to a strange call and response. Now they're speaking—Arabic?

"Ready for what?" And did they just say Beelzebub?

"Now!" Dylan starts jumping and drops my hand so he can play air guitar properly while bopping his head back and forth. I start jumping up and down along with Dylan. I don't play air guitar, but I do laugh.

This is by far the weirdest song I've ever heard.

For all that build up, too soon the music trails off, returning to its original slower tempo. A curt knock on the door interrupts us. At first, I think it might be part of the song but as Dylan leaps from the bed and says, "Oh, shit," I realize it isn't.

He motions for me to hide behind the room divider wall while he mutes his phone and then rushes toward the door. "Did they mention doing night time room checks?" He whispers.

They didn't. Oh no. Oh no. Oh no.

A flood of light enters the room when Dylan tugs open the door and I hear a stern male voice on the other side. No accent though, so it's definitely not Brooks. "Pardon me, uh, sir. Do you mind keeping it down a bit? I've got a pretty early flight out in the morning."

Dylan apologizes and says something about jet lag, concocting some story about how he's all amped up because he just flew in from Japan. I cover my mouth to hide my giggle.

The guy in the hallway sympathizes and mentions a few remedies. Booze, some type of pills. "If all else fails, Pay Per View porn. *Incidentals*, amiright?"

Dylan laughs awkwardly and I sneak a peek around the corner of the wall to see his back illuminated by the light of the hallway. His pants hang low on his hips and I glance away. I should *not* be thinking about Dylan or anyone like this.

When I hear the click of the lock, I scramble from my hiding spot back to the couch.

"Well, that was interesting." Dylan reenters the room. "Never a dull moment around you."

He flops back on his bed and laughs. "Probably don't tell your boyfriend our bed noises disturbed our neighbor."

Er. "Not a problem since I don't have one."

"Huh. I thought you were the going steady, 'wear my pin' type."

"Uh. No. I'm not supposed to date at all."

"Really? Huh." He pauses. "So like, will you have an arranged marriage?"

I groan. "Not exactly. I mean, we're supposed to court instead." I'm fumbling for words and once again thankful for the cover of darkness.

"Court?"

"You know. Sort of like dating but there's a purpose. And not until you're ready for it to end. Ideally in marriage."

"Wow. That sounds... intense."

Does it? It's all I've ever known and the idea is to protect yourself from heartbreak and vulnerability. I've never really thought about any drawbacks until recently. Until him.

"Dylan?" I whisper after he's quiet for a while.

"Hmm?" he says but I can tell he's half asleep.

With the exception of my brother, which soooooo doesn't count, I've never shared a room with a boy before and though this isn't quite how I pictured it, there are butterflies in my stomach just the same.

Before long, his breathing relaxes back into a soft rhythm again. Sleepiness has finally caught up with him and I wish it would catch me, too. But if I couldn't sleep before, there is no way I'm going to now. Or so I think but the next thing I know, there's this faint humming noise. It's a tune I don't recognize. It's coming from the radio of the car I'm driving. Hey wait, I don't have a car. Or a license. I open my eyes and realize that the tune is coming from a buzzing cell phone on the nightstand. I don't have a cell phone.

Wait. Where am I?

Across from my line of sight, a person stretches and groans. "Morning sunshine."

Dylan.

Oh. My. Gosh.

"Morning." I squeak as I bolt upright. "What time is it?"

He yawns. "It's six."

"Six?" As in a.m.? "Why is your alarm going off?"

"Well, I wondered if you'd be up for a little adventure this morning." He hops out of bed and grabs my now dry skirt off the back of the chair and tosses it at me. "Get dressed. We don't have much time."

Wait. "Adventure?" I think I've had enough adventure to last a lifetime last night. And that we went out last night without getting caught is truly a miracle. Why press our luck?

"Yup. Come on." He disappears to the bathroom for a minute and then comes back, brushing his teeth. What I wouldn't give to brush my teeth. "Let's go!"

I want to resist, I should resist, but somehow, I can't. He's standing there all excited and eager and even though I have no idea what he could possibly have planned at 5 a.m., I really want to find out.

"Give me three minutes." I scramble to the bathroom. Okay, more like five. The light is way too bright and it takes my eyes at least a whole minute to adjust. My hair is a mess; I have crease marks on my face. I do the best I can with the hotel-provided lotion, a splash of water and a squeeze of Dylan's toothpaste on my finger.

"Ready?" He tugs me from the room before I can even get my, thankfully dry, jacket on.

"Where are we going?"

"It's a surprise." He leads me out the same way we came in last night. We head down Michigan Avenue, back toward the pub from last night.

"It better not be another bar."

"Never can tell," he says.

Even though it's early morning, the streets are already alive, filling up with people coming and going. Taxis speed by and honk at each other and pedestrians who dart out between them randomly.

We cross Michigan, same as we did last night, dodging cabs and cars like pros. Well, Dylan does it like a pro, I just hang closely at his side. "Seriously, where are we going?" Do we have time to get there and back before our absence is discovered?

Dylan doesn't say anything but a block or so later he stops abruptly. "Ta da."

"Here?" I look up at the massive stone church that simultaneously looks so natural and so completely out of place in the middle of downtown Chicago. It's an oasis of stone and ivy surrounded by office skyscrapers, retailers and tourist hot spots. A single steeple reaches toward the sky.

"I think that's how a church should be," he says, like he's reading my thoughts. "Surrounded by life."

"How did you...?" I can't even finish, I'm too taken aback.

"I saw the way you were looking at it last night. Since we goaded you to going out on the promise that we might stop in, I figured I should make good on that promise."

He was practically carrying people, very drunk people, up the street, how did he possibly notice me eying the church? "C'mon." We head to the wooden front doors but find both sets locked. "It's okay," I say. I'm sure it's beautiful inside and I would love to see it, but just Dylan having brought me here is amazing enough.

"Oh, we're not giving up that easily." He grabs my hand and leads me through an archway to a small path along the side of the building. There's another door at the end of the walk and when he tries the handle, it gives way. "Hello?"

No answer.

The empty hallway leads to several doors. Dylan heads right instinctively. "This way, I think." Down the hall, there's another wooden door and that one also opens for us. We step through and find we're near the altar of the sanctuary. It's enormous—wood rafters, great stone buttresses and massive chandeliers. The morning sun filters through the intricate glass windows that line the sides, front and back of the sanctuary. "It's beautiful," I say. Like the great churches of Europe. Or so I've heard.

Dylan's footsteps echo on the stone floor as he walks toward the altar, checking out the pulpit and the wood inlays. I sit on the nearest pew and just take it all in. Our church is nothing like this. It's basically an old commercial office space that's been converted to a gathering space. Wood paneled walls, a bunch of mismatched pews we salvaged from junkyards and other churches that underwent remodels, a lectern that serves as the pulpit and still has the crusty glue outline where the University's seal used to be attached. Even though I know wherever two or more are gathered God is also present, I can only imagine what it would be like to worship God in this space. I'd probably be a lot more likely to pay attention. Or maybe I'd be more distracted by all the beauty.

Dylan sits next to me and looks up at the windows. "Such amazing use of color."

"Excuse me?" A woman's voice says through the doorway we entered just moments ago. She's weighed down by two overfilled totes and a stack of papers. "Can I help you?"

We scramble to our feet. Dylan looks to me and then to her. "We were just looking at the church." He grabs my hand. "For our, uh, wedding."

She looks confused. "Oh dear, did you have an appointment?"

"Umm, not exactly." Dylan says. He starts spinning some story about missing a plane and our appointment yesterday. "The door was open so we thought we'd just take a peek." His hand moves to the small of my back and he guides me toward the exit.

The woman is not unkind, but it's clear we're not supposed to be here. She fumbles through one of her tote bags and hands Dylan a brochure. "I'm not sure how much information you have. Weddings are held on Saturdays at noon, 2:30 and 5:00. If you'd like to make another appointment to speak with our wedding coordinator in more detail and get a full tour, I can certainly arrange that."

"Sounds great," Dylan says. He tugs me toward the door. "I'll have my people call shortly."

And just like that, we're back out on the street again.

"Umm, thanks again, for everything," I say as we stand there awkwardly, after we get off the elevator on the eighth floor. "I, uh, better get back to my room and get ready for, for today."

We each return toward our rooms, but Dylan waits outside his door and watches to make sure I actually get in my room this time. I try to open the door to find it's still dead-bolted, but this time, I pound on it. Hard. And in a few moments, it opens and I push my way inside.

"Ohmygod, Piper I am so sorry," Ashley moans when I burst into the room. She's wearing nothing but a towel and her boyfriend is tugging on his pants and looks at me shamefaced. I'm relieved when I notice my bed is still made up and my book bag is resting on top of it. Not that it matters now since I certainly won't be sleeping in it.

I look to Ashley then to the boy once more. "A plague on both your houses," I yell, slamming the door to the bathroom.

CHAPTER FIFTEEN

I'm sitting at a table in the lobby, waiting for the rest of our group to materialize when Jenn comes up to me. She's wearing sunglasses and hands me a mega-sized cup and a bag filled with an assortment of pastries.

"Piper, I am so sorry about last night," she whispers.

I take the cup from her. She looks like a hot mess, which I guess is fitting punishment.

"It's a triple mocha," she says. "I didn't know what you drink or how you take it so I guessed."

I don't drink coffee, but I also don't want to be rude so I pretend to take a sip but when I lift the cup to my lips, it smells like hot chocolate. Oh, one sip won't hurt.

"Did you sleep at all?" she croaks, sitting next to me.

"Umm. No, not really." I debate telling her about getting locked out and how I spent the night in Dylan's room. But I know that's how rumors get started. First, someone says we stayed in the same room and the next thing you know, people will be saying I'm pregnant with his love child or something. It probably wouldn't matter that I'm, well, me. Rumors are rumors.

Chloe is eying me suspiciously from her table, which confirms it: I need to keep my trap shut. "Hotels, you know? All those weird sounds and an unfamiliar bed."

Dylan eases into the chair next to me and reaches for a croissant from the bag. He has a big cup of coffee in his hand, too. "Did you have a nice night, Jenn?" He peels off a thin layer of pastry and pops it in his mouth.

She flops her head down on the table and moans, "Too loud."

"How about you Dylan?" Greg asks.

"A good night, yes. But a better morning." Dylan winks while he takes another drink of his coffee.

When we get to the Art Institute, Dylan catches up with me as I'm kind of aimlessly wandering. "So I've decided to give you a personal tour of the Art Institute." He shoves his hands in his pockets.

Memories of last night and this morning flash through my mind, and it takes everything I have not to melt into a soggy little puddle right there on the tile floor. They could turn it into an installation, a cross between performance art and sculpture. *Girl: verklempt.*

I take a deep breath. "I would like that, thanks."

He smiles and shakes the hair out of his eyes. "Well, all right then. Where do you want to start?"

We're standing in the Arms and Armor section, but before I can answer, Dylan waves at someone coming around the corner toward us. A girl who smiles when she sees us. No, when she sees Dylan. He practically breaks into a run to get by a glass display encasing some chain mail vests and swords. Within seconds, they are a tangled mess of arms and hands, and I am forgotten.

Finally, he pulls away. He glances at my shoes, over the top of my head, everywhere but actually at me. "Piper, this is my, uh, girlfriend, Ava. Ava, Piper."

Girlfriend?

Dylan has a girlfriend?

Dylan has a girlfriend.

Of course he does. I saw him *with* a girl that night in the park, didn't I? Not to mention Dylan's totally the type to have a girlfriend. And even though it doesn't matter—it's not like I was actually going to date him, after all—I still can't help feeling like a boulder has dropped in my stomach. Plunk.

I keep my face as friendly as possible as she smiles at me and extends her hand, smeared with pencil or charcoal or ink or something. I shake it anyway and glance at her face, counting at least six piercings, only three of which are in her ears. And her entire left arm from shoulder to wrist is covered in a sleeve of a tattoo, just like Dylan's, only hers blooms in full color.

I recognize the tattoo from when I'd caught it in the beam of my flashlight. An elaborate bird—a peacock—wraps around her bicep.

"Nice to meet you," she says brightly. Genuinely.

Dylan explains that Ava is from Ridgedale. She went to Immaculate, the remaining private high school in town, and graduated last year. Now she's getting a BFA in Interior Architecture.

"You told me you were busy today." He laces his fingers into hers. She holds his hand for a moment or two, then drops it, tugging away. Must not be big into PDA.

"Oh, yeah. I found some time after all. So you've got what, two hours? What do you want to see?"

I start to back away.

"Piper, was it? You can come along, too, if you'd like."

I take another step backward and avoid looking at Dylan, though when I catch his face in the periphery I'm relieved to see a mixture of emotions there. The flare to his cheeks says embarrassment is probably front and center.

"I wouldn't want to intrude," I say.

"You wouldn't be. It's not like we can make out all over the place." She smiles again. "Well, we could find a way, I guess, but for your sake, we won't."

I feel my face redden and Dylan's matches suit.

"Come on. The more the merrier." She tugs my arm with one hand and Dylan's with the other so Ava is squarely in between the two of us. "What do you want to see?"

I shrug. "What's your favorite exhibit?"

Dylan groans playfully. "Hers is architectural drawings."

Oh. That sounds, erm, thrilling. I purse my lips, determined to go with the flow even if it does sound boring.

"Oh, Piper. Your expression says it all." Ava laughs. "How about we start with American Modern Art? Then we can swing through Impressionism and onto the Contemporary galleries and finish with the traveling exhibit you all are probably supposed to see?"

As we walk, Dylan explains to Ava how I'm in the spring drama and I'm Romeo.

"No shit?" she says. "I leave Ridgedale for a few months and suddenly the town liberals up?"

I laugh out loud at this. "What Dylan here neglected to mention is I'm one of the Ryan kids." She looks at me blankly. "Mt. Sinai Church?"

I can tell the moment it she works it out. "Oh, no way. As in Brother Ryan? The anti-gay guy's *daughter* is *Romeo*? You've got to be kidding me."

He's not—we're not—anti-gay, necessarily. We're just pro-God's design.

"Well, good luck to you sweetie. Something tells me you're going to need it." She turns down the hallway, slightly ahead of Dylan and me.

Dylan and I trail behind, deliberately not looking at each other. Or at least I'm being deliberate about it. We stop in front of one of the most famous paintings ever. *American Gothic*.

"Did you know"—Ava points to the farmer—"that people always make an erroneous assumption about that nature of their relationship? Can you guess what it is?"

"It's not his wife; it's his spinster daughter." I shrug and move on to the next painting. That's common knowledge. You don't have to be an artist to appreciate art. Or to know random facts like that. I mean, even I know how to use Google.

Next up is my favorite painting in the Modern Gallery. *Black Cross, New Mexico* by Georgia O'Keefe. Ava starts to say something no doubt about the artist or the history of the painting, but I hold up my hand. Sometimes, words just aren't necessary; the moment itself is enough.

Dylan and Ava move on but I just want to stand there and take it in.

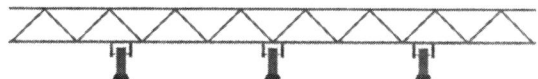

We head off to the traveling exhibit, the reason we've come to the Art Institute in the first place as apparently, the AP English students are in the middle of a section on Victorian English Literature and this exhibit features Victorian painters' works.

I can definitely see the trend toward romanticism, and these images are beautiful. Flowery and poetic, really. I round a corner and come upon a canvas that is familiar even though I can't recall ever seeing it. The plaque says it's by Sir Frank Dicksee and I don't have to read any further to know exactly what I'm looking at. Or rather, whom.

"It's Romeo and Juliet," Dylan whispers.

I nod and step up closer to study it, paying special attention to the artist's use of light, the way it seems to reflect off of Juliet's nightgown and makes her face glow. *The brightness of her cheek would shame those stars.*

"Victorians," Ava groans. "So sentimental and saccharine." She skulks off down the row and Dylan rocks back on his feet to follow.

"You coming?" he asks, walking away.

"In a sec."

"What we know and they don't is that it's the last time they'll see each other," a guy behind me says. I glance from the painting to see Tony grinning back at me. "Well, alive anyway."

I study the way Romeo leans into the kiss, halfway onto the balcony and yet turned back, wanting more. Needing more.

"*Farewell, farewell. One kiss and I'll descend,*" I whisper.

Tony decides to head to lunch with us and I'm grateful to no longer be the third wheel even if I'm still not sure how to *be* around either of these boys right now.

The weather is nice, decent at least, so we opt to sit outside in the garden patio area. While Dylan, Tony and I are in line buying soups and sandwiches, Ava volunteers to grab one of these tables with big green umbrellas.

"I got this." Tony winks at me and thrusts his card to the woman behind the register before I can even pull my money out.

"Tony, you don't have to buy me lunch."

"Obviously. But I got it anyway. I owe ya."

Owe me? For what? He thinks I've been accepting of him after his big reveal, but that's only because I'm apparently a better actress than I thought. Well that and he can't read my mind.

Dylan's standing at the next register over and his face crumples up a bit, like he just smelled something foul. He glances at Tony and then away quickly, turning his attention back to his tray and the guy behind the register, who's calculating the total.

Throughout lunch, Tony and Ava hit it off, laughing at practically everything the other says and finishing each others' sentences as they recall obscure current events. They laugh together, slapping their knees. Tony puts his arm around my chair and it takes everything I have not to shift away.

"Funny, isn't it?" he asks.

I didn't hear what they were talking about, but I smile and look to Dylan who's busy narrowing his eyes at Tony like he's scrutinizing him. Evaluating every movement as if he could be a threat. Ridiculous, of course, since not only have Ava and Tony just met, but Tony couldn't be less interested in Dylan's girlfriend. At least, not as a girlfriend.

When it's time to board the bus to go back home, Dylan has disappeared. Probably off making out with Ava. Unlike last summer, I'll be sure not to interrupt them this time. Because I so don't care to see any more of *that*. I climb on the bus and squeeze into another window seat. Tony is still standing outside the bus talking to some guy. One of the seniors who was out with us last night. I tap on the window to get his attention and point to the seat next to me asking if he wants to sit by me. He nods and holds up one finger as I plop into the seat next to the window.

I pull out my magazine and start on an article about a newly discovered drug-resistant bacteria when someone pushes past the people clustered in the aisle. A mini-chorus of "oomphs" and "heys" erupts in his wake as this same someone flops into the seat next to me.

Not someone. I look up at Dylan sitting beside me in what had been Tony's seat.

For his part, Tony is standing there in the aisle with a goofy grin on his face looking to Dylan and back to me. He winks and gives me a discreet thumbs-up as he slides into a seat two rows in front of me.

"So, did you enjoy the museum?" Dylan asks.

"I like art, so, yeah." I'm determined to be as nonchalant as possible. I flip the page. Because I Don't Care About His Girlfriend. I want to get mad but I can't really, can I? Clearly, he sees me as a friend. I don't have a lot of friends, so I guess I can work with that.

"What's wrong?" he asks.

I shake my head and smile. "Nothing. Reading this article." I hold up the magazine. "Did you know that your body contains more bacteria cells than human ones?"

He makes a face. "You're full of weird information."

I tap my head. "Like a sponge."

He grins and pops his earphones in, but I quickly yank his phone from his knee and scroll through his playlist. It's mostly top forty and oldies. "You have dreadful taste in music." Coming from me that's saying something.

"I do not," he says, too loudly since he's still got the earphones in.

Somewhere around Joliet, I must fall asleep, because the last highway billboard I remember seeing was for a Route 66 diner in town. The few sips of that coffee and the contraband diet coke I had at lunch are still no match for my tiredness. I wake up as we're pulling into Ridgedale. Dylan's jacket is draped over me; it smells like him and now I do, too.

"Oh God, I'm sorry." I sit up and rub my eyes, realizing I've probably been leaning against his shoulder this whole time.

"It's fine." He smiles.

And then I notice the massive drool spot on his shirt.

CHAPTER SIXTEEN

When we get back from the trip, it feels like there's this *thing* that happened. Two things really, and keeping my mouth shut about both of them is nearly impossible. I know I shouldn't need to talk about Dylan since it's truly no big deal, but I kind of have to process at least one of them or I might explode. So of course, I tell Jodi.

"You? Wait. *You* shacked up with Dylan Miller?" Her voice gets all high-pitched and squealy. "Like *shacked up with him* shacked up with him?" Her eyes go wide and she punches my shoulder. "It's like I don't even know you anymore."

We're having ice cream sundaes at Scoopz, which has been a weekly ritual of ours since we were old enough to bike here by ourselves. It hasn't been so weekly lately though with my rehearsal schedule. I still tell my dad we're going to Scoopz, but those afternoons, I've actually been running lines and working on blocking. I'm in desperate need of some Jodi QT.

Tonight, Jodi needed a break from studying for a pre-calc test and I needed a break from trying to memorize my lines, because turns out I have a lot of them. Like seven hundred. Anyway, tonight, it's mint chocolate chip with hot fudge for her, pralines and cream with caramel sauce for me.

"No!" Laughing, I flick some whipped cream that lands on the tip of her button nose. "He let me stay in his room because I was locked out of mine."

"But you slept there? With him?" She wipes the whipped cream off with her finger, licks it, and stares at me, her top lip twitching a smidge.

Man, when she says it like that, it does sound sort of scandalous.

"Technically, yes. But he was on the bed and I was on the couch. And we were really far apart. Like, several Holy Spirits apart." Growing up, my older sisters went to homeschool co-op dances and the chaperones would always insist they leave room for the Holy Spirit between dance partners.

Jodi clicks her teeth.

An eye roll seems insufficient, but I shoot her one anyway. "Dylan has a girlfriend. And like I said, *nothing* happened. I was locked out because Ashley Maygold and her boyfriend were too *busy* to remember to unlock the deadbolt. And Jenn Thompson ralphed all over me, so I was beyond desperate."

"Uh huh," Jodi says, still wearing a huge grin.

Before I can further defend myself, Tony walks in and makes a beeline toward our table. "Hey." He slides into the booth next to me. Jodi shoots me a look but doesn't say anything. "You about ready?"

"Jodi, you know Tony, right?" She nods curtly. I know ice cream dates have always been *our* thing, and now I'm inviting a boy to intrude. But it's just Tony. And we're meeting up after this and it's not like I can tell him to come over to my house for that. Especially not now. My dad would probably corner him and suss out his homosexuality in a few minutes of conversation. Then I'd probably never be allowed to leave the house again.

"Ready for what? You aren't coming over after?" Jodi asks.

Shoot. I completely forgot. "Oh, umm. Tony and I are going to run lines."

"Run lines? Here?" Jodi asks.

"No, at my house," Tony says. He dips his pinky into my caramel sauce and licks it off.

"Sorry," I say. "I completely forgot to mention it."

"Oh, sure. No big," she says. She can't fool me, though. The coolness in her voice and twitch in her upper lip tells me that she does mind. At least a little bit.

"You can come along if you want," I offer.

She narrows her eyes, focusing on Tony for a beat too long. "Thrilling as that sounds, I think I'll pass."

"So which scene you want to run first?" Tony picks at the bottom of his sneaker, plucking a piece of rubber from the edge of the sole. He flicks it toward the trash can by his desk and even makes it in. I keep glancing around his room for signs of his lifestyle choices, but it looks like a normal guy's bedroom, just like my brother's except it's about ten times bigger. As the only boy, Peter's been relegated to what used to be a storage closet so the older girls could take over what was supposed to have been the boys' room. Plural.

A soccer poster hangs on the wall by the closet and a couple band posters are tacked up above his desk. He even has a worn out stuffed dog in the middle of his bed, which he tries to hide with a pillow when he catches me eying it.

"Samuel Spaniel," he says sheepishly. He shakes his head and then pulls the stuffed animal from behind the pillow and tosses it into his closet. "Like Mercutio. I am also a heartless badass."

"Heartless? Would we say Mercutio is heartless?"

"Compared to Romeo, yes."

I shrug and we decide to start with Act I, since Mercutio and Romeo are still pretty much inseparable at that point. Tony stumbles over the Queen Mab monologue and asks for a line at least six times before he's finished.

"Gah! What does this even mean?" he groans. "Maybe if I understood it, I'd be able to recite it better."

"Beats me," I say. "And I don't know that understanding it will help all that much. I mean, I still don't completely 'get' Romeo."

"What do you mean you don't 'get' him?"

"Later on, after he meets Juliet, he feels more real to me, more honest. But before that, all the pining over Rosaline? It just seems so silly." I wave my hand like I'm shooing a fly. "Seriously. Who wants to be in love so badly that it causes them to tailspin into an existential crisis? I'm not even convinced he's in love so much as he wants to have sex. With someone. The who is less important, I think. If he has to marry her to do it then so be it."

"Come on. You've never been lovesick?" Tony asks.

"Umm, no..." I chew my lip and try to think of the word. Love. Sick. Shouldn't love, real love, make you the opposite of sick?

"Petrarchan?" Tony looks up from his script.

"Huh?"

"Shakespeare was mocking the romantic cliché of the day. You know, Petrarch. He was a Renaissance poet who wrote a lot of really lame love poems about the unattainable ideal of love."

"Okay. Well, I was going to say superficial."

"You sound like Mercutio. Maybe we should switch roles." He grins and flicks a napkin my direction. "Come on. We've got lines to memorize."

After Tony drops me off, I reheat some mac and cheese and attempt to tackle the growing mound of laundry that's piled up. Usually I try to stay on top of it better, but usually I have more free time. Laundry is my task and I hate it. *Hate* it. Next year, Paula gets it while I get bathrooms, and I seriously cannot wait. I would rather clean Peter's bathroom than do laundry, which probably shows exactly how much I hate it.

When I've determined which shirts belong to Dad and which belong to Peter (Peter's are a size larger and perpetually pitted out—gross), I take Peter's stack to his room.

"You can put them in the top drawer," Peter says coming in behind me. "I like them stacked five high."

I stare at him and then set them on his bed lop-sided. "Have at it, then."

He grabs my arm. "You better clean that up."

THIS ABOVE ALL

Tugging my arm free from his grip, I not-so-accidentally knock his neatly folded shirts over in the process, making sure to keep my dad's stack secure under my other arm. "Oops. My bad."

I make a hasty retreat before he can do anything else. He scoots off down the hall, trying to moan and tattle to Dad, but I smile when I hear Dad mention his lack of a servant heart. Satisfied, I head down the hall to my dad's room, taking care to put his shirts in the drawer. As I turn to leave, I notice the light is on in the closet. Dad must have forgotten it in his rush to get ready for whatever function or meeting he has tonight. I shake my head and open the door further so I can reach in and grab the chain.

I gasp when I see Mom's side of the walk-in, all of her stuff still on hangers, exactly as she left it. She died in the winter—Pammy's birthday is January 10th—so most of the clothes she had out are sweaters and long skirts. A small layer of dust has settled on the shoulders and creases of them, but otherwise they look the same as I've remembered, except that they are limp and sagging instead of filled up with her body, her life.

Why did Dad just leave it like this? I thought my Aunt Sue helped him clean out Mom's stuff ages ago. They were going to donate to the women's shelter or something. Instead, I realize, he's been looking at them every day, an ever-present reminder that my mom is gone. I wonder if seeing her side of the closet empty would be worse. At least looking at the closet this way, a part of me is almost fooled into believing she could come back, could have use for this stuff again. Or at least, that she's not completely gone.

A box on the shelf catches my eye. It's so different from everything else in this entire house. It's dusty, but clearly fine wood, ornately carved. I reach to grab it and blow the dust from the lid. I crack it open, just to peek, but when I lift the lid, the hinge is so tight that I can't help but open it all the way. Inside are an assortment of photographs and mementos. My mom in what looks like a brightly colored bikini with a feathered headpiece. What in the world? She's standing in a line with a bunch of other young women all dressed the same way. They look like…

harlots. But as I flip through the photos and find another couple where she's wearing brightly colored dresses, her shoulders or back bare. Then there's a photo of her and my dad. Now she's wearing a Western-style long skirt and blouse. She smiles, still, but it's a different sort of smile. The stack has a dozen or so other pictures, her pregnant, her holding a baby, her with my grandmother. She looks happy in all of them but she's not radiating joy like in the first photos, the harlot ones. She's more subdued in the recent ones, like sepia toned instead of full, vibrant colors.

Beneath the stack of photos are a couple dried flowers and a well-worn paperback book. *The Collected Works of William Shakespeare*. The cover has been taped and re-taped several times, even now as I open it, the front of it slides off. Inside, the pages are aged and yellow. Half of *Hamlet* flutters to my feet. I flip to *Romeo and Juliet* and find she's made notes in the margins. When Romeo and Juliet first kiss, she's got a note "By the book" circled three times.

Carefully, I close the box back up and slide it back into place. I'm going to hang onto the book for now. No ones opened this box in years and so probably won't notice it missing. Maybe my mom has some insights that will be helpful for my Romeo.

My hand runs over a sweater, one I remember her wearing often. I pull it off the hanger, a drapey black thing. My mom used to pair it with a skirt and leggings and wore it all the time. I bring it to my nose and breathe deeply. Beneath the veneer of dust and time I can still smell her, the faint remnant of her citrusy perfume and face soap. I fill my greedy lungs with as much of her as I can get. As much as they can take before they threaten to explode.

I try to hold the air in, hold her in as long as I can, but my lungs chest starts to burn and ache. I do it again. And again. Each time, taking a hit off of the sweater, hoping that the momentary high will sustain me longer than it possibly can. I finger a couple of other pieces. A flowing silk top, a pair of wool tights. A tweed skirt I don't remember her ever wearing. Her shoes are stacked neatly at the bottom of the closet, ordered by color and style. Mostly sensible, dark flats and boots but in the corner, under a pair of sneakers is one pair of red, alligator heels. They're way flashier than anything I ever remember her wearing and I snag them and slip my feet into them. Mom's feet were a touch bigger than mine, but with a strip of moleskin on my heel, I can probably make them work. I point and flex my toe. What would Mom have had these for, anyway? I don't recall ever seeing them much less seeing her in them. They feel like the kind of shoes that make things happen. I put them on and I feel like someone else entirely.

I pivot and teeter toward the door, my newly acquired heels sinking into the plush carpet and making it difficult to walk. I have to reach out and grab the door to keep from toppling over and as I catch myself, my face stops just short of my dad's tie rack. Dozens of colorful silk ties greet me. Does he wear all of these? I tug on one hanging near the bottom of the rack, pale yellow with gray and sky-blue stripes. It feels cool as it slips through my fingers. The tie Dad wore to Mom's funeral. At that point, he was so messed up that he couldn't steady his hands long enough to complete a Windsor knot. Phoebe and I had to help him, which meant using the church computer to Google "how to tie a tie." I watched a YouTube instructional video twice before I could get it right.

I wrap the tie around my neck and leave the wide end longer than the narrow. I pull the tie around and bring the end up through the loop I've created. Am I supposed to bring it down and under? Or down and over? I try for under and then bring the end back up again. Then across and back up again, taking care to tuck it through the knot I've created. I pull it snug and glance in the mirror hanging next to the door. I'm a sight—shruggy, oversized black sweater, flaming red heels and a sloppy-looking tie.

I undo the tie knot and try once more, flipping the fabric this way and that, taking care to leave a long enough tail. This time when I pull it tight, it looks pretty good. It doesn't make me look like a man, but strangely, it feels manly. Foreign, at least.

A rustling noise outside the door makes me jump.

"Gracious, Piper," Dad shouts as he doubles back from the closet. "What are you doing?" His eyes scan the heels and especially, the tie.

"I, uh." What *am* I doing? With my toe, I slide *The Collected Works of William Shakespeare* under the shoe shelf hoping my dad won't notice it.

"Are those your mother's?" he asks.

I nod and glance away, ashamed to have been caught in this reverie.

"You know, I'm growing concerned about you. Is there anything you need to talk about? Have you been keeping up with your prayer partner?"

I bite my lip. I can't lie outright and say I have because my next oldest sister Pearl is supposed to be mine but we haven't talked in a month, at least. Not really, anyway. "There's nothing wrong."

"You sure? Because that's how he'll get you, you know. Wait until you've grown weak and complacent and then." He claps in my face, causing me to flinch. "He'll have you right where he wants you. Jesus knocks and waits to enter but not him. Nope. He'll barge right into whatever cracked window you leave."

The 'he' he's talking about here is Satan. Satan will get me in his clutches and once you've fallen for his lies and traps, it's incredibly difficult to come back from that.

"Well," Dad says. His face crumples up and then he turns away. "Put everything back how you found it, please. Especially the tie. If you wear that, someone will think you're *confused*."

I hang the sweater back in its spot and put the tie back in its place.

"Actually," he says, startling me as he steps back into the small space. "You should keep those shoes. They were your mom's favorite and you're a lady now. You should have them."

CHAPTER SEVENTEEN

We're starting blocking today and meeting in the auditorium after school. Before rehearsal begins, I slink over to where Dylan and his crew are working on set pieces, mostly cutting plywood.

"Here." I hand him a drawstring bag. In it are his t-shirt and shorts, freshly washed. Monday, I'm determined not to let things be all awkward between Dylan and me. Because nothing happened. Not really.

He cocks his head and peeks inside. "Ah, thanks." He reaches back to his bag. "I have something of yours, too." He pulls out a small, handled paper bag that's folded in half and stapled at the top.

I take it and raise an eyebrow.

"I didn't wash it because I, uh, wasn't sure if you're supposed to." I see his face warm with the faintest hint of color. "And I wasn't about to ask my mom."

I take the bag and rejoin Tony, plopping down by my stuff while we wait for rehearsals to start. I peek in the bag and am mortified to see my bra inside. What? Did I leave it in Dylan's hotel room? I don't even remember taking it off.

"Scandalous," Tony whispers, looking over my shoulder.

It would be except it so isn't. Just mortifying is all. I cannot believe Dylan Miller has been carrying my bra around *all day*. It's official: I want to die. Which is good, I guess, because that's what we're working on today. Death scenes.

"People." Brooks claps a few times to get our attention. "I know you all think that last weekend was about fun, but it wasn't. I want you to take what you saw in Chicago and apply it here." He taps the stage floor for effect. Great. No big deal. Not like I can't live up to *that* standard.

Brooks turns to me. "Piper. Chloe. You're up."

Chloe flicks her hair in my face as she walks in front of me toward the stage.

This is the moment everyone's been waiting for so even the people who don't have to be here today are here, watching and waiting for Chloe and I to... kiss each other.

There's this haunting moment right before the poison kills him, when Romeo kisses Juliet. I mean he literally says, "Thus with a kiss, I die." Even if we fake the other love scenes, we cannot fake this one. I will have to kiss Chloe.

I. Will. Have. To. Kiss. Chloe.

Brooks had a long chat with the whole cast about it; about how it's not about titillation; it's about pain. Passion. Love. But judging by the number of people gathered as close to the stage as possible, it's still about titillation.

"You better not pull any lesbo stunts," Chloe whispers to me before mounting her makeshift altar which, for the moment, is a plain plywood box.

I don't plan to kiss her at all, of course. I plan to "die" just before I can. It's the only way I can justify doing this scene, this play. So I square my shoulders back, the way I gleaned from Dylan, the way I've been practicing in the hopes that I will be a believable male. When I'm holding Juliet in my arms, she starts to giggle, causing me to break character. Obviously.

"I'm sorry," she squeaks. "It's just, it's *Piper*, you know? This is probably her first kiss!" She erupts into a fit of laughter.

Like me, Brooks doesn't see the humor. "Miss Wennert, I expect more professionalism from you."

"Fine," she groans and tries to collect herself.

"Take it from Romeo's soliloquy. 'In faith, I will,'" Brooks says.

THIS ABOVE ALL

I repeat the monologue about the nature of death and timing. How it has stolen the breath from my love, but not her beauty. I leap up on the stage and cradle Chloe's body in my arms. "*Eyes, look your last. Arms, take your last embrace!*"

"*O true apothecary! Thy drugs are quick.*" Keeping my shoulders squared, I pull her closer and brush the hair from her face as tenderly as I can. "*Thus with a kiss I die.*" I lean in and crumple over just before an actual kiss.

I shift my weight so that Chloe can rise as the freshly woken Juliet. I gotta say, she nails her part. I can't see her, of course, since my eyes are closed. But I *feel* it. And the way the hush falls over the room, I just know. She really is good.

The rest of the cast, our audience for the moment, erupts in applause and whoops.

"Brilliant!" Brooks claps. "Piper, I can tell you're really starting to feel Romeo. Whatever you're doing, keep it up." I flush and glance toward where Dylan is working on his set piece. He doesn't look at me, but I can tell he's smiling.

Chloe sits up and scowls at me. Then she makes this big production of pulling a travel bottle of Listerine from her purse and swigging it.

Please. I only got as close as her cheek. And my mouth was closed the whole dang time.

"All right people. With the exception of group E, that's enough for today. The rest of the afternoon is yours. A few of you would be wise to use it memorizing your lines," he chides, eyeing Ashley and Greg pointedly.

Since we now have a free hour to kill, Tony and I decide to go hang out.

"How about the Underground?" he suggests. It's a coffee house in the basement of some big office building on Ash Street, so there are only a few street level windows, which gives the place a cozy, cave-like feel to it. Oversized leather couches crowded around the crackling fireplace and the strings of white twinkle lights wrapped around the exposed pipes on the ceiling further enhance the coziness. I've only been in there once or twice, and never to hang out, so I'm excited.

Two people sit on one couch, cupping their latte mugs and playing a game of checkers on the coffee table. And some group of guys—a band or something—is setting up to play. Behind the espresso bar is a giant chalkboard listing all the café's drink offerings. I opt for something called the Cambridge—an Earl Grey tea bag steeped in milk and topped with honey, which sounds better than coffee. The girl behind the counter hands Tony a mug and points him toward the self-serve coffee bar. When he's filled his mug, we grab a seat at a table near the fireplace.

"So..." Tony blows on his mug of coffee plus cream and stares toward the fireplace.

I hold mine and let it warm my fingers. "So..."

I'm quiet. He asked me to hang out, so I feel like I should let him choose the topic of conversation, but I'm not really good with silence. At least, not silence with someone like Tony. Jodi and I can sit together for hours and not say a word. But we've known each other for ages.

"How's Mercutio treating you?" I ask, finally when I can't stand the silence anymore.

"He's fine," but the way he's chewing his thumbnail tells me he's hesitating. "Except I can't help but wonder—" He shakes his head.

"Wonder what?" I ask, sipping my tea. ...

"Well." He sets his mug on the table and folds his arms in front of him. "Have you read much into Mercutio, as a character?"

"Umm." Not really. He's the prince's relative, neither a Montague nor a Capulet, so he gets invited to hang with both, though he clearly prefers the Montagues since they're his friends. I shrug. "What do you mean?"

"It's probably stupid, but I wonder if..." He keeps speaking, but a familiar frame making his way over to the coffee counter distracts me. He jumps behind the bar and starts fixing himself some kind of drink. While he's steaming some milk, he looks up and his eyes lock on mine.

Dylan.

It figures that of the hundreds of times I've come here and never seen him, the one day when I'd rather not, he's here.

"So what do you think?" Tony asks. "Am I being totally paranoid?"

"Oh. Umm." My face gets hot.

"You weren't paying attention, were you?" He eyes Dylan across the room. He looks to me and then back to Dylan. "You *like* him, don't you?"

"What? No. No!" I say.

"You're an amazing actor, but a really terrible liar," he says. "Horrible, actually."

I wave as flippantly as I can manage. "He has a girlfriend. And I'm not even allowed to date."

"You're not allowed to do a lot of things and yet you seem to be doing them."

It's true. I've spent the better part of the past month doing all sorts of things my dad would flip out over. "I don't want to date him. I just find him... intriguing is all."

He gives me this look that says I-still-don't-believe-you-but-if-you-want-to-keep-fooling-yourself-fine.

"So, you were saying something important?"

He scoffs. "Not really. I was wondering if you think the reason Mr. Brooks cast me as Mercutio is because of the whole sexuality thing." His voice gets hushed when he says sexuality. So much so that he doesn't really verbalize the word, just sort of mouths it.

"Sexuality thing?"

"You know, how Mercutio is supposedly the homo-erotic character?" He looks at me to see if I follow but since I don't he sighs. "You weren't paying attention at all."

"Sorry," I say. I truly am. I hate when people do that. "Tell me now."

"Mercutio is supposedly the gay character. I mean, Baz Lurman ran with it and made him dress in freaking drag."

"Wait, who is Baz Lurman?" I ask. This is the second time I've heard Tony mention him.

Tony laughs. "Oh, Piper. I love you. A director. He did a modern version of *Romeo and Juliet* set in like Venice Beach. Guns instead of swords and daggers. Modern clothes and cars but Shakespeare's language." He shakes his head. "Anyway, even more subtly, it's there. And I wonder if I'm so obvious that that's why Brooks gave me the part."

"Why do you care?" I take a sip of my Cambridge, which is creamy and honey sweet.

He scoffs. "Easy for you to say, Piper."

"I'm sorry. That's not how I meant it." How do I mean it? This is the sort of moment my dad has spent my whole life preparing me for, one where I can really hit Tony with the truth and pull him back from the brink. I don't even have to use any of the confrontational stuff because he's already a captive audience. I could start by explaining that the wages of sin, what Tony has earned himself is death, and how God wants to throw him into eternal damnation, but Jesus provides a way out. I know looking at the desperation in his eyes that if I lay it out for him like this, it will haunt him for a long time. It will be what my dad calls planting seeds for God to harvest later. But I also know that if I wallop him like this, it will change everything between us.

And it will crush him.

And, if I'm being honest, I think it might crush me, too.

I take a sip of my drink and say nothing, ignoring every instinct I have.

Tony glances at his coffee and takes a deep breath. "The worst part is that I've become a total effing cliché."

"You've started listening to Barbra exclusively and are suddenly full of sassy quips?"

The corners of his mouth turn up. But only slightly. "Ha ha. And how do you even know who Barbra is? It's just…" He stares into his mug as if he's reading the dredges of his coffee instead of tea leaves.

"Look, Tony. I think Brooks gave you the part because it's *your* part. Maybe there is something in you that is like Mercutio, but it probably has less to do with the transparency of your sexuality and more to do with you as an actor. It doesn't mean you're exactly like him or that people know about… you."

"You think?"

"If you had to be exactly like the character you're portraying, well then I'd be impulsive, oversexed and rebellious. And I'm none of those things. Also, I don't have a penis."

He laughs. Genuinely.

"So, if you don't mind me asking, why don't you want to let people know about it?"

"It's complicated." He runs his index finger around the rim of his coffee mug. "For one thing, my parents would probably kill me. Disown me at least."

"Seriously?" Not that I should be surprised. I think of my siblings. None of them are gay that I know of, but if they were, they'd probably try to hide it, too. Would my dad disown one of us? Honestly? Yes. But he'd give us a chance to repent first. I think.

He looks at me. "They're really old-school, first generation Italians and all that. What's funny is, I'm pretty sure my Nonna totally knows and she's Sicilian. Like, lives there. It's the Catholic thing, mostly."

Ah. Now that is more familiar territory for me. My dad thinks Catholics are heretics, but theology aside, the religious pressures to be a certain way, to act a certain way, I get.

"I'm pretty sure my parents would think I'm going to hell, and maybe taking them down with me. Honor and shame and all that." He gets this faraway look in his eye. I don't have to tell him about the wages of sin because clearly, he already knows. But if he knows, why wouldn't he want to repent? But I look at Tony and wonder how God would condemn someone as kind and earnest as him simply because of who he's attracted to. And, again why would God create homosexual people if he didn't want them to be that way? By that logic, either God made a mistake or God is a jerk and either way, I have to wonder if that is really the God I believe in. Truly?

"My second cousin in Brooklyn got sent to gay rehab." He takes a deep breath and lets it out slowly. At this point, I know I'm supposed to act surprised that gay rehab is an actual thing, but I'm not surprised because I know exactly what it is. My dad is on the board for a center in Wisconsin.

"They sent him away and wouldn't let him come home until he was 'cured.'"

"Was he?" My dad has all these success stories about people who've learned to circumvent their sexuality or at least learn to live in celibacy, not to act upon their *urges*.

"His current girlfriend's name is Teresa... And his boyfriend's name is Marco." A ghost of a smile spreads across his face. "What do *you* think, Piper? I mean really. I know how your family comes down on this. But what about you?"

He's holding the door wide open for me. All I have to do is walk through it, lay out the Scripture I know so well. The condemnation of homosexuals. The redemption of Jesus. But I try to open my mouth, to say the words I know so well, the ones I've screamed a hundred times before and... and once again, I just can't.

"Do you know how many times love is mentioned in the Bible?" I say. I'm not really asking him so much as myself.

"Uh, no."

"Upwards of 700. Know how many times homosexuality is mentioned?"

He shakes his head.

"A mere handful." I take another sip of the tea. "I'm not an expert in theology or anything," I say. Hardly. I've memorized more scripture than most, but I'm no apologist. "But you know what I think? I think there's too much hate in the world already."

"Care to come explain this to my parents?" He laughs and lets out a long, exaggerated sigh.

"Care to explain it to mine?" If my dad were here right now, hearing me process these things, these doubts, out loud and in the presence of a non-believing homosexual no less, he'd probably lock me away. Forever.

"Someday I know I'll have to tell them. But hopefully, that day is a long, long ways off. Like, maybe after they're dead. Plus, this town is not exactly gay-friendly."

I look to the floor. My family and our church haven't exactly helped in that regard. Which makes me feel like a total hypocrite. Here I am telling Tony one thing but when I go home? When I go home, it will be different. It has to be. "Does anyone else know?"

He shakes his head. "Not really. A couple friends of mine. And you. That's it."

I'm kind of flattered that he felt like he could tell me. And also kind of confused. We've had classes together for a few years now, but we aren't really friends. At least, not the kind of friends you tell your deepest secrets to.

We weren't anyway. But now maybe we are?

"I dunno. I felt like I could trust you. Plus, I kind of figured you suspected after you saw me eying my ex at lunch the other day. That and my book list."

"Your ex? Book list?"

"At the Burger Shack? He was in line when we were having lunch. And the books on my e-reader? It's practically a textbook list of must-read gay teen literature."

I hadn't noticed. I mean, I saw him eying that guy, but I didn't read into it that way. And the books, well, they're just books, right? I don't read a lot of secular stuff that's not required for school. I shrug and tell him this.

"Oh," he whispers. "Still it feels good to tell someone because my best friend, Jake? I really don't think I could tell him. At least, not yet." Tony stares at his cup.

I wish I had something helpful to offer him. Some words of wisdom or at least something intelligent. But I don't. I have no idea what it feels like to have to hide a huge part of who you are from your family and friends like that. Except I guess now I kind of do, don't I? The further into this acting stuff I've gone, the more I've had to lie and withhold details from my dad, from my family, all the while wondering if who I am around my family and who I really am are becoming two very different things.

It's not the same as what Tony's going through, I know, but in some ways, I do understand. I grab his hand and squeeze it once. He looks up to my eyes and gives me a little half-smile that says at least he knows he's not alone. His expression changes.

"Oh, man. Don't look now, but Mr. Intriguing is headed this direction." Tony nods, looking at something or someone over my shoulder.

Whenever someone tells me not to look, it's the first thing I do, of course. It's Dylan coming toward our table.

"Hey, Tony. Piper," Dylan says.

Tony smiles at Dylan, turns, and practically gapes at me, which I hope Dylan doesn't notice. For good measure, I quietly kick Tony under the table.

Dylan grabs an empty chair, scooting it up to us and edging his way between Tony and me. He flips it around so he's leaning his chest against the backrest. "Post rehearsal debrief?"

"Something like that," Tony says. "You work here, man?"

Dylan takes a sip from his mug, a tiny bit of froth clings to his top lip. "Yup. Not a barista though. I run sound." He gestures at the band setting up on stage. And I'm simultaneously impressed and confused, because I haven't forgotten about his hideous musical leanings.

"Usually we don't have shows on Mondays, but this group is passing through from Nashville and they booked a gig."

"Is that a hammered dulcimer?" I ask. You just don't see those very often.

Dylan nods. "Apparently, they have quite the following. We've been getting calls all week about the show."

An awkward quiet falls over our table. We each take sips of our drinks, nodding periodically as if our beverages are the most mind-boggling of things and require much pondering.

"So how are the sets coming?" Tony asks. And I'm grateful that he thought of something to break the silence.

"Good. It's hard since we have pretty much zero budget, but that inspired some creativity. We're going with an abstract minimalist thing. Lots of black walls and doorframes and corrugated steel that mark space off. I don't want the sets to compete with the real talent." He eyes me as he says this and I lower my gaze to try and hide the pink that's surely blooming in my cheeks. "Seriously. I know I've said it earlier but Piper, you really are amazing."

Tony nods in agreement. "Truth."

"Didn't you spend your summers at Interlochen?" Dylan slurps coffee between his teeth.

"You're thinking of Chloe," I say. "She's gone every year since she was like eight." The sass in my voice is not directed at him, but he shrinks back a bit anyway. Oops. "I've never been in a play before. Not a real one anyway." Try to keep my voice lighter.

"There are fake plays?" Tony teases.

I laugh. "Church musicals. I've been in plenty of those." I don't mention Hell House. Now, the thought of playing the Lesbian with AIDS in Hell House makes me burn with shame.

"There are church musicals?" Dylan asks.

"Definitely not at my church," Tony says.

"Oh yes. You know, kids in ugly smocks with towels on our heads and Birkenstocks on our feet looking like shepherds or disciples or whatever."

Dylan leans back and takes a long sip of his drink. "Like a live nativity?"

"Kind of. But with musical numbers."

Tony laughs. "Nope definitely not at my church. Although once when I was a kid, my older sister and her friends did this liturgical dance-thing during Lent. It was really weird though, and the priest never let it happen again."

I nod. "Like I said, fake plays. Singing lame songs about the tower of Babel or the people of Nineveh hardly counts."

"I'll agree with you on that," Tony says. "Still though, you must have learned something."

"My mom was the church's music director. I guess maybe I learned some stuff from her." I leave out the bit about her reading Shakespeare to me every night. Or the bit about me watching contraband clips on YouTube and mimicking what I saw. Or about how I've recently concluded that my dad takes on a character every time he preaches or evangelizes, and in a way, he's taught us to do the same.

"I knew it," Dylan says. "So what does your mom think of the play?"

"Oh, umm. She died. When I was in eighth grade." I choke down another sip of tea. Most everyone in my grade knows this, but I guess people like Dylan aren't as plugged into the rumor mill.

"I'm sorry," Dylan says. "I mean I'm sorry she died but I'm also sorry to bring it up. I—I didn't know."

"You're one of the few," I say.

The rest of the week is a blur of classes and rehearsals. Chloe and I are doing our best to pretend the other doesn't exist. Which is impossible, of course since I'm Romeo and she's Juliet. Can't have one without the other.

"Watch it," she yelps when I get too close to the makeshift balcony (for now, a ladder) and she toddles a bit, catching herself just before she topples. "Taking me out is definitely not going to help your cause."

My cause? I have no idea what she's talking about so I choose to do what I usually do where Chloe is concerned: ignore her.

That we would both love the chance to clobber one another is apparently lending itself well to our stage chemistry, as backward as that probably sounds. Mr. Brooks seems impressed though. As I finish my balcony soliloquy, he claps.

"Marvelous. But Chloe, remember that for the first bit, you don't know that Piper is there. You've got to be speaking as if to yourself. These are Juliet's innermost thoughts. It's as if you're speaking to a diary or a close confidante." Chloe nods, but when Mr. Brooks turns his back, she gives me the stink eye—as if I have something to do with his notes. Or that she's apparently doing something wrong.

"And Piper?" He turns back and grabs his big binder with the full script. "Remember it's 'liv-er-y' not 'live-ry.'"

I pretend to agree, but I have no idea what a livery is anyway so I make a note to look it up. Of course, Chloe gives me a self-satisfied smile at this. I want to pull her top lip up over her head.

Ordinarily, I am not a violent person, but Chloe seems to bring it out of me. Which begs the question, how will we be able to convincingly play lovers when we aren't even friends? When we can't even stand each other? In rehearsals, we haven't gotten to *those* scenes yet. Just the death one where we have to play *off* of each other but not *with* each other.

I don't know if that's something Mr. Brooks is doing on purpose or if it's luck. But I do know that part of me is dreading it while the other, smaller part of me can't wait to see how it plays out. I get the feeling the rest of the cast feels the same since they probably can't help but notice Chloe and I don't exactly get along.

"Sometimes enemies make the best lovers," Tony says as we're leaving the rehearsal. "Maybe that will be true for the two of you."

Maybe. If the sexual tension were real. Thing is, it definitely is not. I'm not going anywhere though, and I know she feels the same way, so we're going to have to figure out how to make it work.

"It'll be great, you'll see." Tony wraps his arm around my shoulder. "It's like how people always say 'imagine the audience in their underwear.' Well, just imagine Dylan instead of Chloe."

I elbow him and he laughs.

CHAPTER EIGHTEEN

I'm supposed to be at rehearsal in five minutes, but I haven't even stopped by my locker yet because I'm stuck here working on a make-up chemistry experiment I missed the other week for the Chicago trip. I'm so busy watching the clock that I completely space and can't remember which bonds double up. Sigma is single but then what? I scribble something down and hope it's right. Or close to right.

It's not that I don't like chemistry; I do. Admittedly, I haven't been paying much attention to anything outside of drama lately. I need to work on that. Especially with those blasted ACTs and SATs coming up. I'm taking both and soon, but I haven't studied the practice question books in weeks. Too busy memorizing my eleventy billion lines.

I plop the paper on Mr. Jeffrey's desk and scoot down the hall from the science wing toward the auditorium. I don't really have time to stop by my locker, but I do anyway. I'll probably be a minute late, maybe two. But so far, we've never started exactly on time. And anyway, I'm the lead. They can't start without me, right?

Well, I guess they probably can. And I remember the way Brooks dealt with Jenn when she was late on our full-day rehearsal. And his words on day one: you are replaceable. I wonder who would take my place if I got cut? Tony? He's fabulous as Mercutio and it would be natural for him to step into my role and let someone else step into his. Not that Mercutio isn't important. He totally is. It's just, Tony is good.

Really good. And despite Mr. Brooks' opinion, I think Tony probably should have gotten Romeo in the first place.

It's not my call, though, and since Romeo is growing on me, I better hurry and get to practice before I really am late. I charge up the steps, taking them two at a time and head toward the back door of the stage, but when I tug on it, it's locked. Crud. I'll have to go down the hallway and around to the front where it will be infinitely harder to sneak in unnoticed. A walk of shame up the center aisle. Great.

But as I come around the corner, I see a group of my cast mates clustered in the hallway in front of the auditorium doors. And they. Look. Pissed.

Oh no. Am I late? Is Mr. Brooks punishing the lot of us because I'm late to rehearsal? I slide up to Tony, breathless.

"It's not fair." He shakes his head. My shoulders slump. He's right; it's not fair for me to be late like this. I'm not special and regardless of the circumstances, I should have been here on time.

"You're the best for the part," he says. "And they can't step in like this and take it away." And then I blink. Wait, what? Mr. Brooks kicked me out of the cast? Just like that?

I check my watch. "But I was only three minutes late!" It would have been two if the back door hadn't been locked.

"Huh?" Tony looks at me for a moment before returning his attention to the doors, which, I notice for the first time, are still closed. And Mr. Brooks is nowhere in sight.

"Hold on, what's going on?"

"The signs." He points to the door. "They say we can't go on like this."

I step closer and see a Xeroxed letter with the school masthead taped to the door. It's signed by the principal, Mr. Schiffner. *Re: Romeo. Until the part of Romeo is recast appropriately, the spring drama has been canceled.*

Appropriately.

"Someone complained," Greg whispers. "That's what I heard anyway."

"Complained about my acting ability?"

Tony shakes his head and chews his thumbnail. "Piper, someone complained that Romeo is being played by a girl. And Mr. Schiffner is a pansy."

Oh. My stomach falls to the floor with a wooshing thud that I'm sure is audible to everyone around me. I take a step back. And then another. Because it feels like the crowd is closing in on me and I might be crushed under the weight of bodies.

I turn on my heel to get the hell out of there. I need... something. Water? Air? Anything other than the sound of their whispers and muffled conversations, which seems to echo all the way down the hallway.

As I make my way toward the front doors of the school, Mr. Brooks' voice booms over the crowd.

"It's bollocks," he says. "I can't believe he'd have the nerve to—" but his voice fades away as I burst from the building and stand at the top of the steps. I lean over and press my hands into my knees.

"Piper?" a voice says behind me. Without looking up, I know it's Dylan. But I don't want to talk to him. Not now. Not with these tears threatening to burst forth.

"Piper?" another voice says. Tony.

There's an awkward shuffle between the two of them. One backs up and the other steps forward. The door closes, and I feel a hand on my back.

"Piper?"

Tony. Thank God.

"It's going to be okay," he says. "We'll figure this out. It's gotta be some kind of misunderstanding or something."

He sits on the stoop and pulls me down with him. Beside him, really. He wraps his arm around my shoulder and I let myself lean into him.

And then I cry.

CHAPTER NINETEEN

At the Wednesday night service, I'm physically present, but my mind is elsewhere. Dad's launched into a new tirade tonight, one that seems to go on for an hour. I have no way of knowing exactly how long he's been preaching since there isn't a clock in the church sanctuary and I don't own a watch. But judging by the grumbling in my stomach, it has to be close to dinner. One of my favorite things about midweek worship is the potluck we always have afterward.

But Dad doesn't show any signs of slowing. On the contrary, he's gaining momentum, like a train just pulling out of the station. I can almost hear the chug-chug-chug. He shuffles some papers on the podium and nods to where my two oldest sisters, Phoebe and Penelope, are stationed near the side of the platform.

"As it is written in the book of Ezekiel, *Thou hast also committed fornication with thy neighbors, great of flesh; and hast increased thy whoredoms, to provoke me to anger,*" he quotes. Again that word. *Whoredoms.* "The Lord your God is angry." He walks back and forth in front of the podium, pounding his fists in the air on the word anger.

I chew my cheek and keep my eyes lowered to my Bible, flipping through the pages to try and locate the verse. Ezekiel what?

"*Thou hast moreover multiplied thy fornication and yet thou wast not satisfied herewith. Therefore thus says the Lord: 'Your wife shall be a harlot in the city; Your sons and daughters shall fall by the sword; Your land shall be divided by survey line; You shall die in a defiled land.* Can I get an amen?"

"Amen," someone whispers. Another shouts it.

He continues. "In Romans, Paul tells us, '*Therefore God gave them over in the sinful desires of their hearts to sexual impurity for the degrading of their bodies with one another. They exchanged the truth about God for a lie and worships and served created things rather than the Creator- who is forever praised. Amen.*' Does any of that sound familiar?"

A room full of heads bob in unison. I have to admit it does sound a bit like modern society. Materialism. Greed. Lust. Those are definitely still alive and thriving.

"What happened? Paul goes on. He says, '*Because of this God gave them over to shameful lusts. Even their women exchanged natural sexual relations for unnatural ones. In the same way the men also abandoned natural relations with women and were inflamed with lust for one another. Men committed shameful acts with other men, and received in themselves the due penalty for their error.*'"

He takes a long, deep breath and his eyes flick over all of us. "So, what does this mean to us today?" He scans to see who will make eye contact, not that he expects anyone to answer him. But eye contact is a signal that you're paying attention. I look up.

"I'll say it again. The Lord is angry. Did you catch it? He 'gave them over.' Another way you could say that is he said, 'to hell with them.' To hell. With. Them."

"Yes He did!" someone calls out in the back.

"Amen," Peter whispers from behind me.

"And fellow redeemed, we are standing at the edge of the gates of hell. And He is asking you, *Will you stand up for my sovereignty and turn away from your own iniquity*? Or will you be like the Romans and defile yourselves?"

"No!" someone shouts from in front.

"You won't?" My father pauses and takes a dramatic swig of water from his glass. "Because that's not what I see. I see a world that is defecating on the Word of God. A nation that turns its head while fornicators and sexual deviants run rampant! We're practically laying down the red carpet, ushering them into our churches, our home. Even our schools."

I steal a glance at Penelope. She keeps her eyes forward, head bobbing in agreement with my dad's message.

"Brethren, the Lord God has given us a task. And we must take a stand. We must show this nation that we are not afraid. That the Lord is mighty and the Lord will execute His perfect judgment. His holy wrath. And the way to do that effectively is to provoke. To show the world just how vile these behaviors are, to show them what God will give them over to if they don't repent and turn away."

"Amen."

"Praise God."

"Amen," I mouth when his eyes fall on me. But, I realize, I don't mean it. Not even a little bit.

I know it's true what Paul wrote about knowing there's a Creator, about instinct. But instinct also tells me that the Creator doesn't make mistakes in what he creates. So how do I remedy that dichotomy? If God *hates* gays, why did he create them?

"Maybe some of you have heard about this? Just this week, my son informed me that the high school that my children attend is blatantly promoting a homosexual agenda."

I stare at my hands in lap, my face burning with shame. Does he know about my involvement? He must. I steal a glance, but his eyes are not on me, they are scanning the crowd, making sure we're all with him.

"You know what this tells me? It tells me that we need to make sure our voices are heard, that God's presence is known. Seen. Felt." His voice booms.

"How?" someone asks.

I hear a collective gasp and look up to see my father holding a huge sign. "God hates faggots," it reads in giant bold letters. He holds up a second one that shows male stick figures in obscene poses.

"We must confront the fornicators and faggots boldly. Our words, apparently, are not enough. We will engage them with these. And we're going to begin rotating demonstrations, starting tomorrow evening with the University's Gay-Straight Alliance fundraising dinner. An event sanctioned by the University and to be attended by the Chancellor himself. And in addition, we'll ready ourselves, so if our children's school reneges on their promise to remove the homosexual agenda from the drama? We'll make ourselves known there, too. Whatever it takes."

He smiles broadly like this is the best idea he's ever had, the best idea God has ever given him. "If the school holds up, then we'll focus our attention wherever it's needed. The battles are being fought everywhere and the war is far from over. Now, there are materials to make a sign or two for each of you. We will hold them and we will stand against those who stand against God, warning of His impending wrath."

"I didn't tell him it was you, you know." Peter leans forward and whispers behind me. "I figured that you'd want a chance to confess your sins directly. But you better do it soon or else I will tell him."

How could I be so stupid to think my brother wouldn't have heard about the play? That he wouldn't object and tell our dad about it?

I whip around in my seat. "You found out?" I whisper.

He rolls his eyes. "I go to Ridgedale, too, Piper. I'm not blind. Or deaf."

Stupid. I am so, so stupid.

Penelope holds a stack of sign making materials. I pass them down the row and grab my stomach, pretending that I'm getting sick. It's not that hard.

"Back in a minute," I say. "I don't feel so good."

Back in our room and collapse in a heap on my bed, yanking my comforter up over my shoulders. Maybe if I can just tune out the world for a bit, I'll be able to come up with a plan. Or if not a plan, maybe I'll be able to sit still and not cry for more than a minute. I knew my dad, my church, wouldn't approve of me playing Romeo—of *a girl* playing Romeo.

The fury is building behind my eyeballs. I'm so angry. At Mr. Schiffner. And Mr. Brooks for not standing up to Mr. Schiffner. And at myself for ever believing I could be Romeo without something like this happening. Of course this was going to happen. My dad is John Ryan, hater of all things worldly, mouthpiece for God, who also, apparently, hates the world.

Except the first line of scripture I ever memorized was John 3:16. I was three and there were M&Ms involved. *For God so loved the world that he gave his one and only son that whoever believes in him shall not perish but have eternal life.*

God. So. Loved. The. World.

The play aside, I don't know how I can reconcile a God who so loved the world with the God my dad claims to serve. The God he wants me to serve.

My entire life has been built on the premise that God was shaping me into *this* girl. The one who obeys her father in order to further the Kingdom of God.

But if I'm not her or if she is not me, then who am I?

CHAPTER TWENTY

In the morning, on my way out the door, I pass by a stack of signs propped against the wall. There's at least three-dozen of them, each emblazoned with a message more provocative than the last. When my little sister Pammy runs out the door to catch her bus I can't help it, I gently flip the front sign around so that only it's blank backside is visible now.

At school, there are shifty eyes, low voices, averted gazes, and blatant stares. A hush seems to fall over every cluster of students when I pass. People I don't even know. Great. I've gotten used to not being *this* girl. To being able to blend in unnoticed. Only now, it's even worse than when I started. Now, instead of pity or sideshow curiosity, I'm getting looks of ridicule and amusement. Before today, no one really paid any attention to the theater stuff or those who participated. It was just another extracurricular activity in a high school filled with them. But now? Now the play (and by association me) have become a spectacle. Well, a bigger spectacle. And virtually everyone is talking about it.

"Piper?" Tony comes up behind me, breathless. He's been chasing me all morning and I've been narrowly avoiding him, skipping down the hall and around the corner, pretending I don't see or hear him. But not this time. He was waiting for me outside my second period class and he grabs my elbow as if I might bolt. He already knows me too well.

"I've been trying to catch you all morning," he says between breaths.

"Really?" I feign innocence. "I've been in my own world, I guess."

"Listen..." Breath. "There's a cast meeting after school..." Breath. "At Greg's."

"Why would I go? I'm not in the cast anymore." Secretly, I'm wondering who's going to replace me. My money's on Tony, which, frankly, is part of why I've been avoiding him. It's like, I know he'd be a great Romeo, but hearing the news would still kill me. Because that would make it real. I'm out and Tony's in.

How ironic.

"News flash: no one is in the cast anymore."

I shake my head. "That's not true. The ultimatum was for me. There's no reason the rest of you can't continue. The show must go on, right?"

"Bullshit," Tony practically spits. "First of all, *you* are Romeo. And second, this is so much bigger than just you now." He points to the flyer on the door. "Them's fighting words and we've got our answer."

"Our answer?" I am so confused.

Tony takes my hand in his. "Yeah. We say, 'Game on, bitch.'"

Huh? My jaw drops.

"Come to the meeting today. We're meeting at 3:30 at Greg's. He's over in the Ivies."

"The Ivies" is the development next to our neighborhood. The houses are fifty years younger, forty percent bigger, and three hundred percent more expensive.

"Gotta jet," he says over his shoulder as he races down the hall.

I don't understand who is fighting whom or why, but I'm intrigued enough that maybe I will go to this meeting.

Before lunch, I seek a momentary escape in the bathroom. I need to muster up enough courage—or at least fake courage—to go into the commons. I lock the door to the stall and pull my legs up on the seat so no one knows I'm here. Two other girls enter and go over to the sink to apply lip-gloss or fluff hair or whatever.

"So I heard there was this really graphic girl-on-girl sex scene. Like they were pretty much going to do it. On stage."

"Shut up!" the other squeals. "Between Chloe and Piper?"

"Well, the tension between them is palpable." Another laughs.

"So what happened?"

"Well, I hear Piper was really into it, if you know what I mean. I guess all the church-girl stuff has led to some pent up tension? And her dad freaked out."

"I sooooo should have tried out for the spring drama." And then they both laugh as they leave the bathroom.

I knew there were rumors but I didn't know they were so… so graphic. And wrong. Or are they? Is it possible that my dad had something to do with this? Peter's words echo in my head, *"I didn't tell him it was you."*

Could one person really wield that much power?

I decide to skip the commons altogether as my new objective is clear: to keep my head down and my focus on the true task at hand: surviving today. Jodi has been trying to run interference for me as best as possible, but we only have two classes together and she has to go to the track meet tonight mostly to support her team, which means she's in competition mode. Also, she's part of the team now and that means hanging out with them, even if she doesn't ever get to compete. They make her suit up and sit on the bleachers with the rest of the team but usually, she doesn't get to do a single event. If you ask me, that's totally lame and more than that, Jodi is fast and she deserves a chance to prove her stuff. But nobody ever asks me.

She keeps inviting me to come and at least watch practice, but with rehearsal schedule, I haven't been able to. Maybe now I'll actually have the chance.

"Piper, if you need me you better call, you hear?" Jodi holds up her cell phone as she walks backward down the hall, away from me and toward a pack of her track friends. "Anytime."

THIS ABOVE ALL

I'm walking down the hall on my way out when a voice stops me. "Miss Ryan?"

Mr. Brooks. He looks exhausted and disheveled. He's wearing a T-shirt and crumpled khakis instead of his usual tweed coat.

"Mr. Brooks?" As far as I knew, he hadn't been at school today.

"I just stopped by to drop off lesson plans for tomorrow. Personal day. Do you have a moment?" He motions me into his classroom and sits down at his desk, offering me a chair opposite him.

"So," he says, taking a deep breath.

"So?"

"This isn't about you, you know."

"It isn't?" Because it sure feels like it is.

"Sometimes adults forget that children aren't as innocent as we think. And adults aren't as smart as we think, either." He runs a finger through his mustache and I study his face, waiting to see if there is more. "Yours is a real talent and whatever happens, I hope that you won't waste it. Continue to explore opportunities in community theater at least, but I truly believe you could do more, much more, if you wanted to."

I nod and force a smile. "Okay." It is nice to hear. I've always loved the idea of acting on stage, but I never really knew if I could actually *do* it. So to hear him affirm it is, in spite of everything else, nice. I press my lips together to keep the tears at bay. Brooks waves his hand dismissively and clears his throat. "Well. Speaking of community theater, I'm directing *Pygmalion* at the Theater Center this summer. I'd love for you to audition."

He stands and moves toward the door and I'm pretty sure this is my cue to leave.

"Thanks, and hey, there's always next year, right?"

CHAPTER TWENTY-ONE

I**n here," someone calls.**
Tony kicks off his shoes and adds them to the pile by the door before he grabs my hand and leads me toward the back of the house, what I guess to be the living room. It, too, has high ceilings, vaulted with track lights and a massive chandelier.

I'm so busy scoping out the house that I almost miss that all eyes are on me from the moment we enter. Tony ushers me to a spot on the floor, near the back of the sofa. As I glance around the room, it's clear that basically the entire cast and crew are here. Except Mr. Brooks and his assistant, Scott.

Dylan is leaning against a pillar of some sort. I look away when Greg starts to speak.

"Now that we have everyone, let's get started."

I wonder if they really were waiting for me.

"Since clearly, we've been sent a message," Greg says, "one we cannot ignore, I wanted to get everyone together so we can plan our next move. We're on defense here, so our options are limited. But, I've done some research and found..." In my head, his voice gets quieter and quieter, replaced by my thoughts. I look around the room at the faces of my fellow cast mates. Judging by the bags under their eyes and the way they try to stifle yawns, I'm not the only one who didn't get much sleep. And I feel awful they've all been put in this situation in the first place.

I should have just declined the role. How much easier would this all have been if I'd just said no?

"So, who has ideas?" Greg claps, snapping me from my thoughts.

For a long time, no one moves or says anything. So I do. I raise my hand and stand up. "Umm, I think the solution here is pretty clear. I'll just step aside."

Everyone stays quiet and I don't know if it's because they were waiting around for me to say it and don't want to be rude by showing their relief? Probably.

Chloe speaks up. "I mean I totally think she'd be a, umm, decent Romeo or whatever, but maybe Piper is right. There's no need for all of us to suffer." It's not quite smug, but almost. Whatever. I can't blame her. If the tables were turned, who's to say I wouldn't think the same thing?

Greg makes a sound like a buzzer. "Wrong."

"But why? It's simple and that way no one gets hurt," I say.

"Sorry to tell you this Piper, but it's not all about you. I mean, you are a great actor and for that reason alone, we should fight. But this thing is about more than just that. If we allow the administration to shut us down because someone or a group of someones don't like something we've chosen to do, where does it end? What if they decide they don't like a particular line or theme? What if one scene offends them? Or a certain play? How far will it go?"

I see his point, but I've never been a fan of the slippery slope argument. Chalk it up to years of my dad's political forecasting. If the liberals let whatever issue happen, then all hell will break loose and the planet will implode. I'm beginning to see it's probably more prudent to focus on the now. The what *is* not the what *could be*.

"I think we have to fight it," Tony says beside me.

A few people murmur their agreement.

"This amounts to censorship and we need to nip it in the bud now," Ashley says.

A few people clap.

"So if we're in agreement, what do we do?" Greg asks, scanning the room but for what, exactly I'm not sure.

Dylan steps forward. "I think we need to appeal to the school board."

My stomach sinks again, for the eleventy-billionth time in twenty-four hours. I feel my face get hot.

"I like where you're going with this." Greg busts out his laptop and scrunches up his face as he starts typing. "The next meeting is the evening of Monday, April 3. And in order to get on the agenda, we've got to file by end of business Monday, the week before."

"File what?" someone else chirps.

I know the answer to that. Ever since his kids started in the public school system, Dad's church has made a habit of frequenting school board meetings and sponsoring referendums. So I know for certain that the school board meets bi-weekly and in order to present before them, you've got to file a petition. And depending on the nature of the appeal, the petition has to be signed by a whole lot of people. If this issue affects the entire school, as this one arguably does, then we'll need hundreds of student signatures.

"A petition. We gotta collect signatures pronto," Greg says. I hear a printer start up somewhere. Greg gets up and runs down the hall. He returns in a moment carrying a bunch of papers. "Alright." He bites his lip calculating. "We need like 300 signatures."

"By next Monday?"

Greg nods.

And the first thing I feel is relief. There is no way we'll collect 300 student signatures by then. Which means there is no way we'll get to go before the school board. Which means there is no way I'll find myself pitted against my dad or the church.

The image of those outreach signs flashes through my head. I don't think they'd protest a school board meeting with them, but it's not beyond the scope of possibility. Especially if they find out that I'm at the center of this whole thing and Peter's basically assured me that they will.

Greg holds up one page. "Says here we need a spokesperson. Someone to present a summation of our petition to the board."

As soon as the words have left his mouth, another quiet settles over the room. I'm studying the hardwood floor intently, as if it is the most amazing thing I've ever seen. When I finally look up, all eyes are on me. Tony's staring at me, pleading with his eyes. He looks like he might get down on his knees and beg if it comes to it.

"What?" I ask. It comes out as a sort of croak.

"Well, you are the natural choice," Greg says.

Oh no. I can't do that. Don't they understand what they're asking?

"Besides, with you being the daughter of Pastor Ryan and all…" Greg stops mid-sentence, no doubt noticing the horror that must be scrawled across my face.

"That's exactly why I can't do it," I say. The truth is I'm not even sure I want to go to the meeting at all, much less speak. They're basically suggesting I choose between the play and my family. Don't they understand that? The room feels hot and spinney and I know I have to get out of there, get some air. I spring to my feet and make for the door, bursting out onto the patio. I don't take the time to slip on my shoes and the cement is cold against my bare feet. I claw at the collar of my shirt because it feels as if it's choking me.

"Piper?" Dylan's standing there, propping the door open and peeking his head out. "Come back inside. It's cold out here."

"Maybe I want to be cold."

"Okay." He steps out on the patio, barefoot like me. Well, he has on socks.

He's quiet and I know he's waiting for me to speak, but I have nothing to say. I can't do it. That's final.

"You know, in a way, this is a gift."

A gift? He's got to be kidding. "A gift?"

"Of a sort."

"How so?" I can barely keep the incredulity from my voice.

"It's not that *Romeo and Juliet* isn't a good play and all. But now we have the chance to really make it mean something, you know? Something bigger and more lasting than just… than just two people who want to be together but can't."

I steal a glance but he's not watching me, he's looking out across Greg's lawn and down the street. I have to admit that I will miss having an excuse to watch him. For research purposes and all. Of course.

Dylan crosses his arms and presses his hands against the sides of his arms. He's right; it is cold. "Like we're the Montagues and the administration or, umm, whoever, are the Capulets."

Whoever. No, not whoever. My family. Wait. I haven't become like Romeo. I'm like Juliet. I'm hiding this secret, going against my family behind their backs.

"We aren't the Capulets?" I ask.

"We could be, I guess. But I always thought of the Montagues as the good guys." He shrugs. "You have to admit Juliet's dad was kind of an asshole."

True. He did try and marry off his fourteen year-old daughter as if that could be an antidote to the family's grief over Tybalt's death.

"Anyway, I think you should do it. Speak at the meeting, I mean."

I take a deep breath and let it out slowly. I know why he thinks that; I know why everyone thinks that. Of who I am, who my family is, they think that the school board will pay more attention. And they might be right, but I know who else will pay attention: my family. My church.

"But it's my family, you know? And if I push against them like this..." I can't even finish the thought.

"But you aren't pushing against *them*, you're pushing against the system."

"The system that my dad wants to influence. And anyway, he won't see it that way. He'll see it as me rebelling against him. Worse, he'll see it as me rebelling against God." I can't admit that that's my fear, that this whole thing has been one massive rebellion: me against God. There is no way I can win that battle.

"You know," he says, shaking me from my thoughts. "You won't know what your dad thinks unless you talk to him about it. He's supposed to be into 'family' right? Maybe it won't be so bad."

Right.

"Well, think about it." He sighs. "Because I think you're our best hope."

THIS ABOVE ALL

I'm sitting on the stiff couch, enjoying the relative quiet of the empty formal room when Peter plods in carrying a big box. "What are you doing in here?"

I spend a lot of time in here because no one else does. It's the one place in the whole house that I can be alone. Close to alone, anyway. Peter turns on the light and it's so bright I have to blink. The sun has started retreating from the sky and I didn't realize I was sitting in the dark.

"You shouldn't have your feet on the sofa."

I don't move a muscle and he sighs. "You talk to dad yet about... everything? At school?"

"That's not really any of your business, is it?" Why does he care so much? Why is he always trying to boss me around? Practically control everything I do?

"It is, actually. A shepherd's flock is his business."

"Last I checked, you're not a shepherd and I'm definitely not your sheep." And then it hits me. He thinks he's a shepherd? "You want to be the next in line for Dad's ministry."

He tries to keep his face blank, but I can tell by the way his eye twitches that this is exactly what he thinks. "Seriously? It's a pulpit not a throne."

Peter's expression sours. "Piper, you're part of this family, aren't you? Well, the things you do, the choices you make? They affect all of us, whether you like it or not. I'm surprised you were able to carry on as long as you did. That the guilt of disobedience didn't destroy you. Makes me wonder about the state of your salvation. I think you better pray long and hard about that. Get right with God."

"I thought Jesus was supposed to *take away* our guilt."

"Only if you repent and turn away from your sins and take up your cross daily to follow him."

Take up my cross daily. What does that even mean, really? It's the passage in Mark where Jesus is telling his disciples that this is how they follow him. Before Jesus, the cross was a symbol of humiliation and indignity of the grandest order, so the disciples we're probably really confused. Now, you hear people say it like it's a burden or something difficult they have to do. 'Like 'oh that's just my cross to bear.'

I think it means dying daily to ourselves in order to follow Jesus.

I already tried that though, didn't I? I was willing to give up the play—to die a small death to myself—in order to appease everyone, including Jesus. The cast gets their show, my dad gets his obedient daughter, God gets his servant back. Win-win-win. So why didn't it work?

"Well, don't forget to talk to Dad. Soon. Or I will." Peter tsks and turns to go. "Oh, and I made this one just for you to hold tonight." He opens his box and hands me a gigantic foam-core sign. It's neon orange and it says, 'Faggots go to Hell!' in bold angry letters.

CHAPTER TWENTY-TWO

Dad says that this is a good thing, that throngs of students are gathered around cursing us. The more people who react against us, the more effective our work. No, the more righteous we become. By comparison, maybe? Like God might look down on us and see that we were true, and good, attempting to bring his message of truth to a people simply unwilling to hear it. It actually sounds kind of ridiculous to me now.

"*I come not to bring peace, but a sword,*" Dad says, quoting Jesus. "Stand firm. We will not be moved."

So I'm standing here, holding the sign that Peter made just for me but wishing I could be somewhere—anywhere else. Without the drama, this is my life again, I guess. Before, I never would have considered playing hooky, but now I might have to come up with another regular excuse to get out of these events. Is that even a possibility? Or will my family get suspicious and figure me out? All right, so what if they do? Would my dad really cast me out? He thumps his chest with the Bible and points to the sky and my siblings clap and cheer in response.

He might.

The rain let up which makes it only a fraction less miserable. But the angry looks and makeshift counter-protests are spreading like a virus. Girls in sorority letters, guys in jerseys, people dressed up for this fundraising dinner we're protesting, all of them getting as close as the campus police will allow, shouting at us. One girl spits on Penelope. Dad just turns up the sound on his megaphone.

It's not our first confrontational demonstration, obviously, but it's the first time we've used signs this bold and off-putting. Now, the whole point of this is to anger people, to reach phase two faster and more efficiently.

Me? I just want it to be over.

I'm about to shift my sign from one hand to the other when a guy bolts from the crowd of onlookers and trips over the makeshift barricade.

"Watch out," I holler, instinctively reaching my hand out to help block his fall. My sign clatters to the ground and for a moment his eyes—both confused and angry—lock on mine.

"Get the fuck off of him," his friend says, pulling his arm from my hand. The fallen guy gives me an apologetic half-smile before his friend pulls him away. The friend turns my direction once more. "Bitch."

"Faggots," Phoebe yells. If she saw what happened, the whole of what happened, she doesn't say anything. "The Lord will judge your sinful ways." For a second, I wonder if she's talking to them or to me.

I retrieve my sign and hoist it up again to Phoebe's approving look when I look up to see a face in the crowd, one I recognize.

Tony.

He's standing there with who I guess must be his parents. They're all holding programs with the School of Music's logo. A concert or recital, maybe? Tony's gaze flicks from me to my sign, which I turn to the side so he can't read it. Though he keeps his face blank, stoic, his eyes tell a different story. A story, I realize, I can't ignore. He turns away and I swear I see his shoulders slump. I want to run after him, to scream that I don't mean it. I don't mean any of it. But before I can do anything, he's gone. Vanished around the corner of the School of Music with his parents.

"Excuse me," I say. I drop the sign like it's burned my hand.

"Piper?" Phoebe asks.

"Not feeling great." I grab my stomach and then think better of it and put a hand to my mouth like I'm going to puke. Even if I hadn't recently taken up acting, this wouldn't be much of a stretch. I do feel sick. Or more accurately, disgusted. With myself.

"Hurry back," Phoebe says. She turns her attention back to the crowd, joins in with the rest of the church members now singing, "If you're a homo and you know it," at the top of their lungs.

When I get home, I try and call Tony, but he doesn't answer which is maybe just as well. I'm not sure what I would say if he did.

CHAPTER TWENTY-THREE

Friday morning I get to school early, hoping to avoid the whispers and prying eyes since the school drama is all anyone cares about. Jodi picked me up and didn't say anything when I plopped in her car wearing some humongous sunglasses. I used to make fun of my mom for her big sunglasses. "Mom, you look like a bug," I'd say. Now, I'm grateful for them and how much they hide. I know I can't wear them in school without drawing more attention to myself, but at least getting to and from the building I have a mask.

Jodi parks on the street a few blocks from school. We've got a student lot, but only seniors are guaranteed parking spaces. Juniors have to hoof it about a quarter of a mile and around the corner. It's not bad when the weather's nice, but when it's snowy or raining or sweltering, that quarter mile feels a heck of a lot longer.

As we're coming up on the front entrance to the school, I see a group of people with signs and banners out front. And I realize that they're a group of cast members. Tony's holding a megaphone and leading a chant. "We won't be silenced. No, we'll stay! Give us back our play today!"

Jodi looks at me and I know she wants to know if I want to join in. I also know that she'll defer to me—if I want to chant, she'd gladly stand right along side me, screaming at the top of her lungs.

I grab her arm and tug her toward the building, hoping like heck that no one sees me as I pass. If only I could be so lucky. Instead, Tony's yell comes over the megaphone behind me.

"Piper! One, two, three, four, *you* are who we're fighting for."

For a moment, I'm frozen in place, as if my feet have been replaced with cinderblocks. Tony stares at me, as if he can see through me. In a way, he probably can. I'm trying to straddle this line, to stay neutral, and it's not working.

But here's the thing: it's not fair for them to pin their hopes and expectations on me. Yeah, I want to be in the play. But I didn't ask for this, for any of it. All I wanted was to be Juliet. I don't want all the attention, I don't want to start a freaking revolution and most of all, I don't want to be pitted against my family. Against my dad.

Against God.

No way.

I find my footing again and tear off toward the school, zipping past Jodi up the stairs and into the familiar beige hallway, lined with gray and red lockers.

"What was that about?" she asks, trying to keep up. "They're protesting the cancellation, huh?"

"They want to go before the school board," I whisper, shoving my discarded sunglasses into my bag.

"Oh, that's a good idea," she says.

"No. It's a terrible one."

"What? Why?"

I explain about my church, my family, and their increasing interest in protesting anything and everything that promotes the *homosexual agenda*. How the recent change in tide nationally toward tolerance and equal rights has only solidified their stance.

"You don't understand. Now they're holding these signs and chanting... things." Hurtful things. Hateful things. I have to blink away the memory of the look on Tony's face.

I hid my sign in my room, under my bed. I can't hold it again, I won't. I'm not sure there was ever a time I would've gone along with this particular approach to 'win souls,' but I definitely know I can't now. Not when one of my closest friends is a homosexual.

Wait. One of *my* closest friends is gay. When did that happen?

"So you aren't going to join the fight for the play?"

"I can't. I've tried to tell them to drop it. Replace me and move on, but they won't."

Jodi bites her pinky nail and studies me. "But you don't mean it."

"Of course I mean it. I wouldn't say it if I didn't mean it."

"Uh huh. Piper, for as long as I've known you now, you still think I can't tell when you're lying?"

I'm not lying. I really would rather they move on without me. Okay, truthfully, I'd rather they didn't have to make that choice at all. "You're right. I don't want to give up the play. But what choice do I have?"

Jodi stops at a red locker and tucks a note through the vent. It belongs to one of her track friends I think. "You have the choice we all have: fight or flight."

I groan and smack the back of my head against her locker for effect. Which is really stupid because it kind of hurts.

"Have you at least talked to your dad about it? He's not completely unreasonable, you know. Maybe there's no reason to fight at all."

"That's exactly what I told her," Dylan says. He's leaning against a locker watching us. I wonder how long he's been standing there.

"See? At least someone has some sense." Jodi licks her lips and gives me this look that I hope Dylan doesn't notice. With her eyes, she's telling me to remember my night in Chicago, as if I'd forgotten. I frown at her and step away from the locker.

Dylan follows me down the hall toward my locker. "Wait up." He pulls something out of his pack and hands it to me.

"What's this?" I take the paperback. The cover says it's by Sophocles.

"*Electra and Other Plays*," Dylan says.

"I can see that but, erm, why?"

"I think you should read *Electra*."

"What are you my English teacher now?"

"Nah. I could never replace Mrs. D. But I thought you might... connect with it. That's all." He spins on his heel and heads the other way down the hall.

"Will there be a pop quiz later?" I call out after him.

He turns back toward me and just smiles and shrugs. "Never can tell."

On my way to my locker, I pass by Tony. Even though we're the only two people in the hallway, when I try to stop him, he ignores me completely like he can't hear me. Not that I blame him. I'd probably ignore me, too. Or worse.

I sigh and round the corner and come upon my locker, but even if I hadn't been distracted, I wouldn't have been prepared for the sight. At first I think it must be a mistake. I'm on the wrong floor, right? But then I glance at the locker numbers and I know I'm not. A small crowd has formed around locker 1129 and it is covered with obscene graffiti. "Dyke" is written in huge black letters with—is that spray paint? There are dozens of other less-than-flattering phrases and words and crude images scrawled all over the place. I inch closer and the scent of fresh Sharpie and spray paint attacks my nose. The paint is still running down on the "O" of "lesbo" making a serpentine trail of black. Like a slug.

I hear a few people laugh, but time sort of stops as I reach out to touch the paint, to verify that yes, this is real and I'm not hallucinating. Just as my finger connects with the cold metal of my locker, I hear another gasp behind me.

"Oh my God, Piper," Jodi whispers. She and Serene stand there gaping for a moment before they rush forward. Jodi pulls me in for a hug. I don't hug her back though because now my mood has instantly shifted from denial to anger. Still, she keeps her arms wrapped around my tense frame for a minute, holding me like that before she goes into mom-mode and leads me back down the hall toward the main office. "Don't worry. We'll get it taken care of."

Serene echoes her agreement.

We wait in the main office for a few moments. Serene links her arm in mine and Jodi explains the situation to a secretary who then calls in the custodian who hadn't noticed anything last night before he went home.

"Obviously." I hold up my finger, now smudged with the black. "The paint is still wet."

Moments later, the secretary and custodian are speaking with our principal, Mr. Schiffner.

"Wonder if he knows this is his fault," Jodi scoffs.

It's not though, not really. He was a catalyst, sure, but this runs much deeper than Mr. Schiffner.

"Piper, I want you to know that here at Ridgedale, we take defacement of school property very seriously," Mr. Schiffner says. I notice that he doesn't mention *what* was written, just that school property was defaced. "But given the sensitive nature of this particular incident, how about I write a pass for you for this morning's classes? You can have a study hall in the empty back office. Take some time to collect yourself and then, when the custodian has finished cleaning your locker, you can go back to class."

Even if Mr. Johnston removes all traces of what was written there, he can't remove the feeling those words left behind. They're not even true, so why do they affect me so much?

Because they make me feel small and powerless.

Which is probably exactly how we—no, how *I*— made Tony feel last night.

Jodi looks at me in a way that asks if I'll be all right and I nod and give her a strained smile. I'm sure I will be. Eventually. My only consolation is that school hasn't started yet so most people will only see Mr. Johnston cleaning process. But knowing the way rumors spread around this place, I'm sure that everyone will know just exactly what happened before the first bell rings.

What kind of sick person would do this? Why?

The realization hits me so hard I nearly stumble backward. My dad. My dad would do this. Not only would, but he did. Not these actual words scrawled on my locker but those signs the church made, that my brother and sisters waved around said strikingly similar things, didn't they?

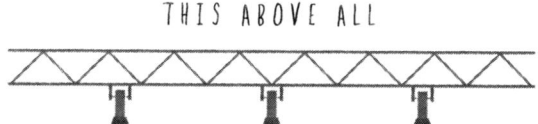

The ticking of the clock on the wall is the only sound to compete with the thoughts in my head. I'm sitting in my makeshift study hall in the vacant back office, right next to Mr. Schiffner's suite trying to keep my mind off the morning's events. Needless to say, it's not going so well. I reach in my bag to grab a pen and feel the book Dylan gave me. I pull it out and open the cover to find a post-it note in Dylan's ragged handwriting.

"This makes me think of you," it says.

So I read it. Okay, I skim it. Because Greek tragedies are even harder than Shakespeare to decipher. Basically, this girl Electra is sad because she thinks her brother is dead (I can't relate to that), but it turns out he isn't; he's pretending to be someone else so he can kill their mother and her lover in order to avenge his father's murder at their hands. Sounds vaguely familiar, but I can't figure out why Dylan wanted me to read it so badly.

By lunch, I'm over the locker thing. Or pretending to be, at least. I'm not gay, those words are vile and hateful, and they aren't true. Whoever wrote them is obviously trying to get to me so I've decided my plan of attack will be to remain strong. Resolute. *It doesn't bother me.* I keep telling myself this, anyway, even as I scrub and scrub at the black residue that lingers on my fingertip.

And it doesn't bother me, so long as I don't think about it.

As a sign of how much I Do. Not. Care, I even slide up behind Dylan as he's standing in line at the vitamin water machine. I wouldn't have pegged him for a fancy water kind of guy. "So, you want me to kill my dad?" I think about what I've read of *Electra*.

He doesn't even turn around, he just laughs and plinks some coins into the machine. "Way to take it literally, Piper."

"How was I supposed to take it?" Even over the swirling odors that permeate the high school commons, the grease-soaked pizza and taco bar and crappucino machine that cranks out "coffee" drinks from powder and water, I can smell him. That mix of boy and detergent and something else. Something that's just him.

"The Greeks were big into symbolism." He chooses plain water, not the fruity kind. "You've read *Hamlet*, right? Well, *Electra* was probably a precursor to *Hamlet*."

I knew it seemed familiar.

"And a theme in both plays, hell in *Romeo and Juliet*, too, is that sometimes, adults or parents mess up. They aren't perfect."

"I know that."

"Do you?" His eyes search out mine. "Also, Electra is as much a complete character as Hamlet. Who cares if the she's a lady or a dude? It matters even less if the actors portraying them are male or female."

"I know that, too."

"Yeah, but do you? Really?" he asks again, keeping his eyes locked on mine.

And now I'm indignant. "Yes, Dylan, I'm not an idiot. Or a baby."

He holds up one of his hands, the one that's not holding the bottle of water. "I didn't say you were."

"Then what are you saying?"

A toothy grin slowly spreads across his face and I notice for the first time since we've been talking that he's sporting a wicked five o'clock shadow. It looks like he hasn't shaved in days. His face is covered in scraggly dark stubble, a bit lighter than his hair color. And I generally detest facial hair on guys, but it looks good on him. He looks simultaneously pulled together and unkempt. Like an artist who shutters himself in a mountain cabin to paint. Or sculpt. Or whatever.

"I'm saying that I think you need to give yourself more credit." We walk toward the other side of the commons where he'll leave and join the artist table and I'll join my friends. "I know you don't want to disappoint your dad or God or whatever and I get that. But I also think that if you sell yourself short here, you'll disappoint yourself. And

THIS ABOVE ALL

that's infinitely worse."

"You don't understand." I sigh.

He steps forward so there is only like a foot and a half between us. And okay, yeah, I don't mind him coming closer, but I'm also keenly aware that we are standing in the middle of the commons. Like a sixth sense, I can feel everyone's eyes on us, boring into him and me and, especially, the tiny space between us.

"Then help me to understand," he says, his voice getting quiet so that I almost have to lean in to hear him.

"I don't know that I can." It's like there's this war going on inside of me. On the one side, my family and their teachings and expectations and on the other, the things I've begun to figure out for myself. What I haven't figured, and what is critically important, is where God factors in all this. My family would say he is squarely and securely on their side, and there was a time when I would have been sure of that, too.

But now? Now I don't know what I think.

He shakes his head and lets out this long sigh as if I'm the most exasperating person he's ever known. "Look, I just want you to think about someone like Jon." He gestures toward his table where Jon, pretty much one of the few openly gay students at our school, sits. "And what this means for him. And other people just like him." He raises his eyebrows. "This could be an opportunity, Piper. A chance to tell the administration exactly how we feel about their policies."

He sighs. "Look, I know your family has some backward ideas about gays and all, and even if you aren't 100% okay with it all, at the very least, I think you're big enough to recognize that it's possible to care about a person even if you don't like all of the things they do." He holds my gaze without blinking and I get the feeling we aren't just talking about Jon anymore.

Dylan steps even closer so that I can almost feel the heat radiating from his chest. My breath catches in my throat. "I really wish you'd reconsider, because I think if you'd just be honest with yourself, you'd admit that you really do want to fight." He steps away, brushing my shoulder with his as he heads to his table.

Be honest? Ha. Coming from him that's especially ironic.

I start toward my friends to see Jodi looking up at me communicating wordlessly that she not only saw the whole exchange but also, *what the heck* was it about?

But before I can get to her, Peter steps out, blocking my path.

"You really should give it up," he says.

"Pete, not today," I grumble as I try to push past him. He steps with me and cuts me off. Again.

"It's just that"—he squishes up his face—"I'd *hate* to see you get hurt when this all blows up in your face. And believe me, it will blow up. In your face. Dad might still think you're his precious little angel, but that can change. Quickly."

He sniggers and shuffles off, leaving me standing there in a wake of his awful deodorant and something else. Something chemically and bitter. Like turpentine maybe? No, like Sharpie. Paint.

I catch up to him and grab one of his hands. There, on his nails, are tiny droplets of black paint, like the kind of splatters you get when you hold a spray can.

"You."

A measured smirk spreads across his face and he shrugs. "Your word against mine."

CHAPTER TWENTY-FOUR

After school, Peter is standing next to my freshly sanitized locker. "Waiting to redecorate my locker again?"

"I'm giving you a ride home."

"I'll walk."

"Come on, Piper. Eventually, we are going to have to talk about all this." He grabs my backpack and starts down the hall, so I have no choice but to chase after him. He throws my pack in the trunk and slams the door before I can protest.

In the car, instead of heading directly home, Peter pulls in the strip mall and parks in front of Scoopz. "I don't have any money with me."

"My treat," he says.

So I order the Grand Tortuga, which is the single most expensive item on the menu even though it's basically a glorified turtle sundae in a parfait cup. He gets one scoop of vanilla on a sugar cone.

"So." We're sitting at the table furthest from the door. I'm want to resolve not to touch my sundae just to spite him, but I can't let perfectly good ice cream go to waste. So I nibble at it, savoring the salted caramel that's drizzled down the inside of the plastic cup.

"Why did you do it?" I ask. I'm pretty sure he won't tell me but I have to try.

"You know why."

"I have no idea, actually." It makes zero sense. He knows I'm not a lesbian and I don't even know where he came up with some of those words. Peter and I have never been close, but I can't say I saw this coming, either.

"To teach you a lesson. To give you a little taste of what would be in store if the play went on."

I laugh. "You've got to be kidding me. How does defacing my locker with obscenities teach me a lesson?"

Peter bites at his ice cream, taking a huge hunk of the cone. He slurps it into his mouth. "That's what people will say about you. It's what some of them have already been saying it behind your back."

"Why do you even care? It's my problem, not yours."

His turn to laugh now. "I already told you—what you do affects all of us. What would that look like for the church? To have a homosexual in our midst?"

I can't believe his logic. Or lack of logic, really. He cares about what a handful of idiots think? "I'm not actually gay, you know. I was cast as a male character, playing opposite a female character." Brooks' words now coming from my mouth.

He scoffs. "Right. Like that makes a difference."

What? "It does make a difference. And anyway, let's say I *was* gay. Would that make me beyond the reach of God's grace?"

He blinks once. Twice. Maybe I've finally gotten through a bit. But nope, because he answers by quoting scripture at me. "*A good tree cannot produce bad fruit.*" The book of Matthew.

"Nor can a bad tree produce good fruit," I counter, finishing the verse. It means that the things of God will bear good fruit or yield results. But what constitutes a 'good' fruit? Is it someone forging a friendship? Someone finding community? Acceptance? Someone feeling loved? Because I've seen that kind of *fruit* come from all this. If good begets good, then which is better: healed relationships, love, justice that can come from accepting people, or pain, suicide, and the tearing apart of families that can come from the condemnation of people who are gay?

"Well, it doesn't matter now anyway. It's over. I just thought it would help you to understand why it has to be this way," he says. "And get you to wise up before you're knocked off of that pedestal Dad's got you on. I could have just told him about all this straight away, you know. I did you a favor."

A favor? He did me a favor? "They're fighting it. The cast, I mean. It could be overturned."

"How?"

And my resolve stiffens, moves from this nebulous intangible feeling to something altogether different. Little does he know, Peter is responsible for that, for the catalyst that has finally pushed me over the razor edge I was trying to navigate. Now that I more fully understand what those labels and words can feel like, now that I have a greater sense of empathy, I have no choice. And Peter gave me that.

I lick some more caramel off my spoon. "They're—we're—going to take it to the school board."

"You can't. You'll have to stand against Dad. Against us. Against the church."

"I know. Believe me, I've thought about that. But then I also thought about the message that this prohibition sends to our school. And to certain members of the student body."

"To who, the fags?" He laughs.

And the word burns. Like, I didn't know it was possible for a single word to literally reach out and slap you in the face, but it does. I feel it sizzle in my gut. And just like that, I'm transported to this morning and my locker. He knows exactly what that word can do. It's why he chose it. It's why my dad chooses it.

It's why now, I choose the opposite.

"Thanks for the ice cream." I stand.

"I'm not done." He gestures to his half-eaten cone.

"Well, I am. And I'm going to walk home." It's a far walk, but there is no way I'm riding in the car with him now.

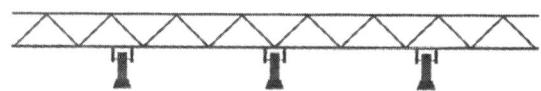

Downtown is lit up in the early evening. A couple years ago, the city council decided that they liked the look of the twinkle-lights in the trees so much that they kept them up even after the holidays. Now, down along the city square they keep all the trees lit year round. It looks like something out of a Norman Rockwell painting full-time.

I should have brought a real coat instead of this lightweight jacket, but then again, I didn't exactly know I'd be walking home. Or meandering around town for hours, avoiding attending another protest. I button my jacket as high as it will go and shove my hands in the pockets, hoping to warm them against my body.

I could call one of my sisters, but, even if they aren't out at another demonstration, I don't because then I'll have to have some kind of explanation. I can't avoid it forever, of course, but I have to figure out what, exactly, I'm going to do. What part I'm going to play, so to speak. And then I'll tell them. And maybe this time they'll listen.

Or not.

I guess it depends on how likely Dad will be to kill me. Scale of one to ten, if I only go to the meeting and sit with everyone else, that's like a two. Dad will shoot me the stink eye for sure, but hey, I'm just a concerned citizen. But if I do what the cast wants and speak before the Board? Well, on the scale of 'thou shalt nots,' that's probably a twelve at least. Definitely a *death to any he that utters them* kind of scenario.

As I'm walking up Ash contemplating all this, I hear the faintest sound of music—a guitar and a voice singing something. The song is familiar and yet not. I stop to listen for a minute and realize it's coming from a cracked window at the Underground. The flier on the menu board outside says Cairo Poppies are playing tonight. Never heard of them but since it's only 7:30, I could stop for a minute and warm up. Plus, if there's live music, it means Dylan might be there. Not that I particularly want to see him in my current state, which is one of tear-stained confusion and cold, but he's like the Bermuda triangle to my personal aircraft: no matter how I try, my internal compass always seems to go haywire around him. One of these days, I just know I'm going to crash.

And burn, probably.

I try not to think about that now as I settle into a seat at the back of cafe. I can't try very hard though because up on the stage, under the spotlight, strumming a ukulele and crooning into the mic is the Bermuda Triangle himself. Dylan.

He's singing a song I vaguely recognize, but then again not. The melody that is vaguely familiar. "'I wish I had a Sylvia Plath,'" he croons and I realize I know the song because he sang it for me, in Chicago. I slip into a table and watch as his fingers deftly dance over the keys.

After the end of his set, the lights come up a bit and the cafe patrons start to chatter and step up to the coffee bar to refill their mugs or order dessert. I'm about to try and slip out the door hopefully unnoticed when I hear my name.

"Piper?" Dylan is standing behind me with his hands in his pockets.

"Oh. Umm. Hi," I say.

"What are you doing here?"

"I was walking by and I heard music so I stopped in. I, uh, didn't know it was you." I glance at the posters on the bulletin board, the ones advertising some band called the Cairo Poppies.

"The band we booked bailed, so I filled in." He smiles.

"You didn't tell me you're an actual musician," I say, remembering my private serenade in Chicago.

"I'm not. Not really."

"Sure had me fooled."

"Just a hobby. For fun. Look, I was going to get a drink. Do you want anything?"

Umm. I'd kill for something warm right now, but I have exactly sixty-seven cents in my pocket and I didn't bring my wallet. I can't tell Dylan this. "I'm okay."

"Well, will you hang for a second? We can chat or something for a bit? If you want?"

"So you can continue beating me over the head with *Electra*?"

"Hey, I gave you fair warning that there could be a quiz."

I shake my head, sit back at the table, and wait. He reappears a moment later with two mugs anyway. "Didn't know what you'd like. It's hot chocolate."

Hot chocolate sounds so good I could cry. I hold it close to my chest and let the mug warm my hands and the steam warm my face. "Thanks."

"So why are you out and about tonight?"

I really don't want to get into what happened with my brother. "Needed to clear my head so I went for a walk."

"And came all the way downtown?"

"Something like that. So how long have you been playing?"

"Since forever and since never." I'm confused and he laughs like he knows what he said doesn't make any sense. "My mom was an artist. Well, kind of. She fancied herself an artist, but never could stick with anything for very long. So we've got oil paint sets and a zillion blank canvases in the attic somewhere, the shed out back was converted into a pottery room. In our basement, we've got everything you'd need for a dark room. There's a baby grand piano in the front room, and the library has like seven shelves of books on writing. But she couldn't ever stick with anything for very long. As soon as she got all the materials to master something, she'd move on to the next thing. My dad's afraid that if my sisters or I take an interest in anything remotely artistic, that means we're going to turn out like her, so he doesn't encourage it. Not the music, and certainly not the visual art."

"So you're self-taught?"

"Kind of. The uke anyway. But Ava's mom is a pianist and I took lessons from her. That's uh, kinda how we met."

"What happened to her? Your mom, I mean." The way his face falls a little makes me regret it, and I trip over myself to recover. "Y-you don't have to talk about it, if you don't want." Of anyone, I should know how awkward this line of questioning is.

"No. It's all right." He takes a big gulp of his hot chocolate before he continues. "She left. My dad wanted her to get help and take meds and she, well, didn't. Said it would 'stifle her light.' So she bounced and my dad got the court to say she was an unfit mother and then we weren't allowed to see her."

"Yuck," I whisper. It sounds like an absolute nightmare. Having a parent die is awful, but at least I know my parents loved each other deeply right up to the end, and I can't imagine having parents who literally wage legal war against one another. "Have you talked to her since?"

He shakes his head. "Not really. She used to call on holidays and my birthday, but that's about it." He sets the mug on the table and looks up at me. "All right, enough of this boring talk. Are you—" The low ringing of his cell phone emanates from his pocket. He pulls it out and frowns at it. "Crap. Do you mind?"

I shake my head. "Of course not."

He answers, and turns away from me and the table, but only slightly. "Hey there." His voice softens out. It must be Ava. His eyes light up and his features relax.

I try to study the artwork currently displayed (and for sale) along the wall of the cafe. Mixed media involving photographs and what looks like papier maché. I swear I'm trying not to eavesdrop, but his voice changes when he talks to her. Then there's a twinge of disappointment.

"You're kidding? It has to be *this* weekend?" He sighs and throws his head back, pinching the bridge of his nose. "No, I understand. Just was really looking forward to seeing you. Okay, call me later?" He clicks the phone shut and turns back to me.

"Ava?" I smile as brightly as I can manage.

He blushes. "God, am I that obvious?"

Yes. And so obviously unavailable.

CHAPTER TWENTY-FIVE

I sneak into school early, mostly to check out my locker and make sure there aren't any more surprises. I grab my books and make my way down the hall, past the front office and the auditorium doors. A copy of Mr. Schiffner's letter is still tacked to the door, though someone keeps ripping them down so the secretaries have to replace them pretty much hourly. I glance behind me and to the left. No one is looking, so I finger the edge of the letter and swiftly lift my hand up. The letter rips off and I crumple it and throw it in the trash can attached to the nearby janitor's cart.

I step toward the door and try the handle. To my surprise, it's unlocked. Probably because the janitor who belongs to this cart was just inside. Or plans to be soon. What's the worst that can happen? The janitor catches me and asks me what I'm doing? I can play dumb.

So I slip through the door into the dark, empty auditorium. I remember the first time I was in here, when this whole mess started. I wander up the aisle and run my hand over the rows of seats as I pass. Four hundred and twenty-five seats down here, another 200 or so in the balcony.

Before I can even make sense of what I'm doing, I hop up on the stage and flick the overhead lights on. There are a few half-finished set pieces clustered upstage. Downstage, on the apron, I notice the tape marks for scene changes. The blue piece is for the balcony scene. My—Romeo's—monologue. I step toward it and look up at the light. *But soft, what light through yonder window breaks?*

THIS ABOVE ALL

The feeling is so much different this time than the first time I said those words on this stage. The first time I was nervous and timid and confused. Now, even though I still don't agree with Romeo's choices, I feel like I at least "get" him. I throw my shoulders back and square my hips the way I've practiced, carrying myself more like a boy. A boy in a skirt, but a boy nonetheless.

"*It is the east and Juliet is the sun,*" I whisper. "*Arise, fair sun, and kill the envious moon who is already sick and pale with grief.*" I press my body against the 'balcony' piece. "*Oh that I were a glove upon that hand, that I might touch that cheek!*"

I close my eyes and let the words hang in the space. It really is a beautiful thought. And the motif of light and dark—taking something that is dark and transforming it into light.

"That was lovely," a voice calls out from the audience, near the auditorium door. I squint to see who's standing there. He steps forward from beneath the balcony's overhang and comes into my view. Mr. Schiffner.

"I, uh. I was just…" I smooth the front of my skirt and fumble for my words, which have suddenly and completely escaped me.

Mr. Schiffner frowns and takes a deep breath, letting it out slowly. Loudly. "You know… You make a fine Romeo."

Err… what? I stare at him dumbfounded. Why is he handing out compliments? I could still make a *fine Romeo* if it weren't for his edict. "But you canceled the show because of me."

He licks his lips and then nods. "Sometimes we are duty-bound to make decisions we might not otherwise make." As if that is sufficient explanation.

I decided to press him. "You're the principal. If it's not up to you, who is it up to?"

He steps back toward the door a bit. "You, I hope."

Me? I'm so confused. He's saying he wants me to fight his decision? Why make it in the first place then? "Is this some kind of reverse psychology thing?" I holler after him.

He laughs as he opens the door and steps into the hallway.

"All right listen up. Today we're going to talk about position papers, but instead of telling you about position papers, I want you to just jump in. So, we're going to take twenty minutes and write one." Mrs. D turns to the board to write.

"What's a position paper?" someone asks.

"Exactly what it sounds like Mr. Jacobs." I love this about Mrs. D. She treats her students like capable adults and expects them to live up to it. "It's a paper where you take a position on an issue. Also known as an argumentative essay. And I will caution you that to craft a fully rounded essay, it is best to consider the opposition's side and address it as well. Your target should be the 'fence-sitters.'" She writes that word on the board. "Those are the people who might know something about the topic but haven't formed a strong opinion either way. You're trying to push them off the fence. Force them to take a side. There will always be people who already agree with your position and those who will never agree no matter what you say. But your objective is to write for is those in the middle. The ones who are sitting on a fence waiting for a strong breeze to knock them off."

She walks back to her desk and sits, setting her timer. "You've got twenty minutes and then we'll read some of them aloud. Ready? Go."

I take out my notebook and try to think of a topic. But I'm totally blanking. I can't think of anything to take a position on at all. The usual suspects run through my head. Abortion, the death penalty, global warming—but none of them stand out to me as particularly worthy. I mean, the issues are worthy I just don't have a definitive stance on them, not anymore. I used to, of course. But lately I feel like I'm lost. I'm not sure what I believe.

I'm not sure what I believe.

The thought terrifies me.

Before I know it, Mrs. D's timer goes off. "Alright, any volunteers?" Mrs. D asks. Now I can only hope she doesn't call on me.

Chloe raises her hand and traipses up to the podium.

"What's the topic?" Mrs. D asks.

"Gender equality, I guess," Chloe says. This oughtta be good.

"It is my personal belief that men and women are not equals," Chloe says, eliciting a muffled gasp from the room.

"Class, Chloe is entitled to her opinion," Mrs. D says, hushing everyone.

"... For the simple reason that men and women are not the same. We have different biology, different strengths and weaknesses, and different needs. We are meant to complement one another in God's perfect plan. Like Yin and Yang."

Way to cross-pollinate cultural philosophies there, Chloe. Christian ideas of God mixed with Eastern philosophy. I try to tune her out because I know it will only make me angry to listen to her drone on. And she's teetering precariously close to talking about homosexuality. I glance at Tony but he has his eyes down, staring intently at something on his desk.

"Take, for example, the famous Shakespearean play *Romeo and Juliet*."

Oh no, she didn't. I perk up and shift in my seat. Out of the corner of my eye, I see Tony is no longer studying his desk, either. Chloe looks pointedly at me before she continues. "The play is perhaps the greatest example we have of the power of true love."

Has she even read the play? Romeo's affections snap from Rosaline to Juliet in a matter of hours, mostly. He can't have Rosaline because she wants to remain chaste.

Romeo loves Juliet, sure, but it's the fiery, lusty, passionate love of youth. They never talk about kids, or getting old or what happens if one of them ends up with cancer and dies leaving the other with twelve kids to raise. Alone. None of the serious stuff that comes with a real and lasting relationship.

They're too focused on getting into each other's pants.

"And that love is between a man and a woman because Romeo and Juliet complement each other. Where one is brash the other is level-headed, where one is weak, the other strong."

The faces of pretty much every other student in the class tell me I'm not the only one who's completely lost in the mire of her logic. Or illogic, as it were.

"That is why, when the play of *Romeo and Juliet* is being performed, it is critical that the male role be played by a male and the female by a female. Shakespeare's original intent is totally lost otherwise."

I curl my fists curl into balls at my side and feel like the collar of my sweater is choking my neck. I reach up and pull it away from my skin a bit. I can't sit there any longer. I shut my notebook and spring to my feet mumbling something about the bathroom. Technically, I need a hall pass, which I haven't requested. But I know right now, Mrs. D won't object. Especially since she can't really interject her own opinion here, not without threat of getting reprimanded. Impartiality is the law of the land for teachers and staff but somehow, that doesn't extend to the district's 15,000 students.

Jodi moves as if she's going to come with me, but I brush her off. I can see the flash of hurt in her eyes, the slump in her shoulders. I'm not being a good friend, I know, but right now, I can't care. I have to get out of here before I explode. I run out of the classroom and slam into the bank of lockers across the hall, leaning my back against them and sinking down to the floor. Whatever I do, I can't cry. I can't let Chloe, of all people, see me cry.

What Chloe doesn't realize, of course, is that if she plays Juliet opposite a guy, it will probably be Tony. And news flash, he's gay.

"Don't listen to her." Tony appears out of nowhere by my side. He's holding a hall pass and he hands me one, too. "Mrs. D said to take our time."

"Hi," I say awkwardly. "I thought you weren't talking to me."

He nods. "I wasn't. Now I guess I am."

"I uh, I owe you—"

Tony hold up his hand. "Look, that was a shit thing you did. And honestly, I don't understand the point. Do you guys think someone is going to see those hurtful signs and be like, 'Of course! I was blind before but your vulgarity has opened my eyes to the sin I've been living in. I will break up with my same sex partner and immediately begin sexual congress with a woman in the confines of biblically sanctioned marriage!" He shakes his head. "No. The problem with those signs, with your family's whole shtick, is that is has nothing to do with the people who you're witnessing' to. It's not about them and where they are, it's about you." He's right, of course. And it makes me cry harder. He plops down on the floor next to me. "But I thought about it and I realized I can't completely blame you. Or at least, I can understand why you did it. So long as you didn't mean it. Did you?"

I shake my head. "No. That's the whole problem. I feel like I'm stuck between what I want to do and what I have to do and I don't know how to walk the line between." If I openly go against my dad's authority, or even just rock the boat, at best, I risk my family turning their attention and scorn on me. At worst, they might actually disown me. But if I don't go against them, am I risking even more?

"Familiar territory," he says. "Don't worry about Chloe. She's just looking for the path of least resistance. If you step aside, she gets to still be Juliet."

"I did back down."

"Correction: you wanted to back down, but we wouldn't let you."

I misjudge how close I am to the locker and my head smacks against the thin metal door. "I'm so tired of all this. What if we just let Chloe have her way? I mean, whatever. I don't care anymore." I'm too tired to care anymore.

Tony turns to me and takes my hand in his. "You can't say that, Piper. So maybe the original catalyst to all this was some stupid edict, but it's become something more now." He smiles a little and I'm reminded of what's at stake for him, too. "It's been building for a while and the play was just the final straw, you know? A tangible cause."

"Well one thing's for sure, in *my* speech I will use actual logic."

"God. Please do. I guess Chloe never heard of the rules of Shakespeare's day."

"You mean about men playing all the parts?"

"Ironic, right?" He shakes his head and chews at a hangnail on his right thumb. "I'm thinking of speaking at the meeting. In addition to your speech, I mean."

"We need more than one?"

"No. But you need an introduction and I thought I would give it."

Ah. An introduction. Duh. "I'd like that. You being my opener, I mean."

He bumps his leg into mine and we sit there for a while longer, listening to the constant hum of the fluorescent lights overhead and the muffled voices behind closed classroom doors. They all sound like Charlie Brown teachers. "Whoaa whaa whoaa whaaan." Every last one of them.

The petition is circulating, the one we need to collect hundreds of signatures on by next Monday. I haven't signed it yet. I've been avoiding it. There's not much harm in just signing the dang thing except that I know that the second I do, I'll be formally committing to the cause. To the fight. In my head, I've already committed. But signing that paper will make it official and I know there will be no going back from that.

I'm still a little afraid that people will think that by fighting this, I'm being selfish. Even though I know, and my cast mates know, that the issue at hand is more than whether or not I am Romeo, I worry that other people won't. They'll see it as this spoiled brat whining because she didn't get her way.

"Screw 'em." Tony comes up next to me as I'm walking down the hallway. "Who cares what they think?"

Jodi steps up next to Tony and smiles. "Good to see you two talking again."

Greg is coming toward us, clipboard in hand. Mr. Schiffner's words echo in my head. "*You, I hope.*" And it's like all these threads are coming together to this one moment, the one where I have to choose. Not who I used to be, not what my family wants me to be, but who do I choose to be? What do I want to do?

I reach out and grab Greg's arm. "Gotta pen?" I ask, no one in particular. They all pat their pockets and fumble through their bags. Tony's first and he hands it to me. A bright blue pen that says "Salvatore's" in white script.

And then I sign it.

Lightning doesn't strike me down. There's no weeping or gnashing of teeth. There's just Tony, my friend, smiling at me.

"Great. Thanks, Piper." Greg grins as he backs away from us. "We're going to kick this thing's ass. You'll see."

I look at Jodi and Tony and wonder why neither of them signed it.

"Already did," Jodi said in her usual mind-reading way. "Ages ago."

CHAPTER TWENTY-SIX

Dad's been so busy with his new line of protesting that it hasn't been too hard to avoid him. I know it's a ticking time bomb and I'm going to have to fess up soon, but I still haven't figured out how. So instead, I'm in distraction-seeking mode.

"There's a party at Mac's tonight," Tony says. "Her parents are in Italy for spring break."

"It's not spring break yet," Jodi says.

"Apparently it's IMSA's," Tony says. "And her mom teaches at Woodfield or something and it's spring break there." Woodfield is the private liberal arts university in the next city over.

"So, you guys wanna go?"

No. I've never been to a party. I've never even considered going to a party. Parties are for kids who date and drink and wear jeans. But then again, I sure as heck don't want to go out to another protest. Jodi smiles and glances at me. "Come on, Piper. It could be fun. Besides, I feel like we never get to hang out anymore." She looks so hopeful and she has a point, with everything going on between the play her track, we haven't hung out like we haven't spent time together like we used to. I owe her this.

"Sure." I sigh. If I'm already going down, may as well go down in a blaze of glory.

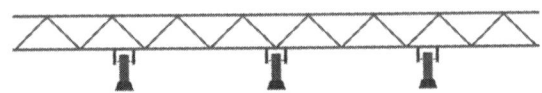

"I'm kind of glad I didn't get to go to the meet this weekend," Jodi says. The way she clicks her teeth as she says it means she's lying, but I indulge her anyway. "I mean, track has been really fun and all, but it's so much pressure. And this is a big meet."

When the team gets invited to away meets that require overnight stays, the whole team doesn't get to go. Only the top varsity team members who'll compete get to go since the school doesn't want to pay for extra hotel rooms.

Jodi leans in and brushes more mascara on her lashes, making a gaping mouth face as she does.

"You should wear a smoky eye tonight," Jodi says, trying to hide her frown at my nearly nude eyelids. Makeup isn't frowned upon in my family, but we are supposed to go for the barely there look. It's more modest.

"Smoky eye?"

"Sit." She points to the toilet lid. I do what she says, and soon she's using all these different brushes to paint my eyes with what feels like twenty different colors of powder. "There." She steps back to admire her work and hands me a mirror.

When I glance at my reflection, I don't even recognize myself. She's used heavy black eyeliner and some kind of dark shimmery powder to make my eyes look like that of a cat. Or a supermodel. Or... something.

"Looks good, huh?" She grins. And I decide to humor her. For tonight, at least, I will be someone else. I will be the kind of girl who has smoky eyes.

After twisting my hair back in a loose knot, we pick out outfits. Jodi pulls out a different options, all of which look great on her curvy figure. She settles on dark skinny jeans and a flouncy striped top that she belts. My options are more limited for one thing, I don't have a lot of 'going out' clothes. Or any, really. And for another, I only brought the one thing I thought could work with me: a tailored denim pencil skirt and my mom's red heels. The heels that feel like they could make things happen.

"Dylan will probably be there." Jodi winds her Civic through Warrington Woods. It's full of pristine pillared houses set up on the hills of fake mini-estates. Supposed to remind you of plantations or something, I think. Even though this is the North and decidedly the land of Lincoln.

I shrug as if I don't care. Because I don't. Or rather, I shouldn't. Outside my window, the houses grow more stately. One house is more massive than the next and in the center of the subdivision there's a big clubhouse with a swimming pool and four tennis courts off the veranda. A sign out front calls it the Estate House Club.

Jodi slows as she nears a cul-de-sac tucked by some 'woods.' We park there and follow a few other people who are also walking up the street. "Well, this must be the place."

"I can't believe we're here!" Jodi yells in my ear but with the pumping bass it sounds more like a whisper.

She's wide-eyed and beaming, like we've just entered some magical alternate universe. I guess in some ways, we have. Only it doesn't seem all that magical. We are pushing our way through a crowd of sloshing cups and too-strong perfume and miniskirts and heels, and of course we get separated.

I stake out a spot near the bay window in the formal living room and lean against it, watching the crowd as more people pack their way in the house while looking for Jodi. Better to stay in one spot and wait than risk passing each other on reverse loops.

There are a handful of girls on the stairwell comforting one of their friends who's crying. To my right, a couple is in the throes of a serious make-out session (get a room) and all around me swarms of people bounce to the music, hitting on each other, and having drunken conversations that they probably won't remember tomorrow. Three guys from my chemistry class seem to be engaged in some kind of heated debate. They are obviously drunk though, because one keeps

THIS ABOVE ALL

slurring his words, and the other two keep giggling. This high-pitched, whiney giggle. I scan the crowd watching for Serene. She was supposed to come with her brother, but since she's got this weird enzyme issue, she doesn't drink. "It's an Asian thing," she always says. She spends a lot of her weekends shuttling people around like an Uber driver. Except without the paycheck.

"Remind me again why we came here?" I ask Jodi when she returns. She's holding two cups and thrusts one at me.

"What is this?" I ask.

"Overpriced keg beer. Natty Light, probably."

I sniff and it tastes the way stale urine smells. "You paid for this?"

"Duh. It's a kegger. You gotta buy a cup. Don't worry, girls get a discount. Two bucks instead of five." Two dollars too much by my estimation.

I set the cup down. A couple of people in front of me make off for the kitchen, leaving me a clear view to the dining room. "How huge is this house?" I say to no one in particular. As I think of it, the drapes and crown molding do have a 'Twelve Oaks' feel to them. Just add a dash of Rhett Butler. Especially that grand staircase in the entryway. It was the second film I ever snuck off to the Senator to see. As my gaze is flitting about the room, taking it all in, my eyes land on another pair I know. Chocolate brown.

Dylan.

He's sitting on a couch in the family room laughing with some of his friends. When his gaze meets mine, he winks and smiles at me. "Cheers," he mouths before raising his cup to his lips.

I give him a quick half-smile of acknowledgment and retreat from the room, toward the back of the house, the kitchen, where I won't be in his line of sight.

Jodi follows at my heels. "What's wrong?"

"Oh. Nothing. I just wanted to check out the kitchen."

"Liar." She laughs. "Tony?"

"What? No. Why, is he around, too?"

"Too? Who else is here, Piper?" She stops then and watches me, carefully. I try to keep my face stoic. Firm. But it's no use. "It's Dylan, isn't it?" She practically squeals and I shush her. "You like him," she sings.

"I do not. And anyway, he has a girlfriend."

"She here?"

I have no idea. "Probably."

"So?"

"Please. I am not the kind of person who goes around stealing other girls' boyfriends." I am not even the type of girl to date at all.

At the front of the house, a crowd has started pushing their way into the foyer. One of them catches my attention because the profile is familiar, too familiar. He turns and I see why: because it's Peter. My brother.

"Whoa," Jodi says, following my gaze. "What is your brother doing here?"

I shake my head. "No clue."

So much for having a responsibility to the church. His eyes narrow when he sees me and his face hardens. He pushes from the group and starts toward me, but luckily, a group of basketball players steps forward at that moment and block his path.

I don't escape him long though, because after I've made my way to the kitchen, Peter's hand falls heavy on my shoulder. "I thought you might be here."

"Clearly," I say. "What are you doing here, Pete?"

"I could ask you the same question." I flare with shame. He's right. He might be a hypocrite, but I'm one, too.

"Look, can we talk?" he says.

Jodi appears then. "You okay?" she whispers, eyeing Peter. He keeps his face firm even as I shift from beneath his hand.

I nod. Peter is harmless.

"Please?" Peter asks again.

"I think you two should talk." Jodi backs away toward a pack of basketball guys including Mike, the guy she's crushed on for a while now. "Holler if you need me." She points to her eyes and then to Peter, attempting to warn him that she'll be watching.

So here I am, stuck for the moment with my older brother. I've never seen him out around non-church people ever. It's kind of freaking me out. "C'mon." I lead him through the keg crowd and back into the main part of the house.

"How about in there?" he asks.

The door across the living room is closed, presumably to keep people out. But even though it's 'locked,' I jiggle the doorknob and hold in the little emergency release button next to the handle with my pinky nail. With so many kids in the house, one of the first things my parents did was replace all the doorknobs to newer ones like this. The lock clicks open and I pull Peter inside, hoping no one else has seen us go. I'll relock it again when we leave because whatever's in here must be important.

Peter flips on the light switch. A massive crystal chandelier illuminates the whole room, which is lined with bookshelves and has a huge baby-grand piano off to the side. A marble fireplace is along the far wall and I'm reminded again of *Gone with the Wind*. Like at any moment, Scarlett herself could come storming in to chuck a crystal vase at my head.

"So what did you want to talk about?" I ask, moving over toward the built in shelves and studying the titles. I've never seen so many books in a personal library before.

"You can't do the play," he says.

"You've already made your feelings *abundantly* clear." I shift my weight a bit and try to pull away from him. His hand is on my arm and he tugs me back until I'm standing right in front of him.

"There's too much at stake." He presses his fingers into my wrist as his face darkens and his eyes get stormy. He's starting to freak me out. "If people think we can't even manage our own, how will we ever effectively witness? You need to remember your place. 'They are to be submissive as the law also says.'"

"You just want to control me," I say. "That's what this is all about?" The realization finally snaps into place. He wants me to be malleable and meek, what he thinks is acceptable, appropriate for a girl. I don't know what kind of girl I am, exactly, but I do know that that's not it.

Maybe I was headed that way once, but definitely not now.

"Let me go, Peter." I try to push him away. His grip on my wrist tightens.

"Make me," he says between clenched teeth. It's like he's released this inner beast he usually keeps under control. But I'm starting to understand that this ugliness is part of the real Peter, what happens when he loses control.

"You're hurting me." I look up at his face. His jaw unhinges, and his gaze is boring into me, cold and steel-like. "Let go!"

"Not until you agree."

"Agree with what?"

"That you won't do it. That you won't jeopardize everything we've been working for." His face softens slightly. "Your rebellion can be forgiven, you know. It's not too late."

He steps forward and I move aside so that he loses his balance and crashes into the bookcase behind me. He looks up at me and wipes the tip of his nose, which has started bleeding. "Bitch."

"Everything all right in here?" someone asks, distracting Peter who turns from me to face the door. I peek out to see Dylan standing there.

"What's it to you?" Peter asks.

"Nothing, I suppose. It's just my mom is pretty particular about this room." His mom? Wait, this is his house?

"I'll take my sister and get outta here, then." Peter tugs me by the wrist as he makes for the door. "She shouldn't be at a party anyway."

"Oh, I'm not going anywhere with you." I try to shake myself free from his pinching grip. I can almost feel the capillaries burst as his fingertips and stubby nails dig into my skin.

"Hey man, be cool," Dylan says, his voice calm but firm. He steps into the room and closes the door a bit.

"You be cool," Peter growls. He lets go of my wrist and steps closer to Dylan like he's going to what, fight him? Dylan backs up to the door a bit like he's going to bolt but when Peter lunges toward him, Dylan opens the door and Peter goes flying out, flailing, caught off guard by the sudden maneuver.

I walk up to the doorway and give Dylan a quick, grateful glance. Pete's sprawled out on the floor of the living room. The music is still pumping, but everyone in the room has taken a collective step back. Peter shakes his head and props himself up on his elbows.

"Too much to drink, buddy?" Someone grabs him by the arm and helps him up.

"Oops." A small smile tugs at Dylan's lips. "You okay?" He shuts the door again and then steps toward me, taking my arm. I try to pull it away. "Hey, hey," he coos. "I just want to look." He turns my hand and lifts the sleeve so the inside of my wrist is exposed. "You're going to have a nasty bruise, I think. That tissue is pretty sensitive."

I can't bring myself meet his eyes. Mostly, I just want to run away. I'm mortified by Peter's behavior, and more so that I allowed it to happen in the first place. Or that anyone, especially Dylan saw it.

"I don't need a rescuer, you know." I twist my arm from his hand.

"I didn't come in here to rescue you. I really was concerned about my mom's stuff. I heard someone went in here and I figured I better check it out." Dylan licks his lip and watches me. "Are you really okay?"

I nod and glance around the room. "So you live here? I thought this was Mac's house?"

Dylan's still quiet, looking at me for a minute longer before he says, "Mackenzie is my sister. Well, stepsister. Didn't I mention that?"

I had no idea. But now that I think about it, in Chicago, he mentioned a stepsister his age. And even called her Mackenzie. And said she goes to IMSA, just like Mac who transferred there last year.

I'm an idiot.

"Most of these books were my real mom's." He shakes his head. "That sounds weird. Real mom as opposed to fake mom? But biological mom sounds so clinical." He shakes his head and runs a hand through his hair, pulled back, but loosely so several pieces frame his face.

We're quiet for a bit; I stare at the door, longing to get the heck out of there. I cross my arms.

"So, what exactly happened tonight?" he asks. "I mean, seriously, should I call someone or something?"

I shake my head. "And ruin your party?"

"Fuck the party," Dylan says. "If you were assaulted, we need to report it."

Assaulted? No. Was I? Peter's my brother. "He's having a hard time with all this."

"That's no excuse."

"I know. I don't mean it to be one. Just an explanation."

"Well, he's also an asshat. And that makes for a wicked volatile combination."

"My family has certain ideas and expectations, and I seem to be breaking them left and right these days. Peter's appointed himself to try to keep me in line, I guess."

"Your own personal Tybalt?"

"Ha. Something like that. Tybalt gets it in the end though. I'm pretty sure that he'll come out of all this just fine. Me on the other hand..."

"What? You're like the best person I know. If you're out of line, I'd hate to think what I would be." Dylan chews the inside of his cheek and studies me quietly. I can't handle the weight of his gaze or the words that linger now between us. *The best person he knows.*

I shift my weight from one foot to the other and look up at the chandelier. "So has anyone ever told you this house is really similar to..."

"*Gone with the Wind*?"

"All that's missing is a tacky gold-framed portrait."

"Oh, we have one. It's tucked away in the basement." Dylan looks at me for a second. "You, uh... You want to see my room?"

I'm not naïve, so I know that at parties that usually means something else. But this is different. For one, as I'm painfully aware, Dylan has a girlfriend. Also, this is his house and 'show you my room' is a legitimate thing to do when you're at a friend's house for the first time.

Isn't it?

CHAPTER TWENTY-SEVEN

As we climb the stairs, I think about that word—*friend*—and wonder if it applies to Dylan and me. Are we friends?

"It's locked to keep the miscreants out." Dylan smiles as he sticks a skeleton key in the lock and side-steps a couple making out in the hallway. He rolls his eyes at them. "I'd say get a room, but this being my house, I really don't want them to," he whispers. He pushes the door open and guides me inside with his hand resting gently on the small of my back. "Home sweet home."

I notice that it's nothing like my brother's room. There's no faintly disguised odor of old socks, Cheetos and stale sheets. It smells fresh, like someone has cleaned it within the last couple days. The massive king-sized bed is made up with a poufy white down comforter and a steel gray coverlet. A host of decorative pillows, all in various shades of graphite, are arranged at the head. Front and center in the pile is a well-worn blue one in the shape of Thomas the Tank. I giggle and Dylan turns to see what I'm looking at. He smiles sheepishly and scratches the back of his neck. "My mom got it for me for my third birthday. I had a thing for trains, apparently."

On the far side of the room is a wood drafting table and a bookshelf full of papers and art supplies. I step over to check out the work in progress that's clipped to the desk. "For your portfolio?"

"Oh, umm. That's uh, something I'm working on." He tries to step between me and the desk but it's too late, I've seen it. A charcoal portrait of a girl. Ava? Her face is mostly in shadows and she's looking off the page, demure somehow. There's a lot of darkness and shadow in the image but even so, her face radiates warmth and light. I step closer and realize that it's not just some girl. It's not even Ava.

It's me.

My nose. My cheekbones. My eyes.

He blushes. "Oh, uh. Yeah. From that day when you guys rehearsed that death scene? There was this one moment, and I haven't been able to shake the image so I had to draw it." He scratches the back of his head and rocks his weight forward. "Sorry, is that weird?"

A little, maybe. But then, I've been using him as my muse, too, haven't I?

He totally got my lips wrong (they're not that full in real life) but at least it's an upgrade.

He looks at me and reaches forward to brush a strand of my hair out of my face. I don't even realize I'm holding my breath until my lungs start to ache. I turn my head away from him just a bit and a collection of photo frames catches my eye. They're mostly filled with pictures of him and Ava and that giddiness dissipates. Poof.

The *girlfriend*.

Not only is he merely an artist looking at me as a subject, but he has a girlfriend. "Who's this one?" I say, stepping toward the shelf and away from him. I pick up a frame with a woman holding a giggling toddler in her arms. "Your mom?"

"Affirmative." He takes the frame from my hands, studying it himself for a moment before putting it back exactly so. "The only one I've got, actually."

"Is that you? In the photo?"

"Yup. Me and Mom."

He looks at the photo for a while and I look at him looking at the photo. I've run out of things to explore and he's run out of things to say.

"So... You sure you're all right? After everything tonight?" He glances at my wrist again where, sure enough, a purplish bruise has started to bloom. I tug at the sleeve of my top to try and hide my wrist.

"I'm fine."

We're both quiet for a bit. Dylan shakes his head and looks to the floor. Is he searching for the conversation I've just killed? He takes a deep breath. "So, uh, what about you and that Tony kid? He seems pretty into you."

I laugh a little because, well, it's Tony. Here I'd figured Dylan suspected something about Tony but I guess not. Tony will be thrilled. "Just friends."

"Really?" Dylan asks, eying me squarely. A little voice in my head starts yelling Abort! Abort! If he doesn't know about Tony, it is not my place to tell him. Or anyone. And if he keeps pressing, he might figure it out and then I'll feel horrible.

"Tell me about your family," I say. "I know about your mom, but what about your dad? Stepmom? Sisters?"

He tells me a bit more about them all. About how his sisters used to make him be their living doll growing up. About how his oldest sister is in law school and hates it but feels trapped now, like she has to finish. About how his stepmom is a history professor at Woodfield.

"And they like, uh, Ava?" I ask. I don't know why.

"Sort of. I guess. Sylvia's not her biggest fan, but she doesn't dislike her, either." He glances at me then back to the dresser. "So, how come I never see you at these things?"

"Things?"

"Parties."

Oh. "I'm not technically allowed."

"You're *not allowed*?" He presses his lips together but he can't hide his amusement. "I bet there's a lot of things you've done lately that you aren't *allowed* to do. Hasn't stopped you though."

That is true. I've been breaking all the rules lately.

"If the standards are so noncompulsory that you're willing to forgo them, I think they probably aren't truly your standards."

"What do you mean?"

"I mean, I think it's one thing to make choices for yourself about what you want to do or what you don't. But to limit yourself based on someone else's ideas about what is or isn't okay? It's tough to sustain. You have to make your own choices and then live with the repercussions, good or bad. *This above all to thine ownself be true.*"

"Wrong play."

"But solid advice."

Dylan scoots closer to me and puts his arm along my back so that my shoulder is almost under the crook of his arm. Almost.

The hum and drone of the party that's happening all around echoes in my ears and I'm having a hard time telling if the pulsing is coming from the party or my heart, which is beating so hard and fast that I'm sure Dylan can hear it. I swallow. Hard.

Dylan grins and shakes his head to flick some hair out of his eyes. I'm keep my face forward, purposely avoiding meeting his gaze because I'm afraid of what will happen if I do. What I might see looking back at me. But when I can't stand it any longer, I turn my head, just a touch, so that his face is in my periphery. And he's staring right at me.

"I've got your lips all wrong," he says.

My stomach melts into a puddle on the floor. Oh man, I want to kiss him. He reaches out and brushes my bottom lip with his thumb, sending lightning bolts tingling down my spine and to my toes. "In my sketch, I mean. The bottom one's not quite so pouty."

"Mm-hmm."

He slides his thumb down the side of my cheek and cups my chin in his fingers. "You're beautiful, you know."

No boy has ever called me beautiful before. Not that I can remember anyway and I'm pretty sure that's not the kind of thing you forget. Kind of like how I also know that no matter what happens, I won't forget this moment right here, right now. *My lips, two blushing pilgrims, ready stand to smooth that rough touch with a tender kiss.* He presses his lips together and my face inches closer to his. And then, I'm kissing him! I press my lips against his, waiting eagerly for his response.

Only he isn't kissing me back. At all. I open my eyes and see that my lips aren't even touching his—they're pressed into his cheek. He must have turned his head at the last second.

I pull back and he turns away further. He opens his mouth to speak.

"I'm sorry," I say, cutting him off. I scramble toward the door. I've totally misinterpreted this. I can't get away fast enough. "I just thought. I mean..." I have no more words. I try to summon some, but to no avail. The latch is tricky and it takes me way longer than I'd like to get it undone, which gives Dylan enough time to get up from the bench and come after me. His hand is on mine, but I tug it away and fly down the hall toward that monstrous staircase.

"Piper, wait," he calls.

"It's okay. Thanks for showing me your, uh, room." I practically trip over the clusters of partiers as I get back to the ground floor.

I'm single-minded: locate Jodi and Serene and get the heck out of here. Unlike the throngs of people around me, I've never felt so sober in my entire life. An emotional slap tends to have that effect, I guess.

I can't believe I was so stupid. He has a girlfriend. Even though we have this sort of... thing, he's never once said he felt like that. About me. Okay yeah, he has this beautiful charcoal drawing of me and I catch him looking at me sometimes, just watching me. But I've been doing that, too, right? And even the other night at the coffee shop, it was pretty clear where his feelings are.

With Ava. Not me.

How could I be so stupid?

Jodi is busy flirting with Mike and he's definitely flirting back. When I ask her if she's ready to go, she shoots me *the* look. Serene isn't much better—she's wrapped up in a game of beer pong. She has a pinch-drinker but she doesn't really need one because she's awesome at it. Maybe it's because she's always sober so her aim is better. It's clear, though, that she's not ready to leave either and I know I can't avoid Dylan much longer. Every time I see him, I duck into another room, but there are only so many places to hide. And this is his house, after all.

Some guy in a tight black t-shirt thrusts a cup at me. "Drink?" he half-asks, half-barks with liquor-laced breath. Yuck.

I push it back at him. "Umm, no thanks."

He downs it in one gulp and belches.

I've had more than enough of this. Of all of it, so I make my way to the front door, careful to avoid Dylan when I see him headed toward the back of the house. One last crowd to push through and then I'm outside. I run down the front steps toward the sidewalk. I shouldn't walk home, but at this point, what choice do I have?

Just as I'm winding down the front walk, Tony drives by in his red deathtrap of a Jeep.

"Piper, what's up?" he asks.

I press my lips together, determined not to lose it completely. "Just on my way home."

"You okay to drive?"

I nod weakly, but my quivering lip soon betrays me. "I don't have a car, so I'm just going to walk."

He shakes his head. "Like hell you are. Get in, I'll take you."

"But you just got here."

"Exactly. I don't know what I'm missing."

I try to open the passenger door, but it's stuck or something.

"Dammit." Tony hops out of the car and comes around the side. As he tugs open the door, I look up to see Chloe standing on the front porch. She raises an eyebrow as she looks to Tony and then me.

"This door is a piece of shit." He holds the handle and tugs it while kicking it near the hinge. "There's a trick to it and you have to do it just right." It opens, and he helps me inside.

"Spill it," He says.

And so I tell him everything. Peter. Dylan. My first kiss that a) wasn't even a real kiss b) wasn't on my wedding day and c) was so hopelessly unrequited.

"Shit. I'm sorry," he whispers. But, I'm quiet. And Tony doesn't push it, which right now, is exactly what I need.

CHAPTER TWENTY-EIGHT

"What time is it?" I wheeze into the phone. It's Jodi's voice on the other end.

"Past eleven. Did I wake you up?"

Past eleven? I shoot up in bed. I glance around to see all of my sisters' bunks are empty. "I have to work on the speech." Midterms are coming up, which means this is one of the last days I'll have time.

"That would probably be a good idea," Jodi says. "So what happened last night? You totally disappeared on us."

Last night? Last night. I think about it and it all comes flooding back. The party. Peter.

Dylan.

"Oh, no," I groan. Tony dropped me off and I crawled into bed, hoping that sleep would erase the whole thing. It didn't. I remember it all as clearly as if it had happened yesterday. Because it did. It definitely did. "Sorry."

"Yeah. Whatever. Want to meet up later?" she asks. "You can read me what you've got and I can like critique it or something."

"How about ice cream?"

"Done. I'll pick you up at three. And bring the speech."

The speech. The speech! I've got to get cracking on it. After a quick shower to wake myself up, I settle into my desk and open a blank document on my laptop. The cursor blinks there, taunting me.

I click save and title the document 'speech.' Then I make another backup and save it to my cloud. But nothing's coming to me. I just stare at the computer where the cursor is still blinking on the blank screen. Surprise. The speech hasn't up and written itself.

Maybe I need something to eat. It's almost lunchtime after all. If my stomach is quiet maybe my head will be able to think. So I head downstairs, stopping to listen for Peter's voice before I go into the kitchen to make myself a turkey sandwich. I end up promising to feed my two littlest siblings in the process. They sit at the counter each waiting for PB&J and carrot sticks.

Dad comes into the kitchen. "Good afternoon." He glances at the clock above the sink to verify that it is, in fact, already afternoon. "How was your evening?"

"Fine." I spread a thin layer of mayo over a slice of bread. Moose has planted himself firmly at my feet, just hoping something will fall.

"I thought you were working at the old folks' home this morning?" He eyes my unkempt hair, my unwashed face. I'd said that to avoid another outreach event.

"They canceled on me. Some stomach bug going around the facility." I make a face for added effect. "So I decided to get a head start on some of my notecards for midterms instead." I marvel at how easily the lies just roll off my tongue now.

Dad doesn't even bat an eyelash. He just takes me at my word and plants himself at the table with a stack of more papers and Bibles. Not wanting to risk running into Peter, I grab a bottle of water from the fridge and decide to take my sandwich to go. I pack up my laptop and lunch and jump on my bike, headed to my favorite thinking place—the old bridge off Mortimer Avenue. It was supposed to be for the railway, but they never finished building it. It's a half-bridge that extends only partway over Chester Lake. And it's one of my favorite places to escape to. Up here, I feel calm, at peace. It's probably stupid, but it's also one of the places I feel closest to God—out here in His creation. I look out over the waters of this narrow inlet, the smooth glassy surface of the lake broken by the occasional fish that flicks its tail and then disappears again.

THIS ABOVE ALL

With renewed energy to tackle this thing, I bust out my laptop and pull on my fingerless gloves. I hope for the words to flow from my fingers without my input or assistance. I will be a vessel. I am a vessel.

As I think about my speech, I try to focus on people like Tony and what this whole ordeal means to them. What it would be like for an organization like my church to swoop in and call who you are and what you stand for an assault on morality, to say that your very existence is offensive. And I think about the nature of censorship, of being told which way of thinking or being is acceptable and which way is not. And how sweeping something (say, gay students) under the rug or pretending they don't exist won't make it go away.

Which is exactly what I'm trying to do with my family, isn't it?

Dang.

"Ready?" Jodi says a few hours later through my phone. I got back home just in time. "'Cause I'm in the driveway."

I bound down the steps with my freshly printed speech and climb into her front seat.

"I called Mike," she says before I've even closed the door. "Get this: he wants to hang out on Friday." I can feel the happiness oozing from her pores. Mike isn't actually named Mike at all. His name is Jordan and he's tall, black, and really good at basketball, so he's earned the nickname "Mike" as in "Wanna be like Mike." Jodi's had a crush on him for months.

"That's great," I say with as much enthusiasm as I can muster. If she wants to hang out with Mike, I should be supportive. Strike that: I will be supportive.

But Jodi's already picked up on it. "You don't sound very happy."

"I am. I've got a lot on my mind today, that's all. I just spent the last couple hours preparing out at Chester Lake."

"Praying?"

I smile and shake my head. "No. Just getting some of my materials ready."

"What is it about you and that bridge?" She shudders. "It's creepy."

"It's not creepy. It's peaceful." I fold and re-fold the paper in my hands. "The meeting's next Monday, you know."

"Of course I know, Piper." The happiness that bubbled up moments ago is gone, replaced by a twinge of anger she seems to be chewing on. Squishing it between her teeth and letting it roll out on her tongue. "But not everything is always about you, you know."

Whoa. Where did this come from? "I didn't say it was." She was the one who practically made me try out for *Romeo and Juliet* in the first place. Come to think of it, if it weren't for her urging and goading, I wouldn't even be in this mess. At all.

"You sure about that? Because ever since you got the lead in the school play, you've had this attitude. Like the whole world revolves around you."

What? That is completely untrue. I've got a lot on my plate right now and it sucks. Where is this coming from? We don't fight. We never fight.

"And I heard about what happened last night," Jodi says. "You and what's his name. So much for saving your lips for marriage."

Dylan? "What do you mean?" I ask slowly.

"How you made out with Tony. It's like I don't even know you anymore." She shakes her head. "And I heard it from Chloe of all people. You could have at least told me yourself."

Wait. Tony? She thinks I made out with Tony?

"I'm not going to tell Stef, but you know she's going to find out." She shakes her head. "You should be the one to tell her."

"I didn't hook up with anyone last night." Okay, yeah I kind of kissed Dylan, tried to anyway. But I definitely didn't hook up with Tony. "Tony just gave me a ride home."

Jodi eyes me over the top of her sunglasses. "Uh huh. Ever since you started this play, you two have been getting awfully close. I guess it makes sense now."

Well, yeah. But not like *that*. "I'm serious. We're just friends. Nothing happened."

"Just like nothing happened last week at school?"

"What are you talking about?"

"You both skipped out on English. For a good *long* while. And I heard you were... You know."

I stare at her blankly. "Seriously, what are you talking about? Tony was comforting me because I was upset."

"*Comforting* you, huh? That's what you call it? Jeez. The girl gets a starring role in the drama and now you can't even be real with your best friend?" She shakes her head. "You know what the problem is, Piper? The problem is you are trying to be two people at once. One, the sweet innocent church mouse who does whatever Daddy says and the other, this wild gender-bending rebel who makes out with boys and doesn't give a damn."

"Not true," I say. Is it?

"It would just be nice if you'd be honest with yourself. Make an actual decision and stand by it. If you want to be the wild rebellious PK then so be it. But this whole two-faced thing isn't working." Jodi huffs. "Look, Piper, I want to be supportive, and if you want to hook up with the Italian Stallion, that's your business. I mean, I get it. You can't have Dylan because he's taken and I've heard how you theater people can be. All hopped up on fake pheromones or whatever."

How *you* theater people can be? Since when am I a *theater person*? "Maybe you're just jealous," I blurt out. I don't know why I say it. It just comes out. "Because I'm spending more time with people like Tony than with you." By all accounts, Tony is several rungs above us on the social ladder I know it and Jodi knows it.

She's really getting heated. I can tell by the way her cheeks puff out slightly. From the right angle, she looks like a chipmunk getting ready for winter. "You think I'd be jealous of *you*?"

I can feel the heat rising up my chest, to my throat, and settling comfortably behind my eyes. If I don't concentrate on breathing, I would probably see spots. "If that's how you feel"—I unclick my seatbelt—"Then we probably shouldn't hang out today."

"Piper, I..." but I don't hang around to let her finish. I hop out at the next intersection, which is only a few blocks from my house. "At least let me drive you home."

"I can walk." I slam the door and start toward my house. For a minute, Jodi looks deflated but she must get over it pretty quick because I'm barely on the sidewalk before she drives off so fast her tires squeal.

CHAPTER TWENTY-NINE

"So what's this about appealing to the school board?" my dad asks. It's the conversation I've been dancing around, dreading ever since that afternoon at Greg's. "Disgusting." There is venom in his voice.

I take a bite of one of my oatmeal chocolate chip pancakes, using my bite as an excuse to consider my words carefully.

"Yes, why don't you tell him what you know." Peter straightens. "Since you're so close to it all. You've practically infiltrated the enemy camp, haven't you?" Peter smirks at me from across the table and then hands Dad a small stack of papers.

"Why was this in your possession?" Dad asks looking from the pages to me and back.

I crane my neck to see that it's a copy of the appeal paperwork we submitted to the school board. How did he... Where did he... I don't have to wonder long because Peter's smirk gives him away. My backpack. The other day when he locked it in the trunk and took it home without me.

Dad furrows his brow as he reads the papers. My other siblings seated around the table go quiet and their eyes all lock on me. "What's this?"

"Well... I mean..." I may as well come out with it. "Dad, *I* was cast in the show."

"You were?" He blinks a few times then looks to Peter, Phoebe and Penelope. "Did we know this?"

Phoebe and Penelope stare back blankly and Peter just shrugs and stares at his plate. He doesn't even try to hide the smile that tugs at his lips.

"But they're doing *Romeo and Juliet*, right?" Dad shakes his head. "Vulgar trash."

Did he just say *Shakespeare* is trash? I press my lips together and square my shoulders. "Well, as a matter of fact, I was the one cast as the lead."

My dad's eyes flicker with recognition. He's quiet then, mulling over what, exactly, I'm telling him. "*You* were the one cast as Romeo? Was this some kind of mistake? A joke, maybe? Surely they didn't want *you* as Romeo."

Part of me gets it. I do. After all, I had those same thoughts once. "Nope. Not a mistake. Not a joke. I am Romeo." As I say the words, I realize they are true. The drama's been 'off' for a while now, but I feel a connection to Romeo in a way I didn't just weeks ago. I *am* Romeo.

"So this is—what, some kind of lesbian play, then?" He's sort of laughing in that we he does when he thinks someone—usually a newscaster on the Liberal Media— is being so completely asinine that they can't possibly be serious. "Have you decided to become a homosexual now?"

"No, Dad. It's not about that. At all."

"Then what is it about?" His tone changes from mocking to something much darker. He's getting angry and I know if I'm not careful, this will teeter precariously close to a personal attack on everything he holds sacred. Everything I hold sacred. Supposedly.

"It's about the best person for the part, which apparently was me."

"But you're a girl."

"Yes." I cross my arms. There it is, the precise thing I've been dreading. "The character of Romeo is male but as you know, I'm not."

I look to Peter who's holding his head a little higher now. He stares at me straight on, an 'I told you so' look.

"Look, you don't have to agree, but you could at least not be against me. I am your daughter, after all."

"Are you? Or are you my son now?" He scoffs.

"It's not like that," I say. "You're completely missing the point."

"The point? The point is this is an affront to all the things we hold dear. There are things of this world and there are things of God. They cannot be both."

"Really? Because I thought God created the world." I don't know why I'm surprised. My dad sees a girl cast in a guy's role and assumes it means something. That I'm gay or that I want to be a guy and the school is endorsing and encouraging that instead of what it actually means: that I was the best person—the best actor—for this role. Period.

Peter opens his mouth as if he's going to say something more, describe the parts of the story that I'm deliberately leaving out so I start talking so he won't get the chance, but Dad cuts me off before either one of us can say anything. He flings the stacks of paper on top of his plate where it lands in a puddle of congealed maple syrup. "You better get right with God, young lady. I shudder to think what would happen if you didn't. And until you repent appropriately, you are grounded. School and home immediately. Extra protest work and housework."

Being grounded is not that big of a deal, it turns out. Especially because since Jodi and I fought, my social life has disintegrated, meaning I'd pretty much be home all the time, anyway.

Jodi and I not only have similar schedules, but she's also staked out our lunch table, the one that contains all of our mutual friends who officially aren't taking sides.

Officially.

But when Stef gets wind of those stupid rumors about me and Tony, it's pretty clear where her loyalties lie. And it's definitely not with me.

This means it's up to me to either be the bigger person and apologize (for something I didn't do) or make alternative plans. So for the past week, I've been staying after class or having lunch in the stacks or hiding out in the bathroom until the warning bell tells me it's acceptable to go to fourth period.

Not ideal, but I don't have much of a choice. I could tell them all it's not true—that Tony and I didn't make out because he's gay, but then I think about the look in his eyes when we talked at the Underground. How completely scared he was. Is. And I know I could never betray his trust like that, even if it means becoming a social pariah. Well, even more of a social pariah.

I try to ignore the hostile stares in the classroom. The whispers in the hallway. It doesn't matter what's true or not. Everyone either believes I'm a lesbian or that I'm a slut who fooled around with Tony multiple times. Never mind that if you stop to think for a second, they can't both be true. How can I simultaneously be a lesbian and be hooking up with Tony?

On Wednesday, I notice Chloe and her friends leaning against the stairwell near my locker. I try to ignore them and focus on the combination. I'm just going to grab my English books and head to the library. But after the lock clicks open, the piece of crap door still won't open. It's like the hinge is stuck on something. I tug a little harder and the door flings open. Dozens of small square foil packages cascade out of the locker, spill onto the floor at my feet. What are these? I pick one up and it becomes clear.

Condoms.

"Geez, Piper." Chloe shakes her head. "You and Tony have some serious plans for the weekend?" She and her friends are laughing at me and capturing the scene on their cellphones. For posterity, I'm sure. Just like I'm sure Chloe had *nothing* to do with this.

Dad is still angry because just as Peter predicted, this is all reflecting poorly on the church. "What kind of a man can't control his own daughter" I overheard someone say after the Wednesday night service. They haven't threatened to burn me at the stake yet, but give it time.

Fortunately, Dylan's been easier to avoid since we have zero classes together, but what really sucks is I've noticed that it seems like he's now avoiding me. I mean, I started it after the botched kiss thing. Now, though, he's giving me the cold shoulder and practically running away whenever he sees me around school.

I catch up with him on Thursday by accident and decide to see if it's true. I get my answer when he pretty much lets me have it.

"What do you want?" His jaw is clenches and unclenches and his keeps glancing around, everywhere but my face.

"I just wanted to say hey." Where is this coming from? I was avoiding him because I was embarrassed, but he's definitely angry. Because of the stupid rumors?

"What does Tony think about that?" He glances toward Tony who approaches us from the side.

Yup. Those stupid rumors. "What? That's completely untrue, you know."

"Really? Because you two have always seemed awfully buddy-buddy to me," he says.

Oh no he didn't. "Tony and I are friends, Dylan. Kind of like how you and I are friends."

"Are we?" He looks at me for the first time, just for a moment before his gaze flicks away. From the expression on his face, it's as if just being in my presence is making him ill. The way his nose crinkles up and his mouth tightens. Like he's repulsed by me.

Fine. I walk away, catching Tony as I do. It's not like he has any right to be mad anyway. Even if I had gone on to hook up with someone else, so what? Dylan made it pretty clear that he didn't want me so it shouldn't be an issue. Plus, he has a girlfriend. I will not let Dylan or Chloe or anyone else make me feel inferior. Especially for something that didn't even happen.

The worst part is that Tony feels guilty because he could, in theory, set the record straight (no pun intended) with a simple admission. But I won't let him. "Forget them. You shouldn't have to out yourself to prove a point. Chloe isn't worth it."

"But what about your friends? Or Dylan?" Tony asks, his expression pained.

"If they need an alibi to know the rumors aren't true, then they're not worth it, either."

So, I continue spending most of my time after school studying, working on my speech and avoiding people.

All the people.

CHAPTER THIRTY

The morning of the meeting, I'm a ball of nerves. It's going to take everything I have just to get through the day. Well, that and the bottle of my dad's wintergreen Tums that I hijacked and have taken to chewing one every twenty minutes. I can't focus on my classes or schoolwork at all. Heck, it's all I can do to avoid the people I'm trying to avoid like Jodi and now, especially, Dylan. Frankly, it's been exhausting.

And at this point, things are so messed up that I wonder if the fight is even worth it anymore. Can we ever get back what we had? And with all this time gone by? The seniors are checking out one by one. At this point, they'll be lucky to focus long enough to study for finals. Much less a silly school play.

But one look at Tony reminds me that it's not about the play anymore. Or whether the show can go on. It's so much more than that.

Tony is at least as nervous as I am today, maybe more so. He's been bumming my stolen Tums all morning. Greg on the other hand is practically throwing a pep rally.

"Big night tonight. You excited?" He sweeps by with an armful of posters that he tapes to every free space in the hallway. He stops when he sees my pained expression. "Dude. You're going to kick so much ass."

I don't have the heart to tell him about what my family's planning and how they're probably going to derail the entire conversation or bully the Board into rejecting our appeal. So I fake it and smile. "You bet."

Anyway, I have more pressing things to focus on. Like not throwing up the half a granola bar I've eaten because I feel like I can hardly keep anything down. I'm standing in front of the vending machine, contemplating a Sprite purchase to help settle my stomach when I hear my name. And without looking I know exactly who's said it.

Dylan.

So I do the most rational, grown-up thing I can think of: I tuck tail and run. I zip around the corner and down the hall toward the gym, but Dylan is close behind. The squeak of the soles of his shoes against the linoleum follow me. "Piper! Wait up, please?" There's no one else around during lunch, so I push through the swinging door to the girls' bathroom. It's the one by the gym that no one ever uses except during basketball games.

"Piper?" he calls from outside the door.

I know I can either pretend not to hear him, as if I'm not even here, or answer. But if I answer, he might wait around until I leave or until the bell rings and smokes me out.

I say nothing. I just stand by the sink and look in the mirror silently. My eyes are puffy from the lack of sleep and my skin has this weird greenish cast today. Probably because I feel like I'm in danger of puking my guts out any moment. Either that or I've OD'd on wintergreen Tums. I take some cold water and splash it on my face, smacking my cheeks to bring a rush of color and hopefully a little life.

Maybe Jodi will help me do my makeup before the thing tonight so I don't look so sickly in front of the board. But then I remember things between Jodi and I are kind of weird right now. Gah!

I'm still bent over the sink when the door flies open.

"Well, if you won't come out," a male voice says and I blink through the drips of water to see that of course, it's Dylan.

"This is the girls' bathroom," I hiss.

"You don't say." He hands me a paper towel.

"You could get expelled." I reach past his outstretched hand to grab my own towel, *thankyouverymuch*.

"For going into the girls' room? I highly doubt that. Besides, this area is off limits during lunch hour, so if I'm going down, I'm taking you with me."

It's true. I'm not supposed to be here, either. Though we probably wouldn't even get detention. Still, I feel like I'm backed into a corner here and all I want to do is run.

"You're avoiding me," he says.

Duh. Because the last time I tried to talk to him, he let me know exactly how he felt. And made me feel about two feet tall. Why go through that again?

"I think you started avoiding me first. Maybe I'm just returning the favor," I say flatly. I grab my bag and stalk past him back toward the door.

"Will you just talk to me? For a minute? Please?" He looks kind of sad. He has his greasy hair tucked under one of his knit caps and clearly, he hasn't shaved for a couple days. There are dark circles under his eyes, too.

"I tried to talk to you the other day, and you made it abundantly clear where you stand." Regardless of if it was entirely in my head or whether the rumors about me and Tony are true or not, the way he treated me the other day was pretty awful. I don't know if I can get past that.

"Tony told me," he whispers.

I freeze. "Told you what?"

"That he didn't… I mean that you guys haven't…" Dylan shifts his weight from one foot to the other, and I feel a tiny flicker of hope. "I asked him if it was true."

The flicker fizzles out. "You had to ask?"

CHAPTER THIRTY-ONE

The Ridgedale School District offices are in a small brick building adjacent to one of the elementary schools. I think the building used to be the elementary school until it expanded to more than a handful of classrooms. This explains why the toilets in the restrooms are only like twelve inches from the ground. I would know because I've spent the better part of the last ten minutes draped over one, afraid I'm going to make some serious sacrifices to the porcelain gods. But nothing comes up. So now I'm hanging by the sink again running cool water over my wrists. Tony's here with me, marking the second time in one day when I've been in the ladies' room with a boy.

He holds up a small flask and instructs me to take a drink and of course, I shoot him a look. This doesn't exactly seem like the time for that.

"Just a little. To take the edge off." He takes one swig himself and passes it. "It's what the new, improved Rebel Piper would do. Well, that and wear pants."

The grainy smell of whatever's in there is about enough to make me throw up.

"You don't breathe; you just drink."

"No thanks," I say. "That is nasty."

"I know. I *borrowed* a tiny bit from like three different bottles in my parents' cabinet."

"They here tonight?" I ask.

He takes another massive gulp, much bigger than the last one. "Yup."

The clock says we've got ten minutes before the meeting starts, so we make our way back to the conference room.

When I first got there a half an hour ago, there were about a dozen people milling around. Now, there aren't any, which seems totally weird. It's deserted. Tony points to a sign on the door that tells us that due to the increased attendance, the meeting has been moved across the street to the gym.

"Oh man." He wiggles his eyebrows. "You know what that means: packed house."

We scramble down the stairs and to the door, crossing the street. But Tony stops in his tracks because there, along the sidewalk is a handful of my family and church members. Holding their signs and singing some song about burning in hellfire to the tune of "Mary Had a Little Lamb."

"What... is that?" Tony asks. His face pales and his shoulders slump as he looks over their signs.

"That is my family." I say. "Come on, chin up. Don't let them get to you." I grab his arm and lace mine through it, leading him through the gauntlet but never once leaving his side.

The hallways of the school are quiet and the smells of peanut butter, bleach and sour milk hang in the air. I breathe through my mouth to keep the nausea from getting worse. When we walk in the gym door, I stop in my tracks because there are so many people crammed in there. Like a hundred, at least. Because I've stopped, Tony bumps into me and I hear him gasp as he surveys the scene.

"They weren't kidding about overflow," he whispers.

Peter sits by the side aisle next to Phoebe and a few of the littler kids. They must be taking turns protesting and listening. Two security guards check people at the entrance and a couple of people from my church are turned away when they try to bring their signs inside. Also present are some of our neighbors and what seems like half of my school. Okay not half, but several dozen students are here. Some I know and some I don't. I casually glance over their faces looking for

Jodi, but I don't see her and I refuse to study the crowd too closely, just in case she is there. I don't want to look desperate even if I am.

Since we're both designated as speakers, Tony and I have reserved seats near the mic. Also, I should note, near the door. I try not to read too much into that, though. Tony grabs my hand. Chloe's self-satisfied grin radiates from her perch across the room.

"Fuck the rumors," he whispers into my ear as he calmly leads me toward our seats.

The folding seat creaks beneath my weight and I'm seriously afraid it might collapse under me, which would be awesome. Or not. Tony nudges me and gestures toward the cluster of our fellow cast members. They're wearing matching t-shirts that say 'Free Piper' above a picture of my face. They make eye contact and give us the thumbs up. Well, all of them except Chloe who's still sitting with her arms crossed looking as pissed off as ever.

"Seriously. Screw her," Tony whispers. He winks.

To distract myself, I open and close the folder I brought and double and triple check to make sure the print out of my speech is still there. After the incident with Jodi, I decided not to let anyone read or hear it before tonight. Which might be really stupid of me, but too late now. I also glance over the agenda under our seats and notice that our issue is being reviewed last. Probably because if they don't get to the other stuff first, they never will. Either that or everyone here will leave after us and disrupt the rest of the meeting.

I'm shuffling the papers when I feel a hand on my shoulder. Dylan. Oh please don't let him try to *talk* to me. Not now; it will totally throw me off my game.

He leans in and whispers to both Tony and me, "Kick some ass," as he walks behind our row and takes his place next to Greg and the others.

I force myself to push it from my mind, though. I also try to silence the hushed murmurs of those who've gathered tonight for the meeting. Because of my family, I've been to these things before. Usually there are like a handful of people who come and most of them are regulars and the same people who write letters to the editor of our local paper and would willingly volunteer for jury duty, if it were possible. Like Mrs. Stagner who lives across the street from Serene. She's this kooky old lady who apparently makes trick-or-treaters answer questions about Illinois history before she'd hand over any Halloween treats. If you don't know the answer to your question, you get a "treat" from the other box, which usually includes little packs of oyster crackers or duck sauce that she's probably been storing up all year from her takeout meals.

The president stands at the front of the makeshift podium, a half-sized lectern that's been set in the center of some folding tables. The other board members take their seats and adjust the microphones that have been set up in front of them.

My dad is stationed next to Peter, front and center. He avoids my gaze but I've taken the opposite approach; I've been staring him down since I got here. It's so unlike me. Well, unlike the old me. I can't help but think maybe if my mom were here, she wouldn't be avoiding me. Maybe she'd be sitting next to me instead.

Someone reads the minutes from last week and they're approved. Then a few other minor issues are addressed and discussed. Something about upcoming union negotiations and an issue about the expense of two-ply toilet paper in the elementary schools. Finally, the president turns toward Tony and me. "Next we'll hear an appeal from students at Ridgedale High School regarding the cancellation of the spring drama."

Tony squeezes my knee as he stands to take his place at the mic where he's supposed to introduce me and why I've been 'chosen' to represent our cause. The board faces the audience full on, but the podium is set so that the speaker is half-facing the board and half-facing the audience. I nibble my pinky nail and watch Tony's face as it loses about three shades of color. At this moment, he looks even paler than me. Also, a bit like he might throw up.

"Good evening. My name is Tony and until about a couple weeks ago, I was a member of the cast of Ridgedale High School's production of *Romeo and Juliet*. As many of you probably know by now, our production has been canceled because of a disagreement over casting. The role of Romeo was assigned to Piper Ryan because she was the best person for the part. But since that time, it's taken on a life of its own, especially in light of certain citizens"—he looks pointedly at my dad—"ideas on issues related to sexual orientation. The situation and its implications mean a great deal to me personally for many reasons but particularly because" —he takes a big sip from his water bottle—"because I, myself, am a gay man."

The entire room seems to take a collective gasp. Obviously, I'm not surprised by the revelation, but the way he's decided to make it makes me gasp, too. Especially since I know Tony's parents are here. In this room. Listening. Watching. No wonder he's looked so nervous. And why he kept hinting that the rumors would clear up soon. He's been planning this all along!

I'm not saying he doesn't have the right to come out any way he wants, but I hate that all of this stupid school drama cheapens that for him. This play is important but it's not as important as *someone's life*. Tony presses on but I'm sitting here festering. I was angry before, but now I'm livid. Livid that some group of people could inject themselves into something that's not even their business and in so doing have this kind of power over him. Over all of us.

"That's why it's my esteemed honor to present Piper Ryan to speak on our behalf. In recent weeks, Piper has revealed herself to be an insanely gifted actor and also an incredibly loyal friend. Ladies and gentlemen, Piper Ryan." Tony gestures for me to take my place at the podium. There's clapping and a few whistles as I walk up to the mic, careful not to trip over the cord. Tony squeezes my shoulder as he passes me and retakes his seat.

I take a deep breath. And then another. And then I start my speech. But two sentences into what I'd planned to say, I stop and shake my head, trying to quiet the anger still pulsing in my temple. I clench and unclench my fists then look to the board, then to my dad sitting there with this blank expression on his face. He's not looking at me. He's looking past me, through me, over me. But not at me.

And I glance to the rest of the audience where I spot who must be Tony's parents. His mother is clutching a tissue and her eyes are bloodshot and sullen. His dad looks angry.

"I'm sorry." I bite my lip and take a more few deep breaths to steady myself. I look back to the conference table where the board members are looking at me, expectantly. And I know their expressions are mirrored in the faces of everyone else in the room. The show must go on, right?

"I had a speech I'd prepared," I start. "But I think I'd rather go off book, as we say in theater." A few people shift in their seats. "So. Yeah. Like Tony said, my name is Piper Ryan and I'm a member of the cast of Ridgedale's spring performance of *Romeo and Juliet*. I came here today to plead our case before you. As you probably know, a certain interest group decided that because I'm a girl and I was cast as Romeo that constitutes, what's the term you all use?" I look directly to my dad. "*An assault on the moral fabric of our city*? Something like that. Anyway, our school's administration bowed to their pressures and decided to suspend the production. I guess I should start by stating, for the record, I am not gay. Not that that should matter. At all. But because some of you are probably wondering, I'm not attracted to Chloe Wennert. Heck, Chloe and I don't even like each other, do we Chloe?" I glance in her direction to find her scowling back. Half the auditorium looks at her, so she shrugs and smiles weakly. Which earns a bit of a laugh.

I continue, "But it's not about that. Because the thing is, we're acting. Pretending to be people we're not. And, spoiler alert, when the curtain falls, both Romeo and Juliet are dead. That doesn't mean that Chloe and I will *actually* be dead. And likewise, neither of us will suddenly be attracted to women."

I sigh and take a moment to collect my thoughts. I was planning to go on this long tirade about the injustice of the administration and the way this whole thing has been handled, but Tony's introduction made me realize that even if I'm trying to deny it, this whole blasted thing really boils down to sexuality, at least in the minds of pretty much everyone in this room. Including the people whose opinions matter the most: the board.

"*Romeo and Juliet* it a play about many things, but it is certainly not a play about rational people making sensible choices. It's about a love that is overwhelming, confusing, passionate and often, erratic, so much so that it leads the characters to take their own lives. Romeo and Juliet's love was quite literally a forbidden one. Which is funny, right? Because that's not completely unlike what many members of the gay community... like Tony here, experience every day. Especially in an environment where they can't even openly discuss their feelings without sending everyone into a conniption."

Everyone's eyes are on me. Except my dad. He's twiddling his pen between his thumb and forefinger, the same thing he does with his fork at dinner. "I'm sure it's not news to anyone that in Shakespeare's day, men played all the parts. Which means that Juliet and Romeo would have both been portrayed by guys. And the fact that Mr. Shakespeare's works have endured and become timeless classics is, I think, a testament to their ability to transcend both time and perhaps, gender. My character is male and I'd be playing him as a male. Just like Juliet is and always has been female, even if she was once played by an actor who happened to be in possession of a penis."

Quiet murmuring fills the silence. Some people even gasp and my dad's face has gone pink. The president taps his makeshift "gavel" against the lectern. The real gavel is mahogany and has an engraved brass plaque. This one is a wooden mallet that's probably used by the kindergarten classes to hammer colored wooden pegs into submission.

"Enough," the Board president tries. He clears his throat. "Order."

I stop for a moment to give the audience time to shut it. When they have, I press on. "Okay, if a bunch of adults can't handle the word penis, then clearly we have bigger some issues." I direct my gaze around the room and keep my face stern. "Anyway, at the heart of all this, *Romeo and Juliet* is a play about an individual railing against social norms and the weight of expectation. So at the very least, whatever you decide, you've given us the opportunity to follow Romeo's example. But I sincerely hope you'll also give us the chance to bring Shakespeare's drama to life."

As soon as I turn to step from the podium, the room erupts in a thunder of applause. Well, part of the room. The part where the cast and those who support the cast are sitting. There is polite applause from some of the other attendees, but nothing like my classmates' display, which includes whoops and hollers and whistles and a slow, rhythmic chanting of my name.

The president steps up to the mic and calls the room to order. He asks if anyone wants to speak for the other side. My dad shifts in his seat, his paper in hand, but does not step forward.

"Very well," the president says. The board takes a few minutes to deliberate amongst themselves. It's pretty clear that our words haven't swayed them, but I notice that several of the cast members have stood and linked arms.

"Let's have the vote," the president says and each board member leans over to a microphone to give their verdict.

CHAPTER THIRTY-TWO

In a move surprising no one (except maybe the more optimistic of my cast mates) the board didn't overturn our principal's decision. The final vote was close though. Well, kind of—7-4. It wasn't a total shutout, at least.

Tony shuffled past me and followed at the heels of his dad who, like mine, bolted from the auditorium as though it were on fire. I grabbed his arm. "Why'd you do that?"

He shrugged. "I was going to have to do it eventually, and I'm tired of the secret having power over me."

When I get home, the house is unnervingly quiet. And my dad is sitting at a table in the darkened kitchen all by himself. He has a glass of bourbon in his hand. I haven't seen him drink since Mom died. I head over to the fridge to grab some water. I'm not thirsty, but I feel the need to *do* something or at least have something to hold in my hands.

It's as if even Moose can feel the tension in the room. Instead of dancing around hoping for a biscuit, he's curled up under the kitchen table pretending to be invisible. Dad's face is firm when he finally looks up at me.

"I can't believe you put me in this impossible position." His voice is barely above a whisper.

I stiffen and set the bottle on the counter. My head is telling me to run away, to back down, to submit, but in my heart I know I can't. Not anymore. "Impossible position?"

"When you were little, you were so helpful. So compassionate. You remember that old oak tree we had chopped down last year? Thing used to drop thousands of acorns into the yard and made it darn near impossible for me to mow without my legs getting pelted. One time, I came in with all these welts and you took one look at my shins and went out to the yard and collected up those acorns. Bag after bag of them. You didn't stop until the entire yard was clear. Took you three days." He gets a faraway look in his eye, wistful, even.

"I'm not a little girl anymore, Dad."

"You will *always* be my little girl."

I stop for a moment and look to him considering my words carefully. In this moment, I realize there is so much I've been holding back, so much I've wanted to say and it's like the speech at the school board opened the floodgate and now there is no going back. "No, I won't. Not really. I may make decisions about what to do with my life, my heart, my body that you wouldn't make. Maybe even decisions that you think God doesn't like. But they're my decisions because it's my life. My body. My relationship with God." He tries to say something but I press on. "You raised us well, Dad. You did. But I'm not a puppet. You can't pull this string and make me move this way or that. Eventually, we all have to make our own choices. And live with the consequences."

"I don't treat you like puppets..."

I hold up my hand to stop him. Out of the corner of my eye, I see shadows flutter under the far doorway. Several of my siblings must be there listening in and for some reason, this empowers me. I raise my voice so they can all hear me better. "You know what I think? No, what I know? We live in a fallen, broken world filled with to the brim with sinners of which, *I am the worst.*" Paul, as in the guy who wrote half the New Testament said that first. And I know my dad will catch it. "But you know what else? In the midst of all that muck and brokenness can come a lot of beauty if you're willing to see it. I wouldn't have the ability to see it if it weren't for you. I just wish you could see it, too." I keep talking, afraid that if I don't get this out there now, I might never get a chance. I feel hot tears start to trickle down.

And the realization slams into me with a force so urgent it nearly knocks me over: the world isn't perfect, I love it anyway.

God loves it anyway.

"You think I don't know that?" He pushes his chair back and it bangs against the wall. I hear a gasp in the hallway.

"I think your head knows it, but your heart is still in denial. And instead, you're channeling all this energy into the church, into trying to right the world by sanitizing it somehow. But that will never right it, will it? Not truly. Because we can't set it right ourselves. And hating people in order to 'love' them seems awfully counterproductive. Wouldn't it just be easier to love them?"

At this, my dad breaks his eye contact with me and stares at the kitchen's Spanish tile floor. He opens his mouth like he's going to say something, but closes it again, and his shoulders and face fall. He leaves the room.

He's a master at confrontation when it's on his own terms, when he's the instigator. But if it isn't? Fight or flight and he'll choose flight. Every time.

I reach into my bag and pull out my mom's worn out copy of the *Complete Works of William Shakespeare* and set it on Dad's placemat.

I make for the back door and wander into the night.

Ordinarily, I'd probably go to Jodi's at a time like this. Not that there's exactly a precedent since my dad and I never really fight, and definitely not like this. In the past, he gives a directive and I've unquestioningly followed it, but I guess that's what this is all about, isn't it? How I've spent the better part of my life being the dutiful daughter, but I'm not sure I can do that anymore.

After strapping my bike pack on and grabbing a scratchy wool blanket off the workbench, I hop on my bike and pedal off somewhere. It's not that I want to become some kind of rebel—I don't. But I also don't want to keep up a charade just because it's the path of least resistance. I've done that for so long and the truth is it's exhausting.

It always looks so much easier on cheesy old TV shows. By this point, we'd be hugging it out and then we'd share some ice cream and play a board game or something. Until the next episode when we'd have to do it all over again. The reality looks like this: My brother has become my biggest enemy. The guy I was crushing on rejected me. My dad and I are back to square one. Tony outed himself for nothing and, oh yeah, the drama is now officially off. I've made a royal mess of things and I can't see any way to fix it.

My body is propelling me toward the exact place I want to be, even though I didn't consciously decide to go there. It's one of my favorite places in the world and I know the way as well as I know my own bedroom. The bridge out by Chester Lake, the same place I spent hours the other day crafting my speech for tonight.

If you go too far out, it can get a little iffy. But closer to the land, the bridge is still secure. More of a platform to nowhere. I always feel *right* here. Even if everything in my world is anything but. I climb up with my pack and as soon as I settle in, it's like the weight of it all crashes into me at once in such a way that I feel dizzy. And sick. I lay back against bridge, thankful that the night air isn't too cool.

The tears come. And this time, I let them.

CHAPTER THIRTY - THREE

I don't know how long I've been laying here, crumpled in a heap of snot and tears but I must have dozed off because I wake to the sound of someone calling my voice. For a split second, I think it might be God.

"Piper?" I hear again so I peek over the edge of the bridge to see Dylan standing below at the water's edge. "Oh my God, Piper!" His voice sounds panicked over the scuffling of his shoes against the bluff.

"Don't jump, okay," he says in a forced sing-song voice. Like he's trying to cajole me.

I roll my eyes but then realize he can't see me in the dark. "I'm not going to jump you, dummy." I'm bummed out, not suicidal.

He's climbs the rusty rungs of the old bridge and crawls toward my spot out further over the lake. "Seriously. Don't jump. It's not worth it."

I shake my head and sigh. The crusty remnants of the tears and snot remind me that I probably look a mess, so I wipe my face as best I can with this scratchy wool blanket that smells like the trunk of our van. I'm quite confident that I officially look like crap. "How'd you know I was out here?" I ask when he's close enough to hear me and not so focused on not falling from his climb.

"Jodi. I stopped her after the meeting and asked her for your home number."

Wait, she was at the meeting? I looked briefly but didn't notice her there. I can't help but feel a glimmer of hope at this. Then again, this is

Jodi we're talking about, even if things are unsettled between us, she's still my best friend. And apparently, I'm still hers.

"She didn't want to give it to me at first. She tried to call you, and when you didn't answer, or when Tony called, she told me some ideas where you might be. She went to Scoopz to look and I chose this place because it seemed like the most pressing." He looks over the edge. "Holy hell, we're high up, aren't we?"

"It's not exactly the Golden Gate Bridge."

He leans out a bit, still holding the metal rail in a death-grip. I sigh and pat the space on the wool blanket next to me.

"So, why are you here?" I ask, taking a swig from my bottle and he sits down beside me. "And how could you be sure I wouldn't be up here screwing Tony?" I don't even try to hide the sarcasm in my voice, but saying his name reminds me that in all of this I'd nearly forgotten about him and how tonight probably rocked his world irreversibly. I should call him and make sure he's all right. If the look on my dad's face was unpleasant, Tony's dad looked downright murderous. Well, judging from the brief glance I stole before his dad stormed out.

"Yeah. About that." Dylan sighs. "Did you know he was gay?"

"He told me. On the Chicago trip."

"See, I never got that vibe from him."

I remember when I thought Dylan knew somehow. Until he bought into the rumors about Tony and me; that made it pretty clear he didn't.

"Why didn't you say anything? With all that stuff going around?"

"I'm not going to out Tony just to dispel some stupid rumors. Besides, people who know me don't need to know Tony is gay to know that whole thing is a lie. Or so I thought, anyway."

This last snip has its intended effect as Dylan retracts a little bit, stung. "You're right. I was just... stupid."

He wasn't the only one. Jodi believed it, too. She's supposed to be my friend, my best friend. "It's just you guys always had this sort of *thing* and so when I heard... well it made sense. I could see it, at least." He shakes his head.

"That thing is called friendship. You should try it sometime," I say, keeping my voice as catty as I can. I'm still mad at him and I want him to know it.

I take another swig of water not because I'm thirsty, but because it's something to do.

"You shouldn't be drinking up this high. And by yourself," he says.

I hand him the bottle. "I don't drink. It's flavored water. That okay with you?"

"Oh." He screws the cap back on and just holds it, turning it over in his hands.

"So are you going to make me ask you again?" I ask. "Why are you here?"

He smiles, and even in the dark, there's a glimmer in his eyes. "Well for one thing, I was worried about you. After the meeting, you ran off so fast I didn't get to say anything and after what happened, when Jodi mentioned a bridge..."

"You thought I was going to kill myself over what, the play?"

"Well, no. Maybe. I don't know. You're family is pretty intense."

"You catch on quick."

"Well. I didn't know so I wanted to make sure."

I shake my head. "I play—*played*— Romeo... It doesn't mean I am becoming him."

"Right. Acting is different." He winks at me. At least I think he does. Hard to tell in the dark. Maybe his eyes are just dry. "And for another thing, I owe you an apology. Several, really, but let's start with this: I shouldn't have listened to stupid gossip."

He's right, that's a start. But even if Tony and I were hooking up, frankly, that's none of his business and I tell him as much.

"You're right. It's just I've always... I mean ever since...." He shakes his head and takes a deep breath. "I like you, okay? And I thought maybe you and Tony had something. You were always hanging out and laughing at your inside jokes and giving each other these looks."

Wait. He likes me?

He likes me!

But he has a girlfriend.

I turn my attention back to what he's saying. "And I know I had no right to be jealous but the fact is, I was. Insanely."

"Jealous?"

"Yeah."

"But you *have* a girlfriend."

"I know. That's why I felt like I couldn't be jealous but it doesn't change the fact that I was. Am."

"Am? You're jealous? Of what, exactly?"

"More like of *whom*. Tony."

"Weren't you there tonight? Obviously, Tony and I are not dating or hooking up. And never have been."

"Well, I know that now. But he got to be there for you today in a way that I couldn't. And he got to stand next to you during it all. So yeah, I'm still jealous."

"Please. I didn't accomplish anything except alienating myself from my family and letting down the cast."

"You're joking, right? What you did makes Romeo look like a pansy."

"Whatever. Romeo had balls and I don't."

"Are we talking literally or figuratively now? Because literally, yes, as has been established Romeo is a dude. But in terms of action or inaction, you definitely have bigger balls."

I sigh. "Romeo knew he wanted something so he went after it, figurative balls to the wall. I'm a coward and only stood up to my family reluctantly, and now they hate me for it."

"Another theme of the play, right? *Deny thy father* and whatnot?" He shifts a little bit. "Look, sometimes parents suck. Believe me, I know. Piper, you aren't Romeo. Or Juliet. Or Electra. You're just you. Sure, your speech was pretty great tonight, but what really took balls or… whatever, was being there for Tony and not saying anything or outing him to defend yourself. Most people would have, you know."

He stares out over the water, away from me. We sit like that for a bit, watching the moonlight ripple on the surface of the lake and listening to the quiet of the night. It's still too cool for the bugs and birds, so the quiet lapping of the water against the rocks and the distant drone of the highway are the only noises.

I shiver, maybe because of the coolness of night air against my flushed face. Or maybe because I'm sitting next to this guy who I've totally fallen for, and it freaks me right out. Especially since he is painfully unavailable.

Dylan unscrews the cap of my water bottle of and lifts it to his lips, taking a long pull. I study his profile. The stubble on his chin, the way his eyelashes flutter against his cheek. Most boys have the same parts, but there's something about his. About him. He turns back toward me and tilts his head. "Well, maybe now you'll finally let me explain about everything? Well, I guess you have to. No where to run."

"Explain what?" I ask though I already know the answer. I sigh and shift uncomfortably. "Look, I'm sorry I shouldn't have—" I start to say, but he holds up a hand stopping me.

"No, I want to explain. The thing is, Ava and I had a really good thing for a while. But we knew we'd be apart for a year so when she left for school, we—well, she really—thought it would be best if we left things open ended. Not a period, a—" He scratches the back of his head and turns his head, like he's literally searching for the word.

"An ellipsis?" I offer.

"Exactly. An ellipsis. The catch was, we were supposed to tell each other if anything ever got serious with someone else. Or started to. She's gone on casual dates with a couple of people and so have I. But anyway, I knew that if I kissed you that would be…"

Serious? He's got to be kidding. I'm the one who's supposed to think a kiss is some big deal thing.

"I don't think a kiss is inherently serious. But honestly, with the way I feel about you, well, it would be. So I felt like I owed it to Ava, you know?"

I nod and what he's saying is hitting. Really hitting. The way he feels about me? So this really wasn't some one-sided thing that I created in my head? He shifts his weight so that his arm brushes mine.

"See the thing is, my dad cheated on my mom and shortly after, she had an episode. A bad one she never really came back from. And then she left. I'm not saying it was because of my dad, but that whole thing didn't help, you know? So anyway, I promised myself I would never be *that* guy. Never be like my dad." His voice is softer. "He's not a bad person, he's just made some dumb decisions. Really dumb decisions."

I move my arm so that I'm still technically using it to support my weight but it really is behind him now. "Was your stepmom—I mean...." I shouldn't even ask but I can't help myself. "Never mind. It's none of my business."

"It's all right. No, I like Gina and if she had been the other woman, there's no way I could say that." Then he laughs, this weird wheezing laugh. "The real trip is that the next morning, after the party? When I called Ava, she was looking at apartments with some guy. They're moving in together after the semester, which is like, as serious as you can get, isn't it? Pretty much, anyway."

Oh, ouch. No wonder he's looked kinda like a bum this week. I've been trying not to pay attention, but it's impossible not to notice. I scoot closer to him and let my arm fall to the side so that it's almost touching him. Not quite.

"Not just some guy. The tattoo artist who did this." He pulls up his sleeve to reveal a rose on the inside of his forearm and I remember seeing it that night in Chicago. "It was my birthday present for Ava. It's a rose because..." He shakes his head and pinches the bridge of his nose. "Because that's her middle name. What a cliché, huh?"

"Not... totally," I lie.

He grabs the water bottle again and turns it in his hands, round and round. "I guess they've been seeing each other since Christmas. Which means when I saw her a couple weeks ago she knew, but she didn't tell me. Didn't even have the decency to write a Dear John email. Or tell me when we talked on the phone. Or even a text. Nothing." He sighs, scrunches his eyebrows together, and pinches the inside bridge of his nose between his thumb and index finger. "I mean I thought she seemed sorta weird that day in Chicago. But she was in the middle of a huge studio project, so I just thought..." He shakes his head. "Anyway, I guess what I'm trying to say in all this is that I think you're great. And

I know the timing is crap and maybe I mucked it up, but the fact remains." He takes a breath and lets it out slowly. "I like you, Piper. I know it makes zero sense and you're not supposed to date or whatever. But I had to tell you because, well because you deserve to hear it."

"There's a lot of things I'm not supposed to do that I've done anyway." I know what my dad's standards are, and as best I can tell, they're impossible for a human to meet. More importantly, I'm still trying to figure out what *my* standards for myself are."

"So what now?" he asks.

"I have no idea."

I look over to see him staring at me. He licks his lips, and I'm careful not to move, not to even breathe for fear of scaring him off again.

Dylan leans in the rest of the way, crossing the divide between us. "Is this okay?" His lips hover so close to mine I can feel the heat coming off of them.

I can't speak but I nod. It's more than okay.

"I'm really new at this," I blurt. Like, insanely new. As in, until recently I thought I wouldn't kiss someone until he was pronounced my husband.

He smiles. "That's okay as long as it's okay with you that I'm, uh, not."

And then he kisses me. A slow, soft kiss, his lips parted, but just barely. I feel it reverberate all the way down in my toes. I am kissing Dylan.

No, *Dylan is kissing me*!

He pulls away and studies my face for a moment pressing his thumb into my bottom lip. "It is fuller than I thought," he whispers.

I'm too stunned to do anything but stare back at him. He leans in and kisses me again, deeper and hungrier than before so that I no longer have a single doubt how he feels about me.

And this time, I kiss him back.

CHAPTER THIRTY-FOUR

This is the part where I'm supposed to imagine them all in their underwear. Or naked. Or... something.

Except I'm standing by myself on this stage and the auditorium is so dark I can't see anyone anyway. It's just me up here beneath one wicked hot spotlight. I'm all alone.

Well, almost all alone. A 'dead' girl is in my arms.

And I have to choose: open my mouth and say the words I've practiced or run.

"*O true apothecary! Thy drugs are quick. Thus with a kiss, I die.*" I whisper, bringing my lips toward the 'dead' girl's, but I keel over just after they meet.

Moments later, the altar my 'body' rests on is wheeled off stage by the stagehands, and I get up and take my place in the wing. The curtains rise and rest of the cast filters out onto the brightly lit stage first, in groups and then some as individuals. Tony grins at me and squeezes my shoulder before he trots out to roaring applause. Chloe goes out a moment before me and curtsies before bowing and stepping aside. I skip out to the middle of the stage and mirror her but in reverse, first bowing then curtsying. We aren't exactly friends now, the two of us. But it turns out whether we like it or not, Juliet needs a Romeo. And Romeo needs a Juliet. Plus, once Chloe figured out the rest of the cast wasn't going to let me go, she basically had to choice but to get on board. Or she'd be the one being replaced.

But it's not like we're besties or anything now. Not even close.

I look out to the audience as the house lights come up and find they are on their feet. All of them. Stef and Jodi are in the very front row, clapping and whooping it up.

After another minute of clapping, as an entire cast we bow and then curtsy (Tony's suggestion) and the curtain falls.

"Romeo, Romeo, wherefore art thou Romeo?" Dylan says from behind me. He's standing there in his black stagehand attire. He holds the most obnoxiously large bouquet of Gerber Daisies. Pink ones.

"Come on, what kind of jerk would I be if I didn't bring my girlfriend flowers on opening night?"

Wait. Girlfriend? I mean we are most definitely dating (and most definitely *not* courting—there's no endgame, just here and now), but he's never called me his girlfriend before.

"You were brilliant." He wraps his arms around me.

No, the school didn't give us our play back, but it worked out okay because Mr. Brooks got the Theatre Center in town to let us use their playhouse instead. Which meant total creative freedom and the ability to add extra performances when the tickets sold out in three days. Which they did. Our show (and yes, the controversy surrounding it) has even been covered by the *Tribune* and the *Post-Dispatch*, and the clip from our local news station has gone viral. *The Today Show* is even lining up an interview for Tuesday morning.

None of that would have happened without my family and our church. That's one way to look at it, at least. And it's the way I'm choosing to look at it because life is just too short to worry about what other people might think or say. Or even do. The only way other people can control you is if you allow them to.

Some of our church members are livid, of course, but once the play moved off public (school) territory and into the realm of community theater there wasn't much they could do. Except protest. Which they did. Well, are. Currently, they're standing outside the theater with signs and chants, and I heard there was even one poster board with an actual photo of my face on it engulfed in cartoon flames.

Dad is the head pastor of a church that basically wants to crucify his daughter. So to say things between my family and me are a bit strained is probably an understatement. They didn't kick me out of the house, but they either give me the cold shoulder or try and witness to me at the breakfast table or in line for the bathroom. I haven't been to a church service since the School Board meeting, and I don't know if I will ever go back. Correction: I haven't been to *their* church service. Jodi's Korean Presbyterian church has welcomed me with open arms, even if I'm not Korean. Or half-Korean. I'm even thinking of checking out a few other churches around town to find the one that fits me best.

I'm talking to a couple audience members in the theater's foyer when I see my dad standing there waiting for his turn to talk to me. Wait. My dad is standing there?

"This is for you." He hands me a single white rose. He rocks back on his feet. Are those tears in his eyes? Echoes of tears, at least. "Piper you were..." He presses his lips together. "You were great, sweetheart."

He wraps his arms around me and squeezes. I can tell by the way his shoulders shake that he's trying not to cry. "I can see why they wanted you for Romeo. You were—you are—wonderful."

"You mean that?"

He nods. "Absolutely. I always knew the Lord had great things in store for you." He's about to say something else. Maybe something about how if only I would use my talents for the church instead of against it. But he takes a deep breath, shakes his head, and for once, holds his tongue.

I finger the rose petals and notice that he's here alone. None of my siblings have come along and as far as I know, members of his church are still outside protesting. But at least he made the effort. And right now?

Right now, maybe that's enough.

ACKNOWLEDGMENTS

Thanks to my agent Amy Tipton for her belief in this story and these characters, and for all her unwavering support over the years. Thanks also to the cast and crew at CQ for their passion, dedication, and diligence in moving this story from a word document on my computer to a real life book.

There are so many writer friends whose encouragement has kept me afloat and whose critiques have kept me humble. All of you have in some way made this book better and have made me a stronger writer. Krystle Carter, Lindsey Satterfield, Sarah Enni, Kara Thomas, also the LBs and the Slack(ers). You know who you are and you know what you've done. I couldn't be more grateful.

Thanks also to my many non-writer friends for putting up with my neurosis and celebrating the rollercoaster that is a publishing journey, even when you had no idea what the heck I was talking about. Sarah Kennedy, Katie VanArendonk, Kellie Zephir, Jennifer Kennedy, Liz Gwinn, Nancy Krelle and Erin Ladd, in particular. This book would look very different without your support.

This is a work of fiction but there are countless people who've lent me their stories, moments, turns of phrase, idiosyncrasies etc. If you know me and you think you recognize yourself in one (or several) of these characters, odds are there's a reason for that. However, none of the characters in this book are based on any one person, living or dead (hear that, Mom? Piper's dad is not Dad. Obviously.). Speaking of, Mom, 'thanks' seems insufficient and as a writer I know I can do better. But there is only so much space here and I could probably fill an entire volume just for you. Same with the rest of my family. Y'all are the literal best.

Finally, my kiddos Carly and Calvin, and my husband, Sam. You might be last on this list, but you're first in my heart. Always.

ABOUT THE AUTHOR

Lindsey Roth Culli writes books for teens and people who used to be teens. She earned her MFA in Creative Writing in 2010. Though she currently calls Baltimore, Maryland home, part of her heart is hidden in the cornfields of Illinois where she grew up.

She is Team Oxford Comma.

Thank You for Reading

© 2016 **Lindsey Roth Culli**

http://www.lindseyrothculli.com

Please visit http://curiosityquills.com/reader-survey to share your reading experience with the author of this book!

Of Pens and Swords, by Rena Rocford

All Cyra wants is a date with Rochan and a chance to prove a one-handed girl can fence in the Olympics. Cyra finds a coach who could take her all the way, but the lessons costs too much. With her dreams slipping away, she agrees to tutor a ballerina with a rich father and a D-minus in English, but the ballerina isn't interested in English, only Rochan. The ballerina threatens to turn her D into a full-fledged F if Cyra doesn't help her win Rochan.

Vinehart Farm, by Lisa Monique Kent

Eva Blanchard knows loss first-hand. But she's determined to make a life for herself on the farm her parents left her. Though she wants to live in peace, community events force her to take action and she's tossed into a whirlwind of conflict. Should she withhold information and keep the status quo, or be truthful and risk losing everyone she holds dear? Follow Eva as she struggles to keep her farm and her home town's respect, while living out the values of integrity and justice her parents instilled in her.

PLEASE VISIT CURIOSITYQUILLS.COM FOR MORE GREAT BOOKS!

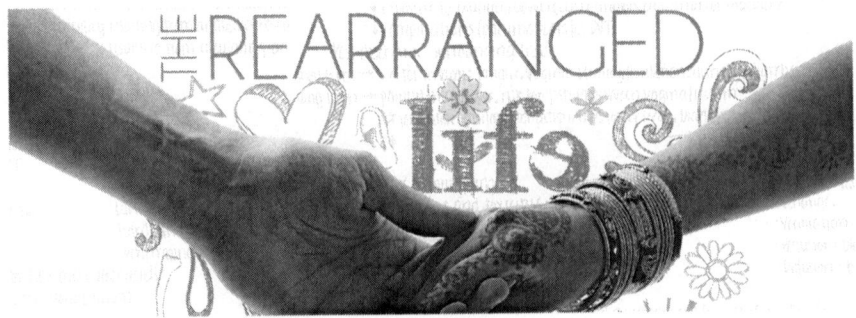

The Rearranged Life, by Annika Sharma

Nithya, an Indian college student with big dreams, unexpectedly falls in love with James, a intelligent and handsome American. Challenging her family's hopes for an arranged marriage, Nithya has a choice to make and the journey changes how she sees her future, her relationships with her loved ones and how she learns to put herself back together when even her best-laid plans fall apart.

Because of You, by RaShelle Workman

It's been seven years since Maddie Martin's parents died. Their killer wasn't just a random stranger, but her best friends' father. Kyle Hadley. The boy she's been in love, the boy she promised all of her firsts to. Worst of all, Kyle's father got away with it, and Maddie hasn't seen Kyle since. That changes on her first day of college. Seeing Kyle again brings back all of her childhood feelings of friendship and love for him, but it also brings back the anger, sorrow, and pain she's been trying to bury because of his father. But there are problems beyond Kyle and Maddie and their old feelings. The two of them are in danger and one or both might end up dead.

CPSIA information can be obtained at www.ICGtesting.com
Printed in the USA
LVOW07s1031021016

507070LV00003B/655/P